MW01493076

The first non-European to win the Nobel prize, Rabindranath Tagore (1861-1941) was a poet, painter, musician and novelist. Tagore wrote poetry as an eight-year-old. At the age of sixteen, he released his first substantial poems. By 1877 he graduated to his first short stories and dramas. As a humanist, universalist, internationalist, and ardent anti-nationalist, he denounced the British Raj and advocated independence from Britain. As an exponent of the Bengal Renaissance, he advanced a vast canon that comprised paintings, sketches and doodles, hundreds of texts, and some two thousand songs; his legacy endures also in the institution he founded, Visva-Bharati University.

Tagore modernised Bengali art by spurning rigid classical forms and resisting linguistic strictures. His novels, stories, songs, dance-dramas, and essays spoke to topics political and personal. Gitanjali , Gora, and Ghare-Baire are his best-known works, and his verse, short stories, and novels were acclaimed for their lyricism, colloquialism, naturalism, and unnatural contemplation. His compositions were chosen by two nations as national anthems: India's Jana Gana Mana and Bangladesh's Amar Shonar Bangla. Tagore renounced his knighthood in response to the Jallianwala Bagh massacre in 1919.

THE VERY BEST SHORT STORIES OF RABINDRANATH TAGORE

Rabindranath Tagore

EMBASSY BOOKS

www.embassybooks.in

The Very Best Short Stories of Rabindranath Tagore
by Rabindranath Tagore

This edition first published in 2017

Published in India by:

Embassy Book Distributors

120, Great Western Building,
Maharashtra Chamber of Commerce Lane,
Fort, Mumbai - 400 023.
Tel : (91-22) 22819546 / 22818567.
Email : info@embassybooks.in
Website : www.embassybooks.in

Distribution Centres:

Mumbai, Ahmedabad, Bangalore, Kolkata,
Chennai, Hyderabad, New Delhi, Pune

ISBN: 978-93-86450-27-2

Page Design and Layout by PSV Kumarasamy

Printed by : Jayant Printery LLP, Mumbai

Contents

The Postmaster

The postmaster first took up his duties in the village of Ulapur. Though the village was a small one, there was an indigo factory near by, and the proprietor, an Englishman, had managed to get a post office established.

Our postmaster belonged to Calcutta. He felt like a fish out of water in this remote village. His office and living-room were in a dark thatched shed, not far from a green, slimy pond, surrounded on all sides by a dense growth.

The men employed in the indigo factory had no leisure; moreover, they were hardly desirable companions for decent folk. Nor is a Calcutta boy an adept in the art of associating with others. Among strangers he appears either proud or ill at ease. At any rate, the postmaster had but little company; nor had he much to do.

At times he tried his hand at writing a verse or two. That the movement of the leaves and the clouds of the sky were enough to fill life with joy – such were the sentiments to which he sought to give expression. But God knows that the poor fellow would have felt it as the gift of a new life, if some genie of the *Arabian Nights* had in one night swept away the trees, leaves and all, and replaced them with a macadamised road, hiding the clouds from view with rows of tall houses.

The postmaster's salary was small. He had to cook his own meals, which he used to share with Ratan, an orphan girl of the village, who did odd jobs for him.

When in the evening the smoke began to curl up from the village cowsheds, and the cicalas chirped in every bush; when the mendicants of the Baül sect sang their shrill songs in their daily meeting-place, when any poet, who had attempted to watch the movement of the leaves in the dense bamboo thickets, would have felt a ghostly shiver run down his back, the postmaster would light his little lamp, and call out "Ratan."

Ratan would sit outside waiting for this call, and, instead of coming in at once, would reply, "Did you call me, sir?"

"What are you doing?" the postmaster would ask.

"I must be going to light the kitchen fire," would be the answer.

And the postmaster would say: "Oh, let the kitchen fire be for awhile; light me my pipe first."

At last Ratan would enter, with puffed-out cheeks, vigorously blowing into a flame a live coal to light the tobacco. This would give the postmaster an opportunity of conversing. "Well, Ratan," perhaps he would begin, "do you remember anything of your mother?" That was a fertile subject. Ratan partly remembered, and partly didn't. Her father had been fonder of her than her mother; him she recollected more vividly. He used to come home in the evening after his work, and one or two evenings stood out more clearly than others, like pictures in her memory. Ratan would sit on the floor near the postmaster's feet, as memories crowded in upon her. She called to mind a little brother that she had – and how on some bygone cloudy day she had played at fishing with him on the edge of the pond, with a twig for a make-believe fishing-rod. Such little incidents would drive out greater events from her mind. Thus, as they talked, it would often get very late, and the postmaster would feel too lazy to do any cooking at all. Ratan would then hastily light the fire, and toast some unleavened bread, which, with the cold remnants of the morning meal, was enough for their supper.

On some evenings, seated at his desk in the corner of the big empty shed, the postmaster too would call up memories of his own home, of his mother and his sister, of those for whom in his exile his heart was sad, – memories which were always haunting him, but which he could not talk about with the men of the factory, though he found himself naturally recalling them aloud in the presence of the simple little girl. And so it came about that the girl would allude to his people as mother, brother, and sister, as if she had known them all her life. In fact, she had a complete picture of each one of them painted in her little heart.

One noon, during a break in the rains, there was a cool soft breeze blowing; the smell of the damp grass and leaves in the hot sun felt like the warm breathing of the tired earth on one's body. A persistent bird went on all the afternoon repeating the burden of its one complaint in Nature's audience chamber.

The postmaster had nothing to do. The shimmer of the freshly washed leaves, and the banked-up remnants of the retreating rain-clouds were sights to see; and the postmaster was watching them and thinking to himself: "Oh, if only some kindred soul were near – just one loving human being whom I could hold near my heart!" This was exactly, he went on to think, what that bird was trying to say, and it was the same feeling which the murmuring leaves were striving to express. But no one knows, or would believe, that such an idea might also take possession of an ill-paid village postmaster in the deep, silent mid-day interval of his work.

The postmaster sighed, and called out "Ratan." Ratan was then sprawling beneath the guava-tree, busily engaged in eating unripe guavas. At the voice of her master, she ran up breathlessly, saying: "Were you calling me, Dada?" "I was thinking," said the postmaster, "of teaching you to read." And then for the rest of the afternoon he taught her the alphabet.

Thus, in a very short time, Ratan had got as far as the double consonants.

It seemed as though the showers of the season would never end. Canals, ditches, and hollows were all overflowing with water. Day and night the patter of rain was heard, and the croaking of frogs. The village roads became impassable, and marketing had to be done in punts.

One heavily clouded morning, the postmaster's little pupil had been long waiting outside the door for her call, but, not hearing it as usual, she took up her dog-eared book, and slowly entered the room. She found her master stretched out on his bed, and, thinking that he was resting, she was about to retire on tip-toe, when she suddenly heard her name – "Ratan!" She turned at once and asked: "Were you sleeping, Dada?" The postmaster in a plaintive voice said: "I am not well. Feel my head; is it very hot?"

In the loneliness of his exile, and in the gloom of the rains, his ailing body needed a little tender nursing. He longed to remember the touch on the forehead of soft hands with tinkling bracelets, to imagine the presence of loving womanhood, the nearness of mother and sister. And the exile was not disappointed. Ratan ceased to be a little girl. She at once stepped into the post of mother, called in the village doctor, gave the patient his pills at the proper intervals, sat up all night by his pillow, cooked his gruel for him, and every now and then asked: "Are you feeling a little better, Dada?"

It was some time before the postmaster, with weakened body, was able to leave his sick-bed. "No more of this," said he with decision. "I must get a transfer." He at once wrote off to Calcutta an application for a transfer, on the ground of the unhealthiness of the place.

Relieved from her duties as nurse, Ratan again took up her old place outside the door. But she no longer heard the same old call. She would sometimes peep inside furtively to find the postmaster sitting on his chair, or stretched on his bed, and staring absent-mindedly into the air. While Ratan was awaiting her call, the postmaster was awaiting a reply to his application. The girl read her old lessons over and over again, – her great fear was lest, when the call came, she might be found wanting in the double consonants. At last, after a week, the call did come one evening. With an overflowing heart Ratan rushed into the room with her – "Were you calling me, Dada?"

The postmaster said: "I am going away to-morrow, Ratan."

"Where are you going, Dada?"

"I am going home."

"When will you come back?"

"I am not coming back."

Ratan asked no other question. The postmaster, of his own accord, went on to tell her that his application for a transfer had been rejected, so he had resigned his post and was going home.

For a long time neither of them spoke another word. The lamp went on dimly burning, and from a leak in one corner of the thatch water dripped steadily into an earthen vessel on the floor beneath it.

After a while Ratan rose, and went off to the kitchen to prepare the meal; but she was not so quick about it as on other days. Many new things to think of had entered her little brain. When the postmaster had finished his supper, the girl suddenly asked him: "Dada, will you take me to your home?"

The postmaster laughed. "What an idea!" said he; but he did not think it necessary to explain to the girl wherein lay the absurdity.

That whole night, in her waking and in her dreams, the postmaster's laughing reply haunted her – "What an idea!"

On getting up in the morning, the postmaster found his bath ready. He had stuck to his Calcutta habit of bathing in water drawn and kept in pitchers, instead of taking a plunge in the river as was the custom of the village. For some reason or other, the girl could not ask him about the time of his departure, so she had fetched the water from the river long before sunrise, that it should be ready as early as he might want it. After the bath came a call for Ratan. She entered noiselessly, and looked silently into her master's face for orders. The master said: "You need not be anxious about my going away, Ratan; I shall tell my successor to look after you." These words were kindly meant, no doubt: but inscrutable are the ways of a woman's heart!

Ratan had borne many a scolding from her master without complaint, but these kind words she could not bear. She burst out weeping, and said: "No, no, you need not tell anybody anything at all about me; I don't want to stay on here."

The postmaster was dumbfounded. He had never seen Ratan like this before.

The new incumbent duly arrived, and the postmaster, having given over charge, prepared to depart. Just before starting he called Ratan and said: "Here is something for you; I hope it will keep you for some little time." He brought out from his pocket the whole of his month's salary, retaining only a trifle for his travelling expenses. Then Ratan fell at his feet and cried: "Oh, Dada, I pray you, don't give me anything, don't in any way trouble about me," and then she ran away out of sight.

The postmaster heaved a sigh, took up his carpet bag, put his umbrella over his shoulder, and, accompanied by a man carrying his many-coloured tin trunk, he slowly made for the boat.

When he got in and the boat was under way, and the rain-swollen river, like a stream of tears welling up from the earth, swirled and sobbed at her bows, then he felt a pain at heart; the grief-stricken face of a village girl seemed to represent for him the great unspoken pervading grief of Mother Earth herself. At one time he had an impulse to go back, and bring away along with him that lonesome waif, forsaken of the world. But the wind had just filled the sails, the boat had got well into the middle of the turbulent current, and already the village was left behind, and its outlying burning-ground came in sight.

So the traveller, borne on the breast of the swift-flowing river, consoled himself with philosophical reflections on the numberless meetings and partings going on in the world – on death, the great parting, from which none returns.

But Ratan had no philosophy. She was wandering about the post office in a flood of tears. It may be that she had still a lurking hope in some corner of her heart that her Dada would return, and that is why she could not tear herself away. Alas for our foolish human nature! Its fond mistakes are persistent. The dictates of reason take a long time to assert their own sway. The surest proofs meanwhile are disbelieved. False hope is clung to with all one's might and main, till a day comes when it has sucked the heart dry and it forcibly breaks through its bonds and departs. After that comes the misery of awakening, and then once again the longing to get back into the maze of the same mistakes.

The Cabuliwallah

My five years' old daughter Mini cannot live without chattering. I really believe that in all her life she has not wasted a minute in silence. Her mother is often vexed at this, and would stop her prattle, but I would not. To see Mini quiet is unnatural, and I cannot bear it long. And so my own talk with her is always lively.

One morning, for instance, when I was in the midst of the seventeenth chapter of my new novel, my little Mini stole into the room, and putting her hand into mine, said: "Father! Ramdayal the door-keeper calls a crow a krow! He doesn't know anything, does he?"

Before I could explain to her the differences of language in this world, she was embarked on the full tide of another subject. "What do you think, Father? Bhola says there is an elephant in the clouds, blowing water out of his trunk, and that is why it rains!"

And then, darting off anew, while I sat still making ready some reply to this last saying: "Father! what relation is Mother to you?"

With a grave face I contrived to say: "Go and play with Bhola, Mini! I am busy!"

The window of my room overlooks the road. The child had seated herself at my feet near my table, and was playing softly, drumming on her knees. I was hard at work on my seventeenth chapter, where Pratap Singh, the hero, had just caught Kanchanlata, the heroine, in his arms, and was about to escape with her by the third-story window of the castle, when all of a sudden Mini left her play, and ran to the window, crying: "A Cabuliwallah! a Cabuliwallah!" Sure enough in the street below was a Cabuliwallah, passing slowly along. He wore the loose, soiled clothing of his people, with a tall turban; there was a bag on his back, and he carried boxes of grapes in his hand.

I cannot tell what were my daughter's feelings at the sight of this man, but she began to call him loudly. "Ah!" I thought, "he will come in, and my seventeenth chapter will never be finished!" At which exact moment the Cabuliwallah turned, and looked up at the child. When she saw this, overcome by terror, she fled to her mother's protection and disappeared. She had a blind belief that inside the bag, which the big man carried, there were perhaps two or three other children like herself. The pedlar meanwhile entered my doorway and greeted me with a smiling face.

So precarious was the position of my hero and my heroine, that my first impulse was to stop and buy something, since the man had been called. I made some small purchases, and a conversation began about Abdurrahman, the Russians, the English, and the Frontier Policy.

As he was about to leave, he asked: "And where is the little girl, sir?"

And I, thinking that Mini must get rid of her false fear, had her brought out.

She stood by my chair, and looked at the Cabuliwallah and his bag. He offered her nuts and raisins, but she would not be tempted, and only clung the closer to me, with all her doubts increased.

This was their first meeting.

One morning, however, not many days later, as I was leaving the house, I was startled to find Mini, seated on a bench near the door, laughing and talking, with the great Cabuliwallah at her feet. In all her life, it appeared, my small daughter had never found so patient a listener, save her father. And already the corner of her little sari was stuffed with almonds and raisins, the gift of her visitor. "Why did you give her those?" I said, and taking out an eight-anna bit, I handed it to him. The man accepted the money without demur, and slipped it into his pocket.

Alas, on my return an hour later, I found the unfortunate coin had made twice its own worth of trouble! For the Cabuliwallah had given it to Mini; and her mother, catching sight of the bright round object, had pounced on the child with: "Where did you get that eight-anna bit?"

"The Cabuliwallah gave it me," said Mini cheerfully.

"The Cabuliwallah gave it you!" cried her mother much shocked. "O Mini! how could you take it from him?"

I, entering at the moment, saved her from impending disaster, and proceeded to make my own inquiries.

It was not the first or second time, I found, that the two had met. The Cabuliwallah had overcome the child's first terror by a judicious bribery of nuts and almonds, and the two were now great friends.

They had many quaint jokes, which afforded them much amusement. Seated in front of him, looking down on his gigantic frame in all her tiny dignity, Mini would ripple her face with laughter and begin: "O Cabuliwallah! Cabuliwallah! what have you got in your bag?"

And he would reply, in the nasal accents of the mountaineer: "An elephant!" Not much cause for merriment, perhaps; but how they both enjoyed the fun! And for me, this child's talk with a grown-up man had always in it something strangely fascinating.

Then the Cabuliwallah, not to be behindhand, would take his turn: "Well, little one, and when are you going to the father-in-law's house?"

Now most small Bengali maidens have heard long ago about the father-in-law's house; but we, being a little new-fangled, had kept these things from our child, and Mini at this question must have been a trifle bewildered. But she would not show it, and with ready tact replied: "Are *you* going there?"

Amongst men of the Cabuliwallah's class, however, it is well known that the words *father-in-law's house* have a double meaning. It is a euphemism for *jail*, the place where we are well cared for, at no expense to ourselves. In this sense would the sturdy pedlar take my daughter's question. "Ah," he would say, shaking his fist at an invisible policeman, "I will thrash my father-in-law!" Hearing this, and picturing the poor discomfited relative, Mini would go off into peals of laughter, in which her formidable friend would join.

These were autumn mornings, the very time of year when kings of old went forth to conquest; and I, never stirring from my little corner in Calcutta, would let my mind wander over the whole world. At the very name of another country, my heart would go out to it, and at the sight of a foreigner in the streets, I would fall to weaving a network of dreams – the mountains, the glens, and the forests of his distant home, with his cottage in its setting, and the free and independent life of far-away wilds. Perhaps the scenes of travel conjure themselves up before me and pass and repass in my imagination all the more vividly, because I lead such a vegetable existence that a call to travel would fall upon me like a thunder-bolt. In the presence of this Cabuliwallah I was immediately transported to the foot of arid mountain peaks, with narrow little defiles twisting in and out amongst their towering heights. I could see the string of camels bearing the merchandise, and the company of turbanned merchants carrying some their queer old firearms, and some their spears, journeying downward towards the plains. I could see. But at some such point Mini's mother would intervene, imploring me to "beware of that man."

Mini's mother is unfortunately a very timid lady. Whenever she hears a noise in the street, or sees people coming towards the house, she always jumps to the conclusion that they are either thieves, or drunkards, or snakes, or tigers, or malaria, or cockroaches, or caterpillars. Even after all these years of experience, she is not able to overcome her terror. So she was full of doubts about the Cabuliwallah, and used to beg me to keep a watchful eye on him.

I tried to laugh her fear gently away, but then she would turn round on me seriously, and ask me solemn questions:

Were children never kidnapped?

Was it, then, not true that there was slavery in Cabul?

Was it so very absurd that this big man should be able to carry off a tiny child?

I urged that, though not impossible, it was highly improbable. But this was not enough, and her dread persisted. As it was indefinite, however, it did not seem right to forbid the man the house, and the intimacy went on unchecked.

Once a year in the middle of January Rahmun, the Cabuliwallah, was in the habit of returning to his country, and as the time approached he would be very busy, going from house to house collecting his debts. This year, however, he could always find time to come and see Mini. It would have seemed to an outsider that there was some conspiracy between the two, for when he could not come in the morning, he would appear in the evening.

Even to me it was a little startling now and then, in the corner of a dark room, suddenly to surprise this tall, loose-garmented, much bebagged man; but when Mini would run in smiling, with her "O Cabuliwallah! Cabuliwallah!" and the two friends, so far apart in age, would subside into their old laughter and their old jokes, I felt reassured.

One morning, a few days before he had made up his mind to go, I was correcting my proof sheets in my study. It was chilly weather. Through the window the rays of the sun touched my feet, and the slight warmth was very welcome. It was almost eight o'clock, and the early pedestrians were returning home with their heads covered. All at once I heard an uproar in the street, and, looking out, saw Rahmun being led away bound between two policemen, and behind them a crowd of curious boys. There were blood-stains on the clothes of the Cabuliwallah, and one of the policemen carried a knife. Hurrying out, I stopped them, and inquired what it all meant. Partly from one, partly from another, I gathered that a certain neighbour had owed the pedlar something for a Rampuri shawl, but had falsely denied having bought it, and that in the course of the quarrel Rahmun had struck him. Now, in the heat of his excitement, the prisoner began calling his enemy all sorts of names, when suddenly in a verandah of my house appeared my little Mini, with her usual exclamation: "O Cabuliwallah! Cabuliwallah!" Rahmun's face lighted up as he turned to her. He had no bag under his arm to-day, so she could not discuss the elephant with him. She at once therefore proceeded to the next question: "Are you going to the father-in-law's house?" Rahmun laughed and said: "Just where I am going, little one!" Then, seeing that the reply did not amuse the child, he held up his fettered hands. "Ah!" he said, "I would have thrashed that old father-in-law, but my hands are bound!"

On a charge of murderous assault, Rahmun was sentenced to some years' imprisonment.

Time passed away and he was not remembered. The accustomed work in the accustomed place was ours, and the thought of the once free mountaineer spending his years in prison seldom or never occurred to us. Even my light-hearted Mini, I am ashamed to say, forgot her old friend. New companions filled her life. As she grew older, she spent more of her time with girls. So much time indeed did she spend with them that she came no more, as she used to do, to her father's room. I was scarcely on speaking terms with her.

Years had passed away. It was once more autumn and we had made arrangements for our Mini's marriage. It was to take place during the Puja Holidays. With Durga returning to Kailas, the light of our home also was to depart to her husband's house, and leave her father's in the shadow.

The morning was bright. After the rains, there was a sense of ablution in the air, and the sun-rays looked like pure gold. So bright were they, that they gave a beautiful radiance even to the sordid brick walls of our Calcutta lanes. Since early dawn that day the wedding-pipes had been sounding, and at each beat my own heart throbbed. The wail of the tune, Bhairavi, seemed to intensify my pain at the approaching separation. My Mini was to be married that night.

From early morning noise and bustle had pervaded the house. In the courtyard the canopy had to be slung on its bamboo poles; the chandeliers with their tinkling sound must be hung in each room and verandah. There was no end of hurry and excitement. I was sitting in my study, looking through the accounts, when some one entered, saluting respectfully, and stood before me. It was Rahmun the Cabuliwallah. At first I did not recognise him. He had no bag, nor the long hair, nor the same vigour that he used to have. But he smiled, and I knew him again.

"When did you come, Rahmun?" I asked him.

"Last evening," he said, "I was released from jail."

The words struck harsh upon my ears. I had never before talked with one who had wounded his fellow, and my heart shrank within itself when I realised this; for I felt that the day would have been better-omened had he not turned up.

"There are ceremonies going on," I said, "and I am busy. Could you perhaps come another day?"

At once he turned to go; but as he reached the door he hesitated, and said: "May I not see the little one, sir, for a moment?" It was his belief that Mini was still the same. He had pictured her running to him as she used, calling "O Cabuliwallah! Cabuliwallah!" He had imagined too that they would laugh and talk together, just as of old. In fact, in memory of former days he had brought, carefully wrapped up in paper, a few almonds and raisins and grapes, obtained somehow from a countryman; for his own little fund was dispersed.

I said again: "There is a ceremony in the house, and you will not be able to see any one to-day."

The man's face fell. He looked wistfully at me for a moment, then said "Good morning," and went out.

I felt a little sorry, and would have called him back, but I found he was returning of his own accord. He came close up to me holding out his offerings with the words: "I brought these few things, sir, for the little one. Will you give them to her?"

I took them and was going to pay him, but he caught my hand and said: "You are very kind, sir! Keep me in your recollection. Do not offer me money! – You have a little girl: I too have one like her in my own home. I think of her, and bring fruits to your child – not to make a profit for myself."

Saying this, he put his hand inside his big loose robe, and brought out a small and dirty piece of paper. With great care he unfolded this, and smoothed it out with both hands on my table. It bore the impression of a little hand. Not a photograph. Not a drawing. The impression of an ink-smeared hand laid flat on the paper. This touch of his own little daughter had been always on his heart, as he had come year after year to Calcutta to sell his wares in the streets.

Tears came to my eyes. I forgot that he was a poor Cabuli fruit-seller, while I was - But no, what was I more than he? He also was a father.

That impression of the hand of his little Pārbati in her distant mountain home reminded me of my own little Mini.

I sent for Mini immediately from the inner apartment. Many difficulties were raised, but I would not listen. Clad in the red silk of her wedding-day, with the sandal paste on her forehead, and adorned as a young bride, Mini came, and stood bashfully before me.

The Cabuliwallah looked a little staggered at the apparition. He could not revive their old friendship. At last he smiled and said: "Little one, are you going to your father-in-law's house?"

But Mini now understood the meaning of the word "father-in-law," and she could not reply to him as of old. She flushed up at the question, and stood before him with her bride-like face turned down.

I remembered the day when the Cabuliwallah and my Mini had first met, and I felt sad. When she had gone, Rahmun heaved a deep sigh, and sat down on the floor. The idea had suddenly come to him that his daughter too must have grown in this long time, and that he would have to make friends with her anew. Assuredly he would not find her as he used to know her. And besides, what might not have happened to her in these eight years?

The marriage-pipes sounded, and the mild autumn sun streamed round us. But Rahmun sat in the little Calcutta lane, and saw before him the barren mountains of Afghanistan.

I took out a bank-note and gave it to him, saying: "Go back to your own daughter, Rahmun, in your own country, and may the happiness of your meeting bring good fortune to my child!"

Having made this present, I had to curtail some of the festivities. I could not have the electric lights I had intended, nor the military band, and the ladies of the house were despondent at it. But to me the wedding-feast was all the brighter for the thought that in a distant land a long-lost father met again with his only child.

Subha

When the girl was given the name of Subhashini, who could have guessed that she would prove dumb? Her two elder sisters were Sukeshini and Suhasini, and for the sake of uniformity her father named his youngest girl Subhashini. She was called Subha for short.

Her two elder sisters had been married with the usual cost and difficulty, and now the youngest daughter lay like a silent weight upon the heart of her parents. All the world seemed to think that, because she did not speak, therefore she did not feel; it discussed her future and its own anxiety freely in her presence. She had understood from her earliest childhood that God had sent her like a curse to her father's house, so she withdrew herself from ordinary people and tried to live apart. If only they would all forget her she felt she could endure it. But who can forget pain? Night and day her parents' minds were aching on her account. Especially her mother looked upon her as a deformity in herself. To a mother a daughter is a more closely intimate part of herself than a son can be; and a fault in her is a source of personal shame. Banikantha, Subha's father, loved her rather better than his other daughters; her mother regarded her with aversion as a stain upon her own body.

If Subha lacked speech, she did not lack a pair of large dark eyes, shaded with long lashes; and her lips trembled like a leaf in response to any thought that rose in her mind.

When we express our thought in words, the medium is not found easily. There must be a process of translation, which is often inexact, and then we fall into error. But black eyes need no translating; the mind itself throws a shadow upon them. In them thought opens or shuts, shines forth or goes out in darkness, hangs steadfast like the setting moon or like the swift and restless lightning illumines all quarters of the sky. They who from birth have had no other speech than the trembling of their lips learn a language of the eyes, endless in expression, deep as the sea, clear as the heavens, wherein play dawn and sunset, light and shadow. The dumb have a lonely grandeur like Nature's own. Wherefore the other children almost dreaded Subha and never played with her. She was silent and companionless as noontide.

The hamlet where she lived was Chandipur. Its river, small for a river of Bengal, kept to its narrow bounds like a daughter of the middle class. This busy streak of water never overflowed its banks, but went about its duties as though it were a member of every family in the villages beside it. On either side were houses and banks shaded with trees. So stepping from her queenly throne, the river-goddess became a garden deity of each home, and forgetful of herself performed her task of endless benediction with swift and cheerful foot.

Banikantha's house looked out upon the stream. Every hut and stack in the place could be seen by the passing boatmen. I know not if amid these signs of worldly wealth any one noticed the little girl who, when her work was done, stole away to the waterside and sat there. But here Nature fulfilled her want of speech and spoke for her. The murmur of the brook, the voice of the village folk, the songs of the boatmen, the crying of the birds and rustle of trees mingled and were one with the trembling of her heart. They became one vast wave of sound which beat upon her restless soul. This murmur and movement of Nature were the dumb girl's language; that speech of the dark eyes, which the long lashes shaded, was the language of the world about her. From the trees, where the cicalas chirped, to the quiet stars there was nothing but signs and gestures, weeping and sighing. And in the deep mid-noon, when the boatmen and fisher-folk had gone to their dinner, when the villagers slept and birds were still, when the ferry-boats were idle, when the great busy world paused in its toil and became suddenly a lonely, awful giant, then beneath the vast impressive heavens there were only dumb Nature and a dumb girl, sitting very silent, - one under the spreading sunlight, the other where a small tree cast its shadow.

But Subha was not altogether without friends. In the stall were two cows, Sarbbashi and Panguli. They had never heard their names from her lips, but they knew her footfall. Though she had no words, she murmured lovingly and they understood her gentle murmuring better than all speech. When she fondled them or scolded or coaxed them, they understood her better than men could do. Subha would come to the shed and throw her arms round Sarbbashi's neck; she would rub her cheek against her friend's, and Panguli would turn her great kind eyes and lick her face. The girl paid them three regular visits every day and others that were irregular. Whenever she heard any words that hurt her, she would come to these dumb friends out of due time. It was as though they guessed her anguish of spirit from her quiet look of sadness. Coming close to her, they would rub their horns softly against her arms, and in dumb, puzzled fashion try to comfort her. Besides these two, there were goats and a kitten; but Subha had not the same equality of friendship with them, though they showed the same attachment. Every time it got a chance, night or day, the kitten would jump into her lap, and settle down to slumber, and show its appreciation of an aid to sleep as Subha drew her soft fingers over its neck and back.

Subha had a comrade also among the higher animals, and it is hard to say what were the girl's relations with him; for he could speak, and his gift of speech left them without any common language. He was the youngest boy of the Gosains, Pratap by name, an idle fellow. After long effort, his parents had abandoned the hope that he would ever make his living. Now losels have this advantage, that, though their own folk disapprove of them, they are generally popular with every one else. Having no work to chain them, they become public property. Just as every town needs an open space where all may breathe, so a village needs two or three gentlemen of leisure, who can give time to all; then, if we are lazy and want a companion, one is to hand.

Pratap's chief ambition was to catch fish. He managed to waste a lot of time this way, and might be seen almost any afternoon so employed. It was thus most often that he met Subha. Whatever he was about, he liked a companion; and, when one is catching fish, a silent companion is best of all. Pratap respected Subha for her taciturnity, and, as every one called her Subha, he showed his affection by calling her Su. Subha used to sit beneath a tamarind, and Pratap, a little distance off, would cast his line. Pratap took with him a small allowance of betel, and Subha prepared it for him. And I think that, sitting and gazing a long while, she desired ardently to bring some great help to Pratap, to be of real aid, to prove by any means that she was not a useless burden to the world. But there was nothing to do. Then she turned to the Creator in prayer for some rare power, that by an astonishing miracle she might startle Pratap into exclaiming: "My! I never dreamt our Su could have done this!"

Only think, if Subha had been a water nymph, she might have risen slowly from the river, bringing the gem of a snake's crown to the landing-place. Then Pratap, leaving his paltry fishing, might dive into the lower world, and see there, on a golden bed in a palace of silver, whom else but dumb little Su, Banikantha's child? Yes, our Su, the only daughter of the king of that shining city of jewels! But that might not be, it was impossible. Not that anything is really impossible, but Su had been born, not into the royal house of Patalpur, but into Banikantha's family, and she knew no means of astonishing the Gosains' boy.

Gradually she grew up. Gradually she began to find herself. A new inexpressible consciousness like a tide from the central places of the sea, when the moon is full, swept through her. She saw herself, questioned herself, but no answer came that she could understand.

Once upon a time, late on a night of full moon, she slowly opened her door and peeped out timidly. Nature, herself at full moon, like lonely Subha, was looking down on the sleeping earth. Her strong young life beat within her; joy and sadness filled her being to its brim; she reached the limits even of her own illimitable loneliness, nay, passed beyond them. Her heart was heavy, and she could not speak. At the skirts of this silent troubled Mother there stood a silent troubled girl.

The thought of her marriage filled her parents with an anxious care. People blamed them, and even talked of making them outcasts. Banikantha was well off; they had fish-curry twice daily; and consequently he did not lack enemies. Then the women interfered, and Bani went away for a few days. Presently he returned and said: "We must go to Calcutta."

They got ready to go to this strange country. Subha's heart was heavy with tears, like a mist-wrapt dawn. With a vague fear that had been gathering for days, she dogged her father and mother like a dumb animal. With her large eyes wide open, she scanned their faces as though she wished to learn something. But not a word did they vouchsafe. One afternoon in the midst of all this, as Pratap was fishing, he laughed: "So then, Su, they have caught your bridegroom, and you are going to be married! Mind you don't forget me altogether!" Then he turned his mind again to his fish. As a stricken doe looks in the hunter's face, asking in silent agony: "What have I done to you?" so Subha looked at Pratap. That day she sat no longer beneath her tree. Banikantha, having finished his nap, was smoking in his bedroom when Subha dropped down at his feet

and burst out weeping as she gazed towards him. Banikantha
tried to comfort her, and his cheek grew wet with tears.

It was settled that on the morrow they should go to
Calcutta. Subha went to the cow-shed to bid farewell to her
childhood's comrades. She fed them with her hand; she clasped
their necks; she looked into their faces, and tears fell fast from
the eyes which spoke for her. That night was the tenth of the
moon. Subha left her room, and flung herself down on her
grassy couch beside her dear river. It was as if she threw her
arms about Earth, her strong silent mother, and tried to say:
"Do not let me leave you, mother. Put your arms about me, as I
have put mine about you, and hold me fast."

One day in a house in Calcutta, Subha's mother dressed
her up with great care. She imprisoned her hair, knotting it
up in laces, she hung her about with ornaments, and did her
best to kill her natural beauty. Subha's eyes filled with tears.
Her mother, fearing they would grow swollen with weeping,
scolded her harshly, but the tears disregarded the scolding.
The bridegroom came with a friend to inspect the bride.
Her parents were dizzy with anxiety and fear when they saw
the god arrive to select the beast for his sacrifice. Behind the
stage, the mother called her instructions aloud, and increased
her daughter's weeping twofold, before she sent her into the
examiner's presence. The great man, after scanning her a long
time, observed: "Not so bad."

He took special note of her tears, and thought she must
have a tender heart. He put it to her credit in the account,
arguing that the heart, which to-day was distressed at leaving
her parents, would presently prove a useful possession. Like
the oyster's pearls, the child's tears only increased her value,
and he made no other comment.

The almanac was consulted, and the marriage took place
on an auspicious day. Having delivered over their dumb girl
into another's hands, Subha's parents returned home. Thank
God! Their caste in this and their safety in the next world were

assured! The bridegroom's work lay in the west, and shortly after the marriage he took his wife thither.

In less than ten days every one knew that the bride was dumb! At least, if any one did not, it was not her fault, for she deceived no one. Her eyes told them everything, though no one understood her. She looked on every hand, she found no speech, she missed the faces, familiar from birth, of those who had understood a dumb girl's language. In her silent heart there sounded an endless, voiceless weeping, which only the Searcher of Hearts could hear.

The Castaway

Towards evening the storm was at its height. From the terrific downpour of rain, the crash of thunder, and the repeated flashes of lightning, you might think that a battle of the gods and demons was raging in the skies. Black clouds waved like the Flags of Doom. The Ganges was lashed into a fury, and the trees of the gardens on either bank swayed from side to side with sighs and groans.

In a closed room of one of the riverside houses at Chandernagore, a husband and his wife were seated on a bed spread on the floor, intently discussing. An earthen lamp burned beside them.

The husband, Sharat, was saying: "I wish you would stay on a few days more; you would then be able to return home quite strong again."

The wife, Kiran, was saying: "I have quite recovered already. It will not, cannot possibly, do me any harm to go home now."

Every married person will at once understand that the conversation was not quite so brief as I have reported it. The matter was not difficult, but the arguments for and against did not advance it towards a solution. Like a rudderless boat, the discussion kept turning round and round the same point; and at last threatened to be overwhelmed in a flood of tears.

Sharat said: "The doctor thinks you should stop here a few days longer."

Kiran replied: "Your doctor knows everything!"

"Well," said Sharat, "you know that just now all sorts of illnesses are abroad. You would do well to stop here a month or two more."

"And at this moment I suppose every one in this place is perfectly well!"

What had happened was this: Kiran was a universal favourite with her family and neighbours, so that, when she fell seriously ill, they were all anxious. The village wiseacres thought it shameless for her husband to make so much fuss about a mere wife and even to suggest a change of air, and asked if Sharat supposed that no woman had ever been ill before, or whether he had found out that the folk of the place to which he meant to take her were immortal. Did he imagine that the writ of Fate did not run there? But Sharat and his mother turned a deaf ear to them, thinking that the little life of their darling was of greater importance than the united wisdom of a village. People are wont to reason thus when danger threatens their loved ones. So Sharat went to Chandernagore, and Kiran recovered, though she was still very weak. There was a pinched look on her face which filled the beholder with pity, and made his heart tremble, as he thought how narrowly she had escaped death.

Kiran was fond of society and amusement; the loneliness of her riverside villa did not suit her at all. There was nothing to do, there were no interesting neighbours, and she hated to be busy all day with medicine and dieting. There was no fun in measuring doses and making fomentations. Such was the subject discussed in their closed room on this stormy evening.

So long as Kiran deigned to argue, there was a chance of a fair fight. When she ceased to reply, and with a toss of her head disconsolately looked the other way, the poor man was disarmed. He was on the point of surrendering unconditionally when a servant shouted a message through the shut door.

Sharat got up and on opening the door learnt that a boat had been upset in the storm, and that one of the occupants, a young Brahmin boy, had succeeded in swimming ashore at their garden.

Kiran was at once her own sweet self and set to work to get out some dry clothes for the boy. She then warmed a cup of milk and invited him to her room.

The boy had long curly hair, big expressive eyes, and no sign yet of hair on the face. Kiran, after getting him to drink some milk asked him all about himself.

He told her that his name was Nilkanta, and that he belonged to a theatrical troupe. They were coming to play in a neighbouring villa when the boat had suddenly foundered in the storm. He had no idea what had become of his companions. He was a good swimmer and had just managed to reach the shore.

The boy stayed with them. His narrow escape from a terrible death made Kiran take a warm interest in him. Sharat thought the boy's appearance at this moment rather a good thing, as his wife would now have something to amuse her, and might be persuaded to stay on for some time longer. Her mother-in-law, too, was pleased at the prospect of profiting their Brahmin guest by her kindness. And Nilkanta himself was delighted at his double escape from his master and from the other world, as well as at finding a home in this wealthy family.

But in a short while Sharat and his mother changed their opinion, and longed for his departure. The boy found a secret pleasure in smoking Sharat's hookahs; he would calmly go off in pouring rain with Sharat's best silk umbrella for a stroll through the village, and make friends with all whom he met. Moreover, he had got hold of a mongrel village dog which he petted so recklessly that it came indoors with muddy paws, and left tokens of its visit on Sharat's spotless bed. Then he gathered about him a devoted band of boys of all sorts and sizes, and the result was that not a solitary mango in the neighbourhood had a chance of ripening that season.

There is no doubt that Kiran had a hand in spoiling the boy. Sharat often warned her about it, but she would not listen to him. She made a dandy of him with Sharat's cast-off clothes, and gave him new ones also. And because she felt drawn towards him, and had a curiosity to know more about him, she was constantly calling him to her own room. After her bath and midday meal Kiran would be seated on the bedstead with her betel-leaf box by her side; and while her maid combed and dried her hair, Nilkanta would stand in front and recite pieces out of his repertory with appropriate gesture and song, his elf-locks waving wildly. Thus the long afternoon hours passed merrily away. Kiran would often try to persuade Sharat to sit with her as one of the audience, but Sharat, who had taken a cordial dislike to the boy, refused; nor could Nilkanta do his part half so well when Sharat was there. His mother would sometimes be lured by the hope of hearing sacred names in the recitation; but love of her mid-day sleep speedily overcame devotion, and she lay lapped in dreams.

The boy often got his ears boxed and pulled by Sharat, but as this was nothing to what he had been used to as a member of the troupe, he did not mind it in the least. In his short experience of the world he had come to the conclusion that, as the earth consisted of land and water, so human life was made up of eatings and beatings, and that the beatings largely predominated.

It was hard to tell Nilkanta's age. If it was about fourteen or fifteen, then his face was too old for his years; if seventeen or eighteen, then it was too young. He was either a man too early or a boy too late. The fact was that, joining the theatrical band when very young, he had played the parts of Radhika, Damayanti, and Sita, and a thoughtful Providence so arranged things that he grew to the exact stature that his manager required, and then growth ceased.

Since every one saw how small Nilkanta was, and he himself felt small, he did not receive due respect for his years. Causes, natural and artificial, combined to make him sometimes seem immature for seventeen years, and at other times a mere lad of fourteen but far too knowing even for seventeen. And as no sign of hair appeared on his face, the confusion became greater. Either because he smoked or because he used language beyond his years, his lips puckered into lines that showed him to be old and hard; but innocence and youth shone in his large eyes. I fancy that his heart remained young, but the hot glare of publicity had been a forcing-house that ripened untimely his outward aspect.

In the quiet shelter of Sharat's house and garden at Chandernagore, Nature had leisure to work her way unimpeded. Nilkanta had lingered in a kind of unnatural youth, but now he silently and swiftly overpassed that stage. His seventeen or eighteen years came to adequate revelation. No one observed the change, and its first sign was this, that when Kiran treated him like a boy, he felt ashamed. When the gay Kiran one day proposed that he should play the part of lady's companion, the idea of woman's dress hurt him, though he could not say why. So now, when she called for him to act over again his old characters, he disappeared.

It never occurred to Nilkanta that he was even now not much more than a lad-of-all-work in a strolling company. He even made up his mind to pick up a little education from Sharat's factor. But, because he was the pet of his master's wife, the factor could not endure the sight of him. Also, his restless training made it impossible for him to keep his mind long engaged; sooner or later, the alphabet did a misty dance before his eyes. He would sit long enough with an open book on his lap, leaning against a *champak* bush beside the Ganges. The waves sighed below, boats floated past, birds flitted and twittered restlessly above. What thoughts passed through his mind as he looked down on that book he alone knew, if indeed he did know. He never advanced from one word to another, but the glorious thought, that he was actually reading a book, filled his soul with exultation. Whenever a boat went by, he lifted his book, and pretended to be reading hard, shouting at the top of his voice. But his energy dropped as soon as the audience was gone.

Formerly he sang his songs automatically, but now their tunes stirred in his mind. Their words were of little import and full of trifling alliteration. Even the feeble meaning they had was beyond his comprehension; yet when he sang –

> *Twice-born bird, ah! wherefore stirred*
> *To wrong our royal lady?*
> *Goose, ah, say why wilt thou slay*
> *Her in forest shady?*

then he felt as if transported to another world and to fear other folk. This familiar earth and his own poor life became music, and he was transformed. That tale of the goose and the king's daughter flung upon the mirror of his mind a picture of surpassing beauty. It is impossible to say what he imagined himself to be, but the destitute little slave of the theatrical troupe faded from his memory.

When with evening the child of want lies down, dirty and hungry, in his squalid home, and hears of prince and princess and fabled gold, then in the dark hovel with its dim flickering candle, his mind springs free from its bonds of poverty and misery and walks in fresh beauty and glowing raiment, strong beyond all fear of hindrance, through that fairy realm where all is possible.

Even so, this drudge of wandering players fashioned himself and his world anew, as he moved in spirit amid his songs. The lapping water, rustling leaves, and calling birds; the goddess who had given shelter to him, the helpless, the God-forsaken; her gracious, lovely face, her exquisite arms with their shining bangles, her rosy feet as soft as flower-petals; all these by some magic became one with the music of his song. When the singing ended, the mirage faded, and the Nilkanta of the stage appeared again, with his wild elf-locks. Fresh from the complaints of his neighbour, the owner of the despoiled mango-orchard, Sharat would come and box his ears and cuff him. The boy Nilkanta, the misleader of adoring youths, went forth once more, to make ever new mischief by land and water and in the branches that are above the earth.

Shortly after the advent of Nilkanta, Sharat's younger brother, Satish, came to spend his college vacation with them. Kiran was hugely pleased at finding a fresh occupation. She and Satish were of the same age, and the time passed pleasantly in games and quarrels and reconciliations and laughter and even tears. Suddenly she would clasp him over the eyes from behind with vermilion-stained hands, or she would write "monkey" on his back, or else she would bolt the door on him from the outside amidst peals of laughter. Satish in his turn did not take things lying down; he would steal her keys and rings; he would put pepper among her betel, he would tie her to the bed when she was not looking.

Meanwhile, heaven only knows what possessed poor Nilkanta. He was suddenly filled with a bitterness which he must avenge on somebody or something. He thrashed his devoted boy-followers for no fault, and sent them away crying. He would kick his pet mongrel till it made the skies resound with its whinings. When he went out for a walk, he would litter his path with twigs and leaves beaten from the roadside shrubs with his cane.

Kiran liked to see people enjoying good fare. Nilkanta had an immense capacity for eating, and never refused a good thing however often it was offered. So Kiran liked to send for him to have his meals in her presence, and ply him with delicacies, happy in the bliss of seeing this Brahmin boy eat to satiety. After Satish's arrival she had much less spare time on her hands, and was seldom present when Nilkanta's meals were served. Before, her absence made no difference to the boy's appetite, and he would not rise till he had drained his cup of milk and rinsed it thoroughly with water.

But now, if Kiran was not present to ask him to try this and that, he was miserable, and nothing tasted right. He would get up, without eating much, and say to the serving-maid in a choking voice: "I am not hungry." He thought in imagination that the news of his repeated refusal, "I am not hungry," would reach Kiran; he pictured her concern, and hoped that she would send for him, and press him to eat. But nothing of the sort happened. Kiran never knew and never sent for him; and the maid finished whatever he left. He would then put out the lamp in his room, and throw himself on his bed in the darkness, burying his head in the pillow in a paroxysm of sobs. What was his grievance? Against whom? And from whom did he expect redress? At last, when no one else came, Mother Sleep soothed with her soft caresses the wounded heart of the motherless lad.

Nilkanta came to the unshakable conviction that Satish was poisoning Kiran's mind against him. If Kiran was absent-minded, and had not her usual smile, he would jump to the conclusion that some trick of Satish had made her angry with him. He took to praying to the gods, with all the fervour of his hate, to make him at the next rebirth Satish, and Satish him. He had an idea that a Brahmin's wrath could never be in vain; and the more he tried to consume Satish with the fire of his curses, the more did his own heart burn within him. And upstairs he would hear Satish laughing and joking with his sister-in-law.

Nilkanta never dared openly to show his enmity to Satish. But he would contrive a hundred petty ways of causing him annoyance. When Satish went for a swim in the river, and left his soap on the steps of the bathing-place, on coming back for it he would find that it had disappeared. Once he found his favourite striped tunic floating past him on the water, and thought it had been blown away by the wind.

One day Kiran, desiring to entertain Satish, sent for Nilkanta to recite as usual, but he stood there in gloomy silence. Quite surprised, Kiran asked him what was the matter. But he remained silent. And when again pressed by her to repeat some particular favourite piece of hers, he answered: "I don't remember," and walked away.

At last the time came for their return home. Everybody was busy packing up. Satish was going with them. But to Nilkanta nobody said a word. The question whether he was to go or not seemed to have occurred to nobody.

The subject, as a matter of fact, had been raised by Kiran, who had proposed to take him along with them. But her husband and his mother and brother had all objected so strenuously that she let the matter drop. A couple of days before they were to start, she sent for the boy, and with kind words advised him to go back to his own home.

So many days had he felt neglected that this touch of kindness was too much for him; he burst into tears. Kiran's eyes were also brimming over. She was filled with remorse at the thought that she had created a tie of affection, which could not be permanent.

But Satish was much annoyed at the blubbering of this overgrown boy. "Why does the fool stand there howling instead of speaking?" said he. When Kiran scolded him for an unfeeling creature, he replied: "My dear sister, you do not understand. You are too good and trustful. This fellow turns up from the Lord knows where, and is treated like a king. Naturally the tiger has no wish to become a mouse again. And he has evidently discovered that there is nothing like a tear or two to soften your heart."

Nilkanta hurriedly left the spot. He felt he would like to be a knife to cut Satish to pieces; a needle to pierce him through and through; a fire to burn him to ashes. But Satish was not even scared. It was only his own heart that bled and bled.

Satish had brought with him from Calcutta a grand inkstand. The inkpot was set in a mother-of-pearl boat drawn by a German-silver goose supporting a penholder. It was a great favourite of his, and he cleaned it carefully every day with an old silk handkerchief. Kiran would laugh, and tapping the silver bird's beak would say –

Twice-born bird, ah! wherefore stirred
To wrong our royal lady?

and the usual war of words would break out between her and her brother-in-law.

The day before they were to start, the inkstand was missing and could nowhere be found. Kiran smiled, and said: "Brother-in-law, your goose has flown off to look for your Damayanti."

But Satish was in a great rage. He was certain that Nilkanta had stolen it – for several people said they had seen him prowling about the room the night before. He had the accused brought before him. Kiran also was there. "You have stolen my inkstand, you thief!" he blurted out. "Bring it back at once." Nilkanta had always taken punishment from Sharat, deserved or undeserved, with perfect equanimity. But, when he was called a thief in Kiran's presence, his eyes blazed with a fierce anger, his breast swelled, and his throat choked. If Satish had said another word, he would have flown at him like a wild cat and used his nails like claws.

Kiran was greatly distressed at the scene, and taking the boy into another room said in her sweet, kind way: "Nilu, if you really have taken that inkstand give it to me quietly, and I shall see that no one says another word to you about it." Big tears coursed down the boy's cheeks, till at last he hid his face in his hands, and wept bitterly. Kiran came back from the room and said: "I am sure Nilkanta has not taken the inkstand." Sharat and Satish were equally positive that no other than Nilkanta could have done it.

But Kiran said determinedly: "Never."

Sharat wanted to cross-examine the boy, but his wife refused to allow it.

Then Satish suggested that his room and box should be searched. And Kiran said: "If you dare do such a thing I will never forgive you. You shall not spy on the poor innocent boy." And as she spoke, her wonderful eyes filled with tears. That settled the matter and effectually prevented any further molestation of Nilkanta.

Kiran's heart overflowed with pity at this attempted outrage on a homeless lad. She got two new suits of clothes and a pair of shoes, and with these and a banknote in her hand she quietly went into Nilkanta's room in the evening. She intended to put these parting presents into his box as a surprise. The box itself had been her gift.

From her bunch of keys she selected one that fitted and noiselessly opened the box. It was so jumbled up with odds and ends that the new clothes would not go in. So she thought she had better take everything out and pack the box for him. At first knives, tops, kite-flying reels, bamboo twigs, polished shells for peeling green mangoes, bottoms of broken tumblers and such like things dear to a boy's heart were discovered. Then there came a layer of linen, clean and otherwise. And from under the linen there emerged the missing inkstand, goose and all.

Kiran, with flushed face, sat down helplessly with the inkstand in her hand, puzzled and wondering.

In the meantime, Nilkanta had come into the room from behind without Kiran knowing it. He had seen the whole thing and thought that Kiran had come like a thief to catch him in his thieving, – and that his deed was out. How could he ever hope to convince her that he was not a thief, and that only revenge had prompted him to take the inkstand, which he meant to throw into the river at the first chance? In a weak moment he had put it in the box instead. "He was not a thief," his heart cried out, "not a thief!" Then what was he? What could he say? That he had stolen, and yet he was not a thief? He could never explain to Kiran how grievously wrong she was. And then, how could he bear the thought that she had tried to spy on him?

At last Kiran with a deep sigh replaced the inkstand in the box, and, as if she were the thief herself, covered it up with the linen and the trinkets as they were before; and at the top she placed the presents, together with the banknote which she had brought for him.

The next day the boy was nowhere to be found. The villagers had not seen him; the police could discover no trace of him. Said Sharat: "Now, as a matter of curiosity, let us have a look at his box." But Kiran was obstinate in her refusal to allow that to be done.

She had the box brought up to her own room; and taking out the inkstand alone, she threw it into the river.

The whole family went home. In a day the garden became desolate. And only that starving mongrel of Nilkanta's remained prowling along the river-bank, whining and whining as if its heart would break.

The Hungry Stones

My kinsman and myself were returning to Calcutta from our Puja trip when we met the man in a train. From his dress and bearing we took him at first for an up-country Mahomedan, but we were puzzled as we heard him talk. He discoursed upon all subjects so confidently that you might think the Disposer of All Things consulted him at all times in all that He did. Hitherto we had been perfectly happy, as we did not know that secret and unheard-of forces were at work, that the Russians had advanced close to us, that the English had deep and secret policies, that confusion among the native chiefs had come to a head. But our newly-acquired friend said with a sly smile: "There happen more things in heaven and earth, Horatio, than are reported in your newspapers." As we had never stirred out of our homes before, the demeanour of the man struck us dumb with wonder. Be the topic ever so trivial, he would quote science, or comment on the Vedas, or repeat quatrains from some Persian poet; and as we had no pretence to a knowledge of science or the Vedas or Persian, our admiration for him went on increasing, and my kinsman, a theosophist, was firmly convinced that our fellow-passenger must have been supernaturally inspired by some strange "magnetism" or "occult power," by an "astral body" or something of that kind. He listened to the tritest saying that fell from the lips of our extraordinary companion with devotional rapture, and secretly took down notes of his conversation. I fancy that the extraordinary man saw this, and was a little pleased with it.

When the train reached the junction, we assembled in the waiting room for the connection. It was then 10 P.M., and as the train, we heard, was likely to be very late, owing to something wrong in the lines, I spread my bed on the table and was about to lie down for a comfortable doze, when the extraordinary person deliberately set about spinning the following yarn. Of course, I could get no sleep that night.

When, owing to a disagreement about some questions of administrative policy, I threw up my post at Junagarh, and entered the service of the Nizam of Hydria, they appointed me at once, as a strong young man, collector of cotton duties at Barich.

Barich is a lovely place. The Susta "chatters over stony ways and babbles on the pebbles," tripping, like a skilful dancing girl, in through the woods below the lonely hills. A flight of 150 steps rises from the river, and above that flight, on the river's brim and at the foot of the hills, there stands a solitary marble palace. Around it there is no habitation of man – the village and the cotton mart of Barich being far off.

About 250 years ago the Emperor Mahmud Shah II. had built this lonely palace for his pleasure and luxury. In his days jets of rose-water spurted from its fountains, and on the cold marble floors of its spray-cooled rooms young Persian damsels would sit, their hair dishevelled before bathing, and, splashing their soft naked feet in the clear water of the reservoirs, would sing, to the tune of the guitar, the ghazals of their vineyards.

The fountains play no longer; the songs have ceased; no longer do snow-white feet step gracefully on the snowy marble. It is but the vast and solitary quarters of cess-collectors like us, men oppressed with solitude and deprived of the society of women. Now, Karim Khan, the old clerk of my office, warned me repeatedly not to take up my abode there. "Pass the day there, if you like," said he, "but never stay the night." I passed it off with a light laugh. The servants said that they would work till dark and go away at night. I gave my ready assent. The house had such a bad name that even thieves would not venture near it after dark.

At first the solitude of the deserted palace weighed upon me like a nightmare. I would stay out, and work hard as long as possible, then return home at night jaded and tired, go to bed and fall asleep.

Before a week had passed, the place began to exert a weird fascination upon me. It is difficult to describe or to induce people to believe; but I felt as if the whole house was like a living organism slowly and imperceptibly digesting me by the action of some stupefying gastric juice.

Perhaps the process had begun as soon as I set my foot in the house, but I distinctly remember the day on which I first was conscious of it.

It was the beginning of summer, and the market being dull I had no work to do. A little before sunset I was sitting in an arm-chair near the water's edge below the steps. The Susta had shrunk and sunk low; a broad patch of sand on the other side glowed with the hues of evening; on this side the pebbles at the bottom of the clear shallow waters were glistening. There was not a breath of wind anywhere, and the still air was laden with an oppressive scent from the spicy shrubs growing on the hills close by.

As the sun sank behind the hill-tops a long dark curtain fell upon the stage of day, and the intervening hills cut short the time in which light and shade mingle at sunset. I thought of going out for a ride, and was about to get up when I heard a footfall on the steps behind. I looked back, but there was no one.

As I sat down again, thinking it to be an illusion, I heard many footfalls, as if a large number of persons were rushing down the steps. A strange thrill of delight, slightly tinged with fear, passed through my frame, and though there was not a figure before my eyes, methought I saw a bevy of joyous maidens coming down the steps to bathe in the Susta in that summer evening. Not a sound was in the valley, in the river, or in the palace, to break the silence, but I distinctly heard the maidens' gay and mirthful laugh, like the gurgle of a spring gushing forth in a hundred cascades, as they ran past me, in quick playful pursuit of each other, towards the river, without noticing me at all. As they were invisible to me, so I was, as it were, invisible to them. The river was perfectly calm, but I felt that its still, shallow, and clear waters were stirred suddenly by the splash of many an arm jingling with bracelets, that the girls laughed and dashed and spattered water at one another, that the feet of the fair swimmers tossed the tiny waves up in showers of pearl.

I felt a thrill at my heart – I cannot say whether the excitement was due to fear or delight or curiosity. I had a strong desire to see them more clearly, but naught was visible before me; I thought I could catch all that they said if I only strained my ears; but however hard I strained them, I heard nothing but the chirping of the cicadas in the woods. It seemed as if a dark curtain of 250 years was hanging before me, and I would fain lift a corner of it tremblingly and peer through, though the assembly on the other side was completely enveloped in darkness.

The oppressive closeness of the evening was broken by a sudden gust of wind, and the still surface of the Suista rippled and curled like the hair of a nymph, and from the woods wrapt in the evening gloom there came forth a simultaneous murmur, as though they were awakening from a black dream. Call it reality or dream, the momentary glimpse of that invisible mirage reflected from a far-off world, 250 years old, vanished in a flash. The mystic forms that brushed past me with their quick unbodied steps, and loud, voiceless laughter, and threw themselves into the river, did not go back wringing their dripping robes as they went. Like fragrance wafted away by the wind they were dispersed by a single breath of the spring.

Then I was filled with a lively fear that it was the Muse that had taken advantage of my solitude and possessed me – the witch had evidently come to ruin a poor devil like myself making a living by collecting cotton duties. I decided to have a good dinner – it is the empty stomach that all sorts of incurable diseases find an easy prey. I sent for my cook and gave orders for a rich, sumptuous moghlai dinner, redolent of spices and ghi.

Next morning the whole affair appeared a queer fantasy. With a light heart I put on a sola hat like the sahebs, and drove out to my work. I was to have written my quarterly report that day, and expected to return late; but before it was dark I was strangely drawn to my house – by what I could not say – I felt they were all waiting, and that I should delay no longer. Leaving my report unfinished I rose, put on my sola hat, and startling the dark, shady, desolate path with the rattle of my carriage, I reached the vast silent palace standing on the gloomy skirts of the hills.

On the first floor the stairs led to a very spacious hall, its roof stretching wide over ornamental arches resting on three rows of massive pillars, and groaning day and night under the weight of its own intense solitude. The day had just closed, and the lamps had not yet been lighted. As I pushed the door open a great bustle seemed to follow within, as if a throng of people had broken up in confusion, and rushed out through the doors and windows and corridors and verandas and rooms, to make its hurried escape.

As I saw no one I stood bewildered, my hair on end in a kind of ecstatic delight, and a faint scent of attar and unguents almost effected by age lingered in my nostrils. Standing in the darkness of that vast desolate hall between the rows of those ancient pillars, I could hear the gurgle of fountains plashing on the marble floor, a strange tune on the guitar, the jingle of ornaments and the tinkle of anklets, the clang of bells tolling the hours, the distant note of nahabat, the din of the crystal pendants of chandeliers shaken by the breeze, the song of bulbuls from the cages in the corridors, the cackle of storks in the gardens, all creating round me a strange unearthly music.

Then I came under such a spell that this intangible, inaccessible, unearthly vision appeared to be the only reality in the world – and all else a mere dream. That I, that is to say, Srijut So-and-so, the eldest son of So-and-so of blessed memory, should be drawing a monthly salary of Rs. 450 by the discharge of my duties as collector of cotton duties, and driving in my dog-cart to my office every day in a short coat and soia hat, appeared to me to be such an astonishingly ludicrous illusion that I burst into a horse-laugh, as I stood in the gloom of that vast silent hall.

At that moment my servant entered with a lighted kerosene lamp in his hand. I do not know whether he thought me mad, but it came back to me at once that I was in very deed Srijut So-and-so, son of So-and-so of blessed memory, and that, while our poets, great and small, alone could say whether inside of or outside the earth there was a region where unseen fountains perpetually played and fairy guitars, struck by invisible fingers, sent forth an eternal harmony, this at any rate was certain, that I collected duties at the cotton market at Banch, and earned thereby Rs. 450 per mensem as my salary. I laughed in great glee at my curious illusion, as I sat over the newspaper at my camp-table, lighted by the kerosene lamp.

After I had finished my paper and eaten my moghlai dinner, I put out the lamp, and lay down on my bed in a small side-room. Through the open window a radiant star, high above the Avalli hills skirted by the darkness of their woods, was gazing intently from millions and millions of miles away in the sky at Mr. Collector lying on a humble camp-bedstead. I wondered and felt amused at the idea, and do not knew when I fell asleep or how long I slept; but I suddenly awoke with a start, though I heard no sound and saw no intruder – only the steady bright star on the hilltop had set, and the dim light of the new moon was stealthily entering the room through the open window, as if ashamed of its intrusion.

I saw nobody, but felt as if some one was gently pushing me. As I awoke she said not a word, but beckoned me with her five fingers bedecked with rings to follow her cautiously. I got up noiselessly, and, though not a soul save myself was there in the countless apartments of that deserted palace with its slumbering sounds and waiting echoes, I feared at every step lest any one should wake up. Most of the rooms of the palace were always kept closed, and I had never entered them.

I followed breathless and with silent steps my invisible guide – I cannot now say where. What endless dark and narrow passages, what long corridors, what silent and solemn audience-chambers and close secret cells I crossed!

Though I could not see my fair guide, her form was not invisible to my mind's eye, – an Arab girl, her arms, hard and smooth as marble, visible through her loose sleeves, a thin veil falling on her face from the fringe of her cap, and a curved dagger at her waist! Methought that one of the thousand and one Arabian Nights had been wafted to me from the world of romance, and that at the dead of night I was wending my way through the dark narrow alleys of slumbering Bagdad to a trysting-place fraught with peril.

At last my fair guide stopped abruptly before a deep blue screen, and seemed to point to something below. There was nothing there, but a sudden dread froze the blood in my heart- methought I saw there on the floor at the foot of the screen a terrible negro eunuch dressed in rich brocade, sitting and dozing with outstretched legs, with a naked sword on his lap. My fair guide lightly tripped over his legs and held up a fringe of the screen. I could catch a glimpse of a part of the room spread with a Persian carpet – some one was sitting inside on a bed – I could not see her, but only caught a glimpse of two exquisite feet in gold-embroidered slippers, hanging out from loose saffron-coloured paijamas and placed idly on the orange-coloured velvet carpet. On one side there was a bluish crystal tray on which a few apples, pears, oranges, and bunches of grapes in plenty, two small cups and a gold-tinted decanter were evidently waiting the guest. A fragrant intoxicating vapour, issuing from a strange sort of incense that burned within, almost overpowered my senses.

As with trembling heart I made an attempt to step across the outstretched legs of the eunuch, he woke up suddenly with a start, and the sword fell from his lap with a sharp clang on the marble floor. A terrific scream made me jump, and I saw I was sitting on that camp-bedstead of mine sweating heavily; and the crescent moon looked pale in the morning light like a weary sleepless patient at dawn; and our crazy Meher Ali was crying out, as is his daily custom, "Stand back! Stand back!!" while he went along the lonely road.

Such was the abrupt close of one of my Arabian Nights; but there were yet a thousand nights left.

Then followed a great discord between my days and nights. During the day I would go to my work worn and tired, cursing the bewitching night and her empty dreams, but as night came my daily life with its bonds and shackles of work would appear a petty, false, ludicrous vanity.

After nightfall I was caught and overwhelmed in the snare of a strange intoxication, I would then be transformed into some unknown personage of a bygone age, playing my part in unwritten history; and my short English coat and tight breeches did not suit me in the least. With a red velvet cap on my head, loose paijamas, an embroidered vest, a long flowing silk gown, and coloured handkerchiefs scented with attar, I would complete my elaborate toilet, sit on a high-cushioned chair, and replace my cigarette with a many-coiled narghileh filled with rose-water, as if in eager expectation of a strange meeting with the beloved one.

I have no power to describe the marvellous incidents that unfolded themselves, as the gloom of the night deepened. I felt as if in the curious apartments of that vast edifice the fragments of a beautiful story, which I could follow for some distance, but of which I could never see the end, flew about in a sudden gust of the vernal breeze. And all the same I would wander from room to room in pursuit of them the whole night long.

Amid the eddy of these dream-fragments, amid the smell of henna and the twanging of the guitar, amid the waves of air charged with fragrant spray, I would catch like a flash of lightning the momentary glimpse of a fair damsel. She it was who had saffron-coloured paijamas, white ruddy soft feet in gold-embroidered slippers with curved toes, a close-fitting bodice wrought with gold, a red cap, from which a golden frill fell on her snowy brow and cheeks.

She had maddened me. In pursuit of her I wandered from room to room, from path to path among the bewildering maze of alleys in the enchanted dreamland of the nether world of sleep.

Sometimes in the evening, while arraying myself carefully as a prince of the blood-royal before a large mirror, with a candle burning on either side, I would see a sudden reflection of the Persian beauty by the side of my own. A swift turn of her neck, a quick eager glance of intense passion and pain glowing in her large dark eyes, just a suspicion of speech on her dainty red lips, her figure, fair and slim crowned with youth like a blossoming creeper, quickly uplifted in her graceful tilting gait, a dazzling flash of pain and craving and ecstasy, a smile and a glance and a blaze of jewels and silk, and she melted away. A wild glist of wind, laden with all the fragrance of hills and woods, would put out my light, and I would fling aside my dress and lie down on my bed, my eyes closed and my body thrilling with delight, and there around me in the breeze, amid all the perfume of the woods and hills, floated through the silent gloom many a caress and many a kiss and many a tender touch of hands, and gentle murmurs in my ears, and fragrant breaths on my brow; or a sweetly-perfumed kerchief was wafted again and again on my cheeks. Then slowly a mysterious serpent would twist her stupefying coils about me; and heaving a heavy sigh, I would lapse into insensibility, and then into a profound slumber.

One evening I decided to go out on my horse – I do not know who implored me to stay-but I would listen to no entreaties that day. My English hat and coat were resting on a rack, and I was about to take them down when a sudden whirlwind, crested with the sands of the Susta and the dead leaves of the Avalli hills, caught them up, and whirled them round and round, while a loud peal of merry laughter rose higher and higher, striking all the chords of mirth till it died away in the land of sunset.

I could not go out for my ride, and the next day I gave up my queer English coat and hat for good.

That day again at dead of night I heard the stifled heart-breaking sobs of some one – as if below the bed, below the floor, below the stony foundation of that gigantic palace, from the depths of a dark damp grave, a voice piteously cried and implored me: "Oh, rescue me! Break through these doors of hard illusion, deathlike slumber and fruitless dreams, place by your side on the saddle, press me to your heart, and, riding through hills and woods and across the river, take me to the warm radiance of your sunny rooms above!"

Who am I? Oh, how can I rescue thee? What drowning beauty, what incarnate passion shall I drag to the shore from this wild eddy of dreams? O lovely ethereal apparition! Where didst thou flourish and when? By what cool spring, under the shade of what date-groves, wast thou born – in the lap of what homeless wanderer in the desert? What Bedouin snatched thee from thy mother's arms, an opening bud plucked from a wild creeper, placed thee on a horse swift as lightning, crossed the burning sands, and took thee to the slave-market of what royal city? And there, what officer of the Badshah, seeing the glory of thy bashful blossoming youth, paid for thee in gold, placed thee in a golden palanquin, and offered thee as a present for the seraglio of his master? And O, the history of that place! The music of the sareng, the jingle of anklets, the occasional flash of daggers and the glowing wine of Shiraz poison, and the piercing flashing glance! What infinite grandeur, what endless servitude!

The slave-girls to thy right and left waved the chamar as diamonds flashed from their bracelets; the Badshah, the king of kings, fell on his knees at thy snowy feet in bejewelled shoes, and outside the terrible Abyssinian eunuch, looking like a messenger of death, but clothed like an angel, stood with a naked sword in his hand! Then, O, thou flower of the desert, swept away by the blood-stained dazzling ocean of grandeur, with its foam of jealousy, its rocks and shoals of intrigue, on what shore of cruel death wast thou cast, or in what other land more splendid and more cruel?

Suddenly at this moment that crazy Meher Ali screamed out: "Stand back! Stand back!! All is false! All is false!!" I opened my eyes and saw that it was already light. My chaprasi came and handed me my letters, and the cook waited with a salam for my orders.

I said; "No, I can stay here no longer." That very day I packed up, and moved to my office. Old Karim Khan smiled a little as he saw me. I felt nettled, but said nothing, and fell to my work.

As evening approached I grew absent-minded; I felt as if I had an appointment to keep; and the work of examining the cotton accounts seemed wholly useless; even the Nizamat of the Nizam did not appear to be of much worth. Whatever belonged to the present, whatever was moving and acting and working for bread seemed trivial, meaningless, and contemptible.

I threw my pen down, closed my ledgers, got into my dog-cart, and drove away. I noticed that it stopped of itself at the gate of the marble palace just at the hour of twilight. With quick steps I climbed the stairs, and entered the room.

A heavy silence was reigning within. The dark rooms were looking sullen as if they had taken offence. My heart was full of contrition, but there was no one to whom I could lay it bare, or of whom I could ask forgiveness. I wandered about the dark rooms with a vacant mind. I wished I had a guitar to which I could sing to the unknown: "O fire, the poor moth that made a vain effort to fly away has come back to thee! Forgive it but this once, burn its wings and consume it in thy flame!"

Suddenly two tear-drops fell from overhead on my brow. Dark masses of clouds overcast the top of the Avalli hills that day. The gloomy woods and the sooty waters of the Susta were waiting in terrible suspense and in an ominous calm. Suddenly land, water, and sky shivered, and a wild tempest-blast rushed howling through the distant pathless woods, showing its lightning-teeth like a raving maniac who had broken his chains. The desolate halls of the palace banged their doors, and moaned in the bitterness of anguish.

The servants were all in the office, and there was no one to light the lamps. The night was cloudy and moonless. In the dense gloom within I could distinctly feel that a woman was lying on her face on the carpet below the bed – clasping and tearing her long dishevelled hair with desperate fingers. Blood was tricking down her fair brow, and she was now laughing a hard, harsh, mirthless laugh, now bursting into violent wringing sobs, now rending her bodice and striking at her bare bosom, as the wind roared in through the open window, and the rain poured in torrents and soaked her through and through.

All night there was no cessation of the storm or of the passionate cry. I wandered from room to room in the dark, with unavailing sorrow. Whom could I console when no one was by? Whose was this intense agony of sorrow? Whence arose this inconsolable grief?

And the mad man cried out: "Stand back! Stand back!! All is false! All is false!!"

I saw that the day had dawned, and Meher Ali was going round and round the palace with his usual cry in that dreadful weather. Suddenly it came to me that perhaps he also had once lived in that house, and that, though he had gone mad, he came there every day, and went round and round, fascinated by the weird spell cast by the marble demon.

Despite the storm and rain I ran to him and asked: "Ho, Meher Ali, what is false?"

The man answered nothing, but pushing me aside went round and round with his frantic cry, like a bird flying fascinated about the jaws of a snake, and made a desperate effort to warn himself by repeating: "Stand back! Stand back!! All is false! All is false!!"

I ran like a mad man through the pelting rain to my office, and asked Karim Khan: "Tell me the meaning of all this!"

What I gathered from that old man was this: That at one time countless unrequited passions and unsatisfied longings and lurid flames of wild blazing pleasure raged within that palace, and that the curse of all the heart-aches and blasted hopes had made its every stone thirsty and hungry, eager to swallow up like a famished ogress any living man who might chance to approach. Not one of those who lived there for three consecutive nights could escape these cruel jaws, save Meher Ali, who had escaped at the cost of his reason.

I asked: "Is there no means whatever of my release?" The old man said: "There is only one means, and that is very difficult. I will tell you what it is, but first you must hear the history of a young Persian girl who once lived in that pleasure-dome. A stranger or a more bitterly heart-rending tragedy was never enacted on this earth."

Just at this moment the coolies announced that the train was coming. So soon? We hurriedly packed up our luggage, as the tram steamed in. An English gentleman, apparently just aroused from slumber, was looking out of a first-class carriage endeavouring to read the name of the station. As soon as he caught sight of our fellow-passenger, he cried, "Hallo," and took him into his own compartment. As we got into a second-class carriage, we had no chance of finding out who the man was nor what was the end of his story.

I said; "The man evidently took us for fools and imposed upon us out of fun. The story is pure fabrication from start to finish." The discussion that followed ended in a lifelong rupture between my theosophist kinsman and myself.

The Son of Rashmani

I

Kalipada's mother was Rashmani, but she had to do the duty of the father as well, because when both of the parents are "mother" then it is bad for the child. Bhavani, her husband, was wholly incapable of keeping his children under discipline. To know why he was bent on spoiling his son, you must hear something of the former history of the family.

Bhavani was born in the famous house of Saniari. His father, Abhaya Charan, had a son, Shyama Charan, by his first wife. When he married again after her death he had himself passed the marriageable age, and his new father-in-law took advantage of the weakness of his position to have a special portion of his estate settled on his daughter. In this way he was satisfied that proper provision had been made, if his daughter should become a widow early in life. She would be independent of the charity of Shyama Charan.

The first part of his anticipation came true. For very soon after the birth of a son, whom she called Bhavani, Abhaya Charan died. It gave the father-in-law great peace and consolation, as he looked forward to his own death, to know that his daughter was properly looked after.

Shyama Charan was quite grown up. In fact his own eldest boy was a year older than Bhavani. He brought up the latter with his own son. In doing this he never took a farthing from the property allotted to his step-mother, and every year he got a receipt from her after submitting detailed accounts. His honesty in this affair surprised the neighbourhood. In fact they thought that such honesty was another name for foolishness. They did not like the idea of a division being made in the undivided ancestral property. If Shyama Charan in some underhand manner had been able to annul the dowry, his neighbours would have admired his sagacity; and there were good advisers ready to hand who could have rendered him material aid in the attainment of such an object. But Shyama Charan, in spite of the risk of crippling his patrimony, strictly set aside the dowry which came to the share of his step-mother; and the widow, Vraja Sundari, being naturally affectionate and trustful, had every confidence in Shyama Charan whom she trusted as her own son. More than once she had chided him for being so particular about her portion of the property. She would tell him that, as she was not going to take her property with her when she died, and as it would in any case revert to the family, it was not necessary to be so very strict about rendering accounts. But he never listened to her.

Shyama Charan was a severe disciplinarian by habit and his children were perfectly aware of the fact. But Bhavani had every possible freedom, and this gave rise to the impression that he was more partial to his step-brother than to his own sons. But Bhavani's education was sadly neglected and he completely relied on Shyama Charan for the management of his share of the property. He merely had to sign documents occasionally without ever spending a thought on their contents. On the other hand, Tarapada, the eldest son of Shyama Charan, was quite an expert in the management of the estate, having to act as an assistant to his father.

After the death of Shyama Charan, Tarapada said to Bhavani, "Uncle, we must not live together as we have done for so long, because some trifling misunderstanding may come at any moment and cause utter disruption."

Bhavani never imagined, even in his dream, that a day might come when he would have to manage his own affairs. The world in which he had been born and bred ever appeared to him complete and entire in itself. It was an incomprehensible calamity to him that there could be a dividing line somewhere and that this world of his could be split into two. When he found that Tarapada was immovable and indifferent to the grief and dishonour that such a step would bring to the family, he began to rack his brain to find out how the property could be divided with the least possible strain.

Tarapada showed surprise at his uncle's anxiety and said that there was no need to trouble about this, because the division had already been made in the life-time of his grandfather. Bhavani said in amazement, "But I know nothing of this!" Tarapada said in answer, "Then you must be the only one in the whole neighbourhood who does not. For, lest there should be ruinous litigation after he had gone, my grandfather had already given a portion of the property to your mother." Bhavani thought this not unlikely and asked, "What about the house?" Tarapada said, "If you wish, you can keep this house to yourself and we shall be contented with the other house in the district town."

As Bhavani had never been to this town-house, he had neither knowledge of it, nor affection for it. He was astounded at the magnanimity of Tarapada for so easily relinquishing his right to the house in the village where they had been brought up. But when Bhavani told everything to his mother, she struck her forehead with her hand and said: "This is preposterous! What I got from my husband was my own dowry and its income is very small. I do not see why you should be deprived of your share in your father's property."

Bhavani said, "Tarapada is quite positive that his grandfather never gave us any thing except this land."

Vraja Sundari was astonished and informed her son that her husband had made two copies of his will, one of which was still lying in her own box. The box was opened and it was found that there was only the deed of gift for the property belonging to the mother and nothing else. The copy of the will had been taken out.

The help of advisers was sought. The man who came to their rescue was Bagala, the son of their family *guru*. It was the profession of the father to look after the spiritual needs of the village; the material side was left to the son. The two of them had divided between themselves the other world and this. Whatever might be the result for others, they themselves had nothing to suffer from this division. Bagala said that, even if the will was missing, the shares in the ancestral property must be equal, as between the brothers.

Just at this time, a copy of a will made its appearance supporting the claims of the other side. In this document there was no mention of Bhavani and the whole property was given to the grandsons at the time when no son was born to Bhavani. With Bagala as his captain Bhavani set out on his voyage across the perilous sea of litigation. When his vessel at last reached harbour his funds were nearly exhausted and the ancestral property was in the hands of the other party. The land which was given to his mother had dwindled to such an extent, that it could barely give them shelter, or keep up the family dignity. Then Tarapada went away to the district town and they never met again.

II

Shyama Charan's treachery pierced the heart of the widow like an assassin's knife. To the end of her life, almost every day she would heave a sigh and say that God would never suffer such an injustice to be done. She was quite firm in her faith when she said to Bhavani, "I do not know your law or your law courts, but I am certain that my husband's true will and testament will someday be recovered. You will find it again."

Because Bhavani was helpless in worldly matters such assurances as these gave him great consolation. He settled down in his inactivity, certain in his own mind that his pious mother's prophecy could never remain unfulfilled. After his mother's death his faith became all the stronger, since the memory of her piety acquired greater radiance through death's mystery. He felt quite unconcerned about the stress of their poverty which became more and more formidable as the years went by. The necessities of life and the maintenance of family traditions, – these seemed to him like play acting on a temporary stage, not real things. When his former expensive clothing was outworn and he had to buy cheap materials in the shop, this amused him almost like a joke. He smiled and said to himself, – "These people do not know that this is only a passing phase of my fortune. Their surprise will be all the greater, when some day I shall celebrate the Puja Festival with unwonted magnificence."

This certainty of future prodigality was so clear to his mind's eye that present penury escaped his attention. His servant, Noto, was the principal companion with whom he had discussions about these things. They used to have animated conversations, in which sometimes his opinion differed from his master's, as to the propriety of bringing down a theatrical troupe from Calcutta for these future occasions. Noto used to get reprimands from Bhavani for his natural miserliness in these items of future expenditure.

While Bhavani's one anxiety was about the absence of an heir, who could inherit his vast possible wealth, a son was born to him. The horoscope plainly indicated that the lost property would come back to this boy.

From the time of the birth of his son, Bhavani's attitude was changed. It became cruelly difficult for him now to bear his poverty with his old amused equanimity, because he felt that he had a duty towards this new representative of the illustrious house of Saniari, who had such a glorious future before him. That the traditional extravagance could not be maintained on the occasion of the birth of his child gave him the keenest sorrow. He felt as if he were cheating his own son. So he compensated his boy with an inordinate amount of spoiling.

Bhavani's wife, Rashmani, had a different temperament from her husband. She never felt any anxiety about the family traditions of the Chowdhuris of Saniari. Bhavani was quite aware of the fact and indulgently smiled to himself, as though nothing better could be expected from a woman who came from a Vaishnava family of very humble lineage. Rashmani frankly acknowledged that she could not share the family sentiments: what concerned her most was the welfare of her own child.

There was hardly an acquaintance in the neighbourhood with whom Bhavani did not discuss the question of the lost will; but he never spoke a word about it to his wife. Once or twice he had tried, but her perfect unconcern had made him drop the subject. She neither paid attention to the past greatness of the family, nor to its future glories, – she kept her mind busy with the actual necessities of the present, and those necessities were not small in number or quality.

When the Goddess of Fortune deserts a house, she usually leaves some of her burdens behind, and this ancient family was still encumbered with its host of dependents, though its own shelter was nearly crumbling to dust. These parasites take it to be an insult if they are asked to do any service. They get head-aches at the least touch of the kitchen smoke. They are visited with sudden rheumatism the moment they are asked to run errands. Therefore all the responsibilities of maintaining the family were laid upon Rashmani herself. Women lose their delicacy of refinement, when they are compelled night and day to haggle with their destiny over things which are pitifully small, and for this they are blamed by those for whom they toil.

Besides her household affairs Rashmani had to keep all the accounts of the little landed property which remained and also to make arrangements for collecting rents. Never before was the estate managed with such strictness. Bhavani had been quite incapable of collecting his dues: Rashmani never made any remission of the least fraction of rent. The tenants, and even her own agents, reviled her behind her back for the meanness of the family from which she came. Even her husband occasionally used to enter his protest against the harsh economy which went against the grain of the world-famed house of Saniari.

Rashmani quite ungrudgingly took the blame of all this upon herself and openly confessed the poverty of her parents. Tying the end of her *sari* tightly round her waist she went on with her household duties in her own vigorous fashion and made herself thoroughly disagreeable both to the inmates of the house and to her neighbours. But nobody ever had the courage to interfere. Only one thing she carefully avoided. She never asked her husband to help her in any work and she was nervously afraid of his taking up any responsibilities. Indeed she was always furiously engaged in keeping her husband idle; and because he had received the best possible training in this direction she was wholly successful in her mission.

Rashmani had attained middle age before her son came. Up to this time all the pent-up tenderness of the mother in her and all the love of the wife had their centre of devotion in this simple-hearted good-for-nothing husband. Bhavani was a child grown up by mistake beyond its natural age. This was the reason why, after the death of her husband's mother, she had to assume the position of mother and mistress in one.

In order to protect her husband from invasions of Bagala, the son of the *guru*, and other calamities, Rashmani adopted such a stern demeanour, that the companions of her husband used to be terribly afraid of her. She never had the opportunity, which a woman usually has, of keeping her fierceness hidden and of softening the keen edge of her words, – maintaining a dignified reserve towards men such as is proper for a woman.

Bhavani meekly accepted his wife's authority with regard to himself, but it became extremely hard for him to obey her when it related to Kalipada, his son. The reason was, that Rashmani never regarded Bhavani's son from the point of view of Bhavani himself. In her heart she pitied her husband and said, "Poor man, it was no fault of his, but his misfortune, to be born into a rich family." That is why she never could expect her husband to be deprived of any comfort to which he had been accustomed. Whatever might be the condition of the household finance, she tried hard to keep him in his habitual ease and luxury. Under her regime all expense was strictly limited except in the case of Bhavani. She would never allow him to notice if some inevitable gap occurred in the preparation of his meals or his apparel. She would blame some imaginary dog for spoiling dishes that were never made and would blame herself for her carelessness. She would attack Noto for letting some fictitious article of dress be stolen or lost. This had the usual effect of rousing Bhavani's sympathy on behalf of his favourite servant and he would take up his defence. Indeed it had often happened that Bhavani had confessed with bare-faced shamelessness that he had used the dress which had never been bought, and for whose loss Noto was blamed; but what happened afterwards, he had not the power to invent and was obliged to rely upon the fertile imagination of his wife who was also the accuser!

Thus Rashmani treated her husband, but she never put her son in the same category. For he was her own child and why should he be allowed to give himself airs? Kalipada had to be content for his breakfast with a few handfuls of puffed rice and some treacle. During the cold weather he had to wrap his body as well as his head with a thick rough cotton *chaddar*. She would call his teacher before her and warn him never to spare her boy, if he was the least neglectful with his lessons. This treatment of his own son was the hardest blow that Bhavani Charan suffered since the days of his destitution. But as he had always acknowledged defeat at the hands of the powerful, he had not the spirit to stand up against his wife in her method of dealing with the boy.

The dress which Rashmani provided for her son, during the Puja festivities, was made of such poor material that in former days the very servants of the house would have rebelled if it had been offered to them. But Rashmani more than once tried her best to explain to her husband that Kalipada, being the most recent addition to the Chowdhuri family, had never known their former splendour and so was quite glad to get what was given to him. But this pathetic innocence of the boy about his own destiny hurt Bhavani more than anything else, and he could not forgive himself for deceiving the child. When Kalipada would dance for joy and rush to him to show him some present from his mother, which was ridiculously trivial, Bhavani's heart would suffer torture.

Bagala, the *guru's* son, was now in an affluent condition owing to his agency in the law suit which had brought about the ruin of Bhavani. With the money which he had in hand he used to buy cheap tinsel wares from Calcutta before the Puja holidays. Invisible ink, – absurd combinations of stick, fishing-rod and umbrella, – letter-paper with pictures in the corner, – silk fabrics bought at auctions, and other things of this kind, attractive to the simple villagers, – these were his stock in trade. All the forward young men of the village vied with one another in rising above their rusticity by purchasing these sweepings of the Calcutta market which, they were told, were absolutely necessary for the city gentry.

Once Bagala had bought a wonderful toy, – a doll in the form of a foreign woman, – which, when wound up, would rise from her chair and begin to fan herself with sudden alacrity. Kalipada was fascinated by it. He had a very good reason to avoid asking his mother about the toy; so he went straight to his father and begged him to purchase it for him. Bhavani answered "yes" at once, but when he heard the price his face fell. Rashmani kept all the money and he went to her as a timid beggar. He began with all sorts of irrelevant remarks and then took a desperate plunge into the subject with startling incoherence.

Rashmani briefly remarked: "Are you mad?" Bhavani Charan sat silent revolving in his mind what to say next.

"Look here," he exclaimed, "I don't think I need milk pudding daily with my dinner."

"Who told you?" said Rashmani sharply.

"The doctor says it's very bad for biliousness."

"The doctor's a fool!"

"But I'm sure that rice agrees with me better than your *luchis*. They are too indigestible."

"I've never seen the least sign of indigestion in you. You have been accustomed to them all your life!"

Bhavani Charan was ready enough to make sacrifices, but there his passage was barred. Butter might rise in price, but the number of his *luchis* never diminished. Milk was quite enough for him at his midday meal, but curds also had to be supplied because that was the family tradition. Rashmani could not have borne seeing him sit down to his meal, if curds were not supplied. Therefore all his attempts to make a breach in his daily provisions, through which the fanning foreign woman might enter, were an utter failure.

Then Bhavani paid a visit to Bagala for no reason whatever, and after a great deal of round about talk asked concerning the foreign doll. Of course his straightened circumstances had long been known to Bagala, yet it was a perfect misery to Bhavani to have to hesitate to buy this doll for his son owing to want of ready money. Swallowing his pride, he brought out from under his arm an expensive old Kashmir shawl, and said in a husky voice: "My circumstances are bad just at present and I haven't got much cash. So I have determined to mortgage this shawl and buy that doll for Kalipada."

If the object offered had been less expensive than this Kashmir shawl, Bagala would at once have closed the bargain. But knowing that it would not be possible for him to take possession of this shawl in face of the village opinion, and still more in face of Rashmani's watchfulness, he refused to accept it; and Bhavani had to go back home disappointed with the Kashmir shawl hidden under his arm.

Kalipada asked every day for that foreign fanning toy, and Bhavani smiled every day and said, – "Wait, a bit, my boy, till the seventh day of the moon comes round." But every new day it became more and more difficult to keep up that smile.

On the fourth day of the moon Bhavani made a sudden inroad upon his wife and said:

"I've noticed that there's something wrong with Kalipada, – something the matter with his health."

"Nonsense," said Rashmani, "he's in the best of health."

"Haven't you noticed him sitting silent for hours together?"

"I should be very greatly relieved if he could sit still for as many minutes."

When all his arrows had missed their mark, and no impression had been made, Bhavani Charan heaved a deep sigh and passing his fingers through his hair went away and sat down on the verandah and began to smoke with fearful assiduity.

On the fifth day, at his morning meal, Bhavani passed by the curds and the milk pudding without touching them. In the evening he simply took one single piece of *sandesh*. The *luchis* were left unheeded. He complained of want of appetite. This time a considerable breach was made in the fortifications.

On the sixth day, Rashmani took Kalipada into the room and sweetly calling him by his pet name said, "Betu, you are old enough to know that it is the halfway house to stealing to desire that which you can't have."

Kalipada whimpered and said, "What do I know about it? Father promised to give me that doll."

Rashmani sat down to explain to him how much lay behind his father's promise, – how much pain, how much affection, how much loss and privation. Rashmani had never in her life before talked thus to Kalipada, because it was her habit to give short and sharp commands. It filled the boy with amazement when he found his mother coaxing him and explaining things at such a length, and mere child though he was, he could fathom something of the deep suffering of his mother's heart. Yet at the same time it will be easily understood, that it was hard for this boy to turn his mind away altogether from that captivating foreign fanning woman. He pulled a long face and began to scratch the ground.

This made Rashmani's heart at once hard, and she said in her severe tone: "Yes, you may weep and cry, or become angry, but you shall never get that which is not for you to have." And she hastened away without another word.

Kalipada went out. Bhavani Charan was still smoking his hookah. Noticing Kalipada from a distance he got up and walked in the opposite direction as if he had some urgent business. Kalipada ran to him and said, – "But that doll?" Bhavani could not raise a smile that day. He put his arm round Kalipada's neck and said:

"Baba, wait a little. I have some pressing business to get through. Let me finish it first, and then we will talk about it." Saying this, he went out of his house.

Kalipada saw him brush a tear from his eyes. He stood at the door and watched his father, and it was quite evident, even to this boy, that he was going nowhere in particular, and that he was dragging the weight of a despair which could not be relieved.

Kalipada at once went back to his mother and said:

"Mother, I don't want that foreign doll."

That morning Bhavani Charan returned late. When he sat down to his meal, after his bath, it was quite evident, by the look on his face, that the curds and the milk pudding would fare no better with him than on the day before, and that the best part of the fish would go to the cat.

Just at this critical juncture Rashmani brought in a card-board box, bound round with twine, and set it before her husband. Her intention had been to reveal the mystery of this packet to her husband when he went to take his nap after his meal. But in order to remove the undeserved neglect of the curds and the milk and the fish, she had to disclose its contents before the time. So the foreign doll came out of the box and without more ado began to fan itself vigorously.

After this, the cat had to go away disappointed. Bhavani remarked to his wife that the cooking was the best he had ever tasted. The fish soup was incomparable: the curds had set themselves with an exactness that was rarely attained, and the milk pudding was superb.

On the seventh day of the moon, Kalipada got the toy for which he had been pining. During the whole of that day he allowed the foreigner to go on fanning herself and thereby made his boy companions jealous. In any other case this performance would have seemed to him monotonously tiresome, but knowing that on the following day he would have to give the toy back, his constancy to it on that single occasion remained unabated. At the rental of two rupees per diem Rashmani had hired it from Bagala.

On the eighth day of the moon, Kalipada heaved a deep sigh and returned the toy, along with the box and twine, to Bagala with his own hands. From that day forward Kalipada began to share the confidences of his mother, and it became so absurdly easy for Bhavani to give expensive presents every year, that it surprised even himself.

When, with the help of his mother, Kalipada came to know that nothing in this world could be gained without paying for it with the inevitable price of suffering, he rapidly grew up in his mind and became a valued assistant to his mother in her daily tasks. It come to be a natural rule of life with him that no one should add to the burden of the world, but that each should try to lighten it.

When Kalipada won a scholarship at the Vernacular examination, Bhavani proposed that he should give up his studies and take in hand the supervision of the estate. Kalipada went to his mother and said, – "I shall never be a man, if I do not complete my education."

The mother said, – "You are right, Baba, you must go to Calcutta."

Kalipada explained to her that it would not be necessary to spend a single pice on him; his scholarship would be sufficient, and he would try to get some work to supplement it.

But it was necessary to convince Bhavani of the wisdom of the course. Rashmani did not wish to employ the argument that there was very little of the estate remaining to require supervision; for she knew how it would hurt him. She said that Kalipada must become a man whom everyone could respect. But all the members of the Chowdhuri family had attained their respectability without ever going a step outside the limits of Saniari. The outer world was as unknown to them as the world beyond the grave. Bhavani, therefore, could not conceive how anybody could think of a boy like Kalipada going to Calcutta. But the cleverest man in the village, Bagala, fortunately agreed with Rashmani.

"It is perfectly clear," he said, "that, one day, Kalipada will become a lawyer; and then he will set matters right concerning the property of which the family has been deprived."

This was a great consolation to Bhavani Charan and he brought out the file of records about the theft of the will and tried to explain the whole thing to Kalipada by dint of daily discussion. But his son was lacking in proper enthusiasm and merely echoed his father's sentiment about this solemn wrong.

The day before Kalipada's departure for Calcutta Rashmani hung round his neck an amulet containing some mantras to protect him from evils. She gave him at the same time a fifty-rupee currency note, advising him to keep it for any special emergency. This note, which was the symbol of his mother's numberless daily acts of self-denial, was the truest amulet of all for Kalipada. He determined to keep it by him and never to spend it, whatever might happen.

III

From this time onward the old interminable discussions about the theft of the will became less frequent on the part of Bhavani. His one topic of conversation was the marvellous adventure of Kalipada in search of his education. Kalipada was actually engaged in his studies in the city of Calcutta! Kalipada knew Calcutta as well as the palm of his hand! Kalipada had been the first to hear the great news that another bridge was going to be built over the Ganges near Hughli! The day on which the father received his son's letter, he would go to every house in the village to read it to his neighbours and he would hardly find time even to take his spectacles from his nose. On arriving at a fresh house he would remove them from their case with the utmost deliberation; then he would wipe them carefully with the end of his *dhoti*; then, word by word, he would slowly read the letter through to one neighbour after another, with something like the following comment: –

"Brother, just listen! What *is* the world coming to? Even the dogs and the jackals are to cross the holy Ganges without washing the dust from their feet! Who could imagine such a sacrilege?"

No doubt it was very deplorable; but all the same it gave Bhavani Charan a peculiar pleasure to communicate at first hand such important news from his own son's letter, and this more than compensated for the spiritual disaster which must surely overtake the numberless creatures of this present age. To everyone he met he solemnly nodded his head and prophesied that the days were soon coming when Mother Ganges would disappear altogether; all the while cherishing the hope that the news of such a momentous event would come to him by letter from his own son in the proper time.

Kalipada, with very great difficulty, scraped together just enough money to pay his expenses till he passed his Matriculation and again won a scholarship. Bhavani at once made up his mind to invite all the village to a feast, for he imagined that his son's good ship of fortune had now reached its haven and there would be no more occasion for economy. But he received no encouragement from Rashmani.

Kalipada was fortunate enough to secure a place of study in a students' lodging house near his college. The proprietor allowed him to occupy a small room on the ground floor which was absolutely useless for other lodgers. In exchange for this and his board, he had to coach the son of the owner of the house. The one great advantage was that there would be no chance of any fellow lodger ever sharing his quarters. So, although ventilation was lacking, his studies were uninterrupted.

Those of the students who paid their rent and lived in the upper story had no concern with Kalipada; but soon it became painfully evident that those who are up above have the power to hurl missiles at those below with all the more deadly force because of their distance. The leader of those above was Sailen.

Sailen was the scion of a rich family. It was unnecessary for him to live in a students' mess, but he successfully convinced his guardians that this would be best for his studies. The real reason was that Sailen was naturally fond of company, and the students' lodging house was an ideal place where he could have all the pleasure of companionship without any of its responsibilities. It was the firm conviction of Sailen that he was a good fellow and a man of feeling. The advantage of harbouring such a conviction was that it needed no proof in practice. Vanity is not like a horse or an elephant requiring expensive fodder.

Nevertheless, as Sailen had plenty of money he did not allow his vanity merely to graze at large; he took special pride in keeping it stall-fed. It must be said to his credit that he had a genuine desire to help people in their need, but the desire in him was of such a character, that if a man in difficulty refused to come to him for help, he would turn round on him and do his best to add to his trouble. His mess mates had their tickets for the theatre bought for them by Sailen, and it cost them nothing to have occasional feasts. They could borrow money from him without meaning to pay it back. When a newly married youth was in doubt about the choice of some gift for his wife, he could fully rely on Sailen's good taste in the matter. On these occasions the love-lorn youth would take Sailen to the shop and pretend to select the cheapest and least suitable presents: then Sailen, with a contemptuous laugh would intervene and select the right thing. At the mention of the price the young husband would pull a long face, but Sailen would always be ready to abide by his own superior choice and to pay the cost.

In this manner Sailen became the acknowledged patron of the students upstairs. It made him intolerant of the insolence of any one who refused to accept his help. Indeed, to help others in this way had become his hobby.

Kalipada, in his tattered jersey, used to sit on a dirty mat in his damp room below and recite his lessons, swinging himself from side to side to the rhythm of the sentence. It was a sheer necessity for him to get that scholarship next year.

Kalipada's mother had made him promise, before he left home for Calcutta that he would avoid the company of rich young men. Therefore he bore the burden of his indigence alone, strictly keeping himself from those who had been more favoured by fortune. But to Sailen, it seemed a sheer impertinence that a student as poor as Kalipada should yet have the pride to keep away from his patronage. Besides this, in his food and dress and everything, Kalipada's poverty was so blatantly exposed, it hurt Sailen's sense of decency. Every time he looked down into Kalipada's room, he was offended by the sight of the cheap clothing, the dingy mosquito net and the tattered bedding. Whenever he passed on his way to his own room in the upper story the sight of these things was unavoidable. To crown it all there was that absurd amulet which Kalipada always had hanging round his neck, and those daily rites of devotion which were so ridiculously out of fashion!

One day Sailen and his followers condescended to invite Kalipada to a feast, thinking that his gratitude would know no bounds. But Kalipada sent an answer saying that his habits were different and it would not be wholesome for him to accept the invitation. Sailen was unaccustomed to such a refusal, and it roused up in him all the ferocity of his insulted benevolence. For some days after this, the noise on the upper story became so loudly insistent that it was impossible for Kalipada to go on with his studies. He was compelled to spend the greater part of his days studying in the Park, and to get up very early and sit down to his work long before it was light.

Owing to his half-starved condition, his mental overwork, and badly-ventilated room, Kalipada began to suffer from continual attacks of headache. There were times when he was obliged to lie down on his bed for three or four days together. But he made no mention of his illness in his letters to his father. Bhavani himself was certain that, just as vegetation grew rank in his village surroundings, so comforts of all kinds sprang up of themselves from the soil of Calcutta. Kalipada never for a moment disabused his mind of that misconception. He did not fail to write to his father, even when suffering from one of these paroxysms of pain. The deliberate rowdiness of the students in the upper story added at such times to his distress.

Kalipada tried to make himself as scarce and small as possible, in order to avoid notice; but this did not bring him relief. One day, he found that a cheap shoe of his own had been taken away and replaced by an expensive foreign one. It was impossible for him to go to college with such an incongruous pair. He made no complaint, however, but bought some old second-hand shoes from the cobbler. One day, a student from the upper story came into his room and asked him:

"Have you, by any mistake, brought away my silver cigarette case with you?"

Kalipada got annoyed and answered:

"I have never been inside your room in my life."

The student stooped down. "Hullo!" he said, "here it is!" And the valuable cigarette case was picked up from the corner of the room.

Kalipada determined to leave this lodging house as soon as ever he had passed his Intermediate Examination, provided only he could get a scholarship to enable him to do so.

Every year the students of the house used to have their annual Saraswati Puja. Though the greater part of the expenses fell to the share of Sailen, every one else contributed according to his means. The year before, they had contemptuously left out Kalipada from the list of contributors; but this year, merely to tease him, they came with their subscription book. Kalipada instantly paid five rupees to the fund, though he had no intention of participating in the feast. His penury had long brought on him the contempt of his fellow lodgers, but this unexpected gift of five rupees became to them insufferable. The Saraswati Puja was performed with great eclat and the five rupees could easily have been spared. It had been hard indeed for Kalipada to part with it. While he took the food given him in his landlord's house he had no control over the time at which it was served. Besides this, since the servants brought him the food, he did not like to criticise the dishes. He preferred to provide himself with some extra things; and after the forced extravagance of his five-rupee subscription he had to forgo all this and suffered in consequence. His paroxysms of headache became more frequent, and though he passed his examination, he failed to obtain the scholarship that he desired.

The loss of the scholarship drove Kalipada to do extra work as a private tutor and to stick to the same unhealthy room in the lodging house. The students overhead had hoped that they would be relieved of his presence. But punctually to the day the room was unlocked on the lower floor. Kalipada entered, clad in the same old dirty check Parsee coat. A coolie from Sealdah Station took down from his head a steel trunk and other miscellaneous packages and laid them on the floor of the room; and a long wrangle ensued as to the proper amount of pice that were due.

In the depths of those packages there were mango chutnies and other condiments which his mother had specially prepared. Kalipada was aware that, in his absence, the upper-story students, in search of a jest, did not scruple to come into his room by stealth.

He was especially anxious to keep these home gifts from their cruel scrutiny. As tokens of home affection they were supremely precious to him; but to the town students, they denoted merely the boorishness of poverty-stricken villagers. The vessels were crude and earthen, fastened up by an earthen lid fixed on with paste of flour. They were neither glass nor porcelain, and therefore sure to be regarded with insolent disdain by rich town-bred people.

Formerly Kalipada used to keep these stores hidden under his bed, covering them up with old newspapers. But this time he took the precaution of always locking up his door, even if he went out for a few minutes. This still further roused the spleen of Sailen and his party. It seemed to them preposterous that the room which was poor enough to draw tears from the eyes of the most hardened burglar should be as carefully guarded as if it were a second Bank of Bengal.

"Does he actually believe," they said among themselves, "that the temptation will be irresistible for us to steal that Parsee coat?"

Sailen had never visited this dark and mildewed room from which the plaster was dropping. The glimpses that he had taken, while going up-stairs, – especially when, in the evening, Kalipada, the upper part of his body bare, would sit poring over his books with a smoky lamp beside him, – were enough to give him a sense of suffocation. Sailen asked his boon companions to explore the room below and find out the treasure which Kalipada had hidden. Everybody felt intensely amused at the proposal.

The lock on Kalipada's door was a cheap one, which had the magnanimity to lend itself to any key. One evening when Kalipada had gone out to his private tuition, two or three of the students with an exuberant sense of humour took a lantern and unlocked the room and entered. It did not need a moment to discover the pots of chutney under the bed, but these hardly seemed valuable enough to demand such watchful care on the part of Kalipada. A further search disclosed a key on a ring under the pillow. They opened the steel trunk with the key and found a few soiled clothes, books and writing material. They were about to shut the box in disgust when they saw, at the very bottom, a packet covered by a dirty handkerchief. On uncovering three or four wrappers they found a currency note of fifty rupees. This made them burst out into peals of laughter. They felt certain that Kalipada was harbouring suspicion against the whole world in his mind because of this fifty rupees!

The meanness of this suspicious precaution deepened the intensity of their contempt for Kalipada. Just then, they heard a foot-step outside. They hastily shut the box, locked the door, and ran upstairs with the note in their possession.

Sailen was vastly amused. Though fifty rupees was a mere trifle, he could never have believed that Kalipada had so much money in his trunk. They all decided to watch the result of this loss upon that queer creature downstairs.

When Kalipada came home that night after his tuition was over, he was too tired to notice any disorder in his room. One of his worst attacks of nervous headache was coming on and he went straight to bed.

The next day, when he brought out his trunk from under the bed and took out his clothes, he found it open. He was naturally careful, but it was not unlikely, he thought, that he had forgotten to lock it on the day before. But when he lifted the lid he found all the contents topsy-turvy, and his heart gave a great thud when he discovered that the note, given to him by his mother, was missing. He searched the box over and over again in the vain hope of finding it, and when his loss was made certain, he flung himself upon his bed and lay like one dead.

Just then, he heard footsteps following one another on the stairs, and every now and then an outburst of laughter from the upper room. It struck him, all of a sudden, that this was not a theft: Sailen and his party must have taken the note to amuse themselves and make laughter out of it. It would have given him less pain if a thief had stolen it. It seemed to him that these young men had laid their impious hands upon his mother herself.

This was the first time that Kalipada had ascended those stairs. He ran to the upper floor, – the old jersey on his shoulders, – his face flushed with anger and the pain of his illness. As it was Sunday, Sailen and his company were seated in the verandah, laughing and talking. Without any warning, Kalipada burst upon them and shouted:

"Give me back my note!"

If he had begged it of them, they would have relented; but the sight of his anger made them furious. They started up from their chairs and exclaimed:

"What do you mean, sir? What do you mean? What note?"

Kalipada shouted: "The note you have taken from my box!"

"How dare you?" they shouted back. "Do you take us to be thieves?"

If Kalipada had held any weapon in his hand at that moment he certainly would have killed some one among them. But when he was about to spring, they fell on him, and four or five of them dragged him down to his room and thrust him inside.

Sailen said to his companions: "Here, take this hundred-rupee note, and throw it to that *dog*!"

They all loudly exclaimed: "No! Let him climb down first and give us a written apology. Then we shall consider it!"

Sailen's party all went to bed at the proper time and slept the sleep of the innocent. In the morning they had almost forgotten Kalipada. But some of them, while passing his room, heard the sound of talking and they thought that possibly he was busy consulting some lawyer. The door was shut from the inside. They tried to overhear, but what they heard had nothing legal about it. It was quite incoherent.

They informed Sailen. He came down and stood with his ear close to the door. The only thing that could be distinctly heard was the word 'Father.' This frightened Sailen. He thought that possibly Kalipada had gone mad on account of the grief of losing that fifty-rupee note. Sailen shouted "Kalipada Babu!" two or three times, but got no answer. Only that muttering sound continued. Sailen called, – "Kalipada Babu, – please open the door. Your note has been found." But still the door was not opened and that muttering sound went on.

Sailen had never anticipated such a result as this. He did not express a word of repentance to his followers, but he felt the sting of it all the same. Some advised him to break open the door: others thought that the police should be called in, – for Kalipada might be in a dangerous state of lunacy. Sailen at once sent for a doctor who lived close at hand. When they burst open the door they found the bedding hanging from the bed and Kalipada lying on the floor unconscious. He was tossing about and throwing up his arms and muttering, with his eyes red and open and his face all flushed. The doctor examined him and asked if there were any relative near at hand; for the case was serious.

Sailen answered that he knew nothing, but would make inquiries. The doctor then advised the removal of the patient at once to an upstairs room and proper nursing arrangements day and night. Sailen took him up to his own room and dismissed his followers. He got some ice and put it on Kalipada's head and began to fan him with his own hand.

Kalipada, fearing that mocking references would be made, had concealed the names and address of his parents from these people with special care. So Sailen had no alternative but to open his box. He found two bundles of letters tied up with ribbon. One of them contained his mother's letters, the other contained his father's. His mother's letters were fewer in number than his father's. Sailen closed the door and began to read the letters. He was startled when he saw the address, – Saniari, the house of the Chowdhuries, – and then the name of the father, Bhavani. He folded up the letters and sat still, gazing at Kalipada's face. Some of his friends had casually mentioned, that there was a resemblance between Kalipada and himself. But he was offended at the remark and did not believe it. To-day he discovered the truth. He knew that his own grandfather, Shyama Charan, had a step-brother named Bhavani; but the later history to the family had remained a secret to him. He did not even know that Bhavani had a son named Kalipada; and he never suspected that Bhavani had come to such an abject state of poverty as this. He now felt not only relieved, but proud of his own relative, Kalipada, that he had refused to enter himself on the list of proteges.

IV

Knowing that his party had insulted Kalipada almost every day, Sailen felt reluctant to keep him in the lodging house with them. So he rented another suitable house and kept him there. Bhavani came down in haste to Calcutta the moment he received a letter from Sailen informing him of his son's illness. Rashmani parted with all her savings giving instructions to her husband to spare no expense upon her son. It was not considered proper for the daughters of the great Chowdhuri family to leave their home and go to Calcutta unless absolutely obliged, and therefore she had to remain behind offering prayers to all the tutelary gods. When Bhavani Charan arrived he found Kalipada still unconscious and delirious. It nearly broke Bhavani's heart when he heard himself called 'Master Mashai.' Kalipada often called him in his delirium and he tried to make himself recognized by his son, but in vain.

The doctor came again and said the fever was getting less. He thought the case was taking a more favourable turn. For Bhavani, it was an impossibility to imagine that his son would not recover. He *must* live: it was his destiny to live. Bhavani was much struck with the behaviour of Sailen. It was difficult to believe that he was not of their own kith and kin. He supposed all this kindness to be due to the town training which Sailen had received. Bhavani spoke to Sailen disparagingly of the country habits which village people like himself got into.

Gradually the fever went down and Kalipada recovered consciousness. He was astonished beyond measure when he saw his father sitting in the room beside him. His first anxiety was lest he should discover the miserable state in which he had been living. But what would be harder still to bear was, if his father with his rustic manners became the butt of the people upstairs. He looked round him, but could not recognize his own room and wondered if he had been dreaming. But he found himself too weak to think.

He supposed that it had been his father who had removed him to this better lodging, but he had no power to calculate how he could possibly bear the expense. The only thing that concerned him at that moment was that he felt he must live, and for that he had a claim upon the world.

Once when his father was absent Sailen came in with a plate of grapes in his hand. Kalipada could not understand this at all and wondered if there was some practical joke behind it. He at once became excited and wondered how he could save his father from annoyance. Sailen set the plate down on the table and touched Kalipada's feet humbly and said: "My offence has been great: pray forgive me."

Kalipada started and sat up on his bed. He could see that Sailen's repentance was sincere and he was greatly moved.

When Kalipada had first come to the students' lodging house he had felt strongly drawn towards this handsome youth. He never missed a chance of looking at his face when Sailen passed by his room on his way upstairs. He would have given all the world to be friends with him, but the barrier was too great to overcome. Now to-day when Sailen brought him the grapes and asked his forgiveness, he silently looked at his face and silently accepted the grapes which spoke of his repentance.

It amused Kalipada greatly when he noticed the intimacy that had sprung up between his father and Sailen. Sailen used to call Bhavani Charan "grandfather" and exercised to the full the grandchild's privilege of joking with him. The principal object of the jokes was the absent "grandmother." Sailen made the confession that he had taken the opportunity of Kalipada's illness to steal all the delicious chutnies which his "grandmother" had made with her own hand. The news of his act of "thieving" gave Kalipada very great joy. He found it easy to deprive himself, if he could find any one who could appreciate the good things made by his mother. Thus this time of his convalescence became the happiest period in the whole of Kalipada's life.

There was only one flaw in this unalloyed happiness. Kalipada had a fierce pride in his poverty which prevented him ever speaking about his family's better days. Therefore when his father used to talk of his former prosperity Kalipada winced. Bhavani could not keep to himself the one great event of his life, – the theft of that will which he was absolutely certain that he would some day recover. Kalipada had always regarded this as a kind of mania of his father's, and in collusion with his mother he had often humoured his father concerning this amiable weakness. But he shrank in shame when his father talked about this to Sailen. He noticed particularly that Sailen did not relish such conversation and that he often tried to prove, with a certain amount of feeling, its absurdity. But Bhavani, who was ready to give in to others in matters much more serious, in this matter was adamant. Kalipada tried to pacify him by saying that there was no great need to worry about it, because those who were enjoying its benefit were almost the same as his own children, since they were his nephews.

Such talk Sailen could not bear for long and he used to leave the room. This pained Kalipada, because he thought that Sailen might get quite a wrong conception of his father and imagine him to be a grasping worldly old man. Sailen would have revealed his own relationship to Kalipada and his father long before, but this discussion about the theft of the will prevented him. It was hard for him to believe that his grandfather or father had stolen the will; on the other hand he could not but think that some cruel injustice had been done in depriving Bhavani of his share of the ancestral property. Therefore he gave up arguing when the subject was brought forward and took some occasion to leave as soon as possible.

Though Kalipada still had headaches in the evening, with a slight rise in temperature, he did not take it at all seriously. He became anxious to resume his studies because he felt it would be a calamity to him if he again missed his scholarship. He secretly began to read once more, without taking any notice of the strict orders of the doctor. Kalipada asked his father to return home, assuring him that he was in the best of health. Bhavani had been all his life fed and nourished and cooked for by his wife; he was pining to get back. He did not therefore wait to be pressed.

On the morning of his intended departure, when he went to say good-bye to Kalipada, he found him very ill indeed, his face red with fever and his whole body burning. He had been committing to memory page after page of his text book of Logic half through the night, and for the remainder he could not sleep at all. The doctor took Sailen aside. "This relapse," he said, "is fatal." Sailen came to Bhavani and said, "The patient requires a mother's nursing: she must be brought to Calcutta."

It was evening when Rashmani came, and she only saw her son alive for a few hours. Not knowing how her husband could survive such a terrible shock she altogether suppressed her own sorrow. Her son was merged in her husband again, and she took up this burden of the dead and the living on her own aching heart. She said to her God, – "It is too much for me to bear." But she did bear it.

V

It was midnight. With the very weariness of her sorrow Rashmani had fallen asleep soon after reaching her own home in the village. But Bhavani had no sleep that night. Tossing on his bed for hours he heaved a deep sigh saying, – "Merciful God!" Then he got up from his bed and went out. He entered the room where Kalipada had been wont to do his lessons in his childhood. The lamp shook as he held it in his hand. On the wooden settle there was still the torn, ink-stained quilt, made long ago by Rashmani herself. On the wall were figures of Euclid and Algebra drawn in charcoal. The remains of a Royal Reader No. III and a few exercise books were lying about; and the one odd slipper of his infancy, which had evaded notice so long, was keeping its place in the dusty obscurity of the corner of the room. To-day it had become so important that nothing in the world, however great, could keep it hidden any longer. Bhavani put the lamp in the niche on the wall and silently sat on the settle; his eyes were dry, but he felt choked as if with want of breath.

Bhavani opened the shutters on the eastern side and stood still, grasping the iron bars, gazing into the darkness. Through the drizzling rain he could see the outline of the clump of trees at the end of the outer wall. At this spot Kalipada had made his own garden. The passion flowers which he had planted with his own hand had grown densely thick. While he gazed at this Bhavani felt his heart come up into his throat with choking pain. There was nobody now to wait for and expect daily. The summer vacation had come, but no one would come back home to fill the vacant room and use its old familiar furniture.

"O Baba mine!" he cried, "O Baba! O Baba mine!"

He sat down. The rain came faster. A sound of footsteps was heard among the grass and withered leaves. Bhavani's heart stood still. He hoped it was – that which was beyond all hope. He thought it was Kalipada himself come to see his own garden, – and in this downpour of rain how wet he would be! Anxiety about this made him restless. Then somebody stood for a moment in front of the iron window bars. The cloak round his head made it impossible for Bhavani to see his face clearly, but his height was the same as that of Kalipada.

"Darling!" cried Bhavani, "You have come!" and he rushed to open the door.

But when he came outside to the spot where the figure had stood, there was no one to be seen. He walked up and down in the garden through the drenching rain, but no one was there. He stood still for a moment raising his voice and calling, – "Kalipada," but no answer came. The servant, Noto, who was sleeping in the cowshed, heard his cry and came out and coaxed him back to his room.

Next day, in the morning, Noto, while sweeping the room found a bundle just underneath the grated window. He brought it to Bhavani who opened it and found it was an old document. He put on his spectacles and after reading a few lines came rushing in to Rashmani and gave the paper into her hand.

Rashmani asked, "What is it?"

Bhavani replied, "It is the will!"

"Who gave it you?"

"He himself came last night to give it to me."

"What are you going to do with it?"

Bhavani said: "I have no need of it now." And he tore the will to pieces.

When the news reached the village Bagala proudly nodded his head and said: "Didn't I prophesy that the will would be recovered through Kalipada?"

But the grocer Ramcharan replied: "Last night when the ten o'clock train reached the Station a handsome looking young man came to my shop and asked the way to the Chowdhuri's house and I thought he had some kind of bundle in his hand."

"Absurd," said Bagala.

The Babus of Nayanjore

I

Once upon a time the Babus at Nayanjore were famous landholders. They were noted for their princely extravagance. They would tear off the rough border of their Dacca muslin, because it rubbed against their delicate skin. They could spend many thousands of rupees over the wedding of a kitten. And on a certain grand occasion it is alleged that in order to turn night into day they lighted numberless lamps and showered silver threads from the sky to imitate sunlight.

Those were the days before the flood. The flood came. The line of succession among these old-world Babus, with their lordly habits, could not continue for long. Like a lamp with too many wicks burning, the oil flared away quickly, and the light went out.

Kailas Babu, our neighbour, is the last relic of this extinct magnificence. Before he grew up, his family had very nearly reached its lowest ebb. When his father died, there was one dazzling outburst of funeral extravagance, and then insolvency. The property was sold to liquidate the debt. What little ready money was left over was altogether insufficient to keep up the past ancestral splendours.

Kailas Babu left Nayanjore and came to Calcutta. His son did not remain long in this world of faded glory. He died, leaving behind him an only daughter.

In Calcutta we are Kailas Babu's neighbours. Curiously enough our own family history is just the opposite of his. My father got his money by his own exertions, and prided himself on never spending a penny more than was needed. His clothes were those of a working man, and his hands also. He never had any inclination to earn the title of Babu by extravagant display; and I myself, his only son, owe him gratitude for that. He gave me the very best education, and I was able to make my way in the world. I am not ashamed of the fact that I am a self-made man. Crisp bank-notes in my safe are dearer to me than a long pedigree in an empty family chest.

I believe this was why I disliked seeing Kailas Babu drawing his heavy cheques on the public credit from the bankrupt bank of his ancient Babu reputation. I used to fancy that he looked down on me, because my father had earned money with his own hands.

I ought to have noticed that no one showed any vexation towards Kailas Babu except myself. Indeed it would have been difficult to find an old man who did less harm than he. He was always ready with his kindly little acts of courtesy in times of sorrow and joy. He would join in all the ceremonies and religious observances of his neighbours. His familiar smile would greet young and old alike. His politeness in asking details about domestic affairs was untiring. The friends who met him in the street were perforce ready to be button-holed, while a long string of questions of this kind followed one another from his lips:

"My dear friend, I am delighted to see you. Are you quite well? How is Shashi? And Dada – is he all right? Do you know, I've only just heard that Madhu's son has got fever. How is he? Have you heard? And Hari Charan Babu – I have not seen him for a long time – I hope he is not ill. What's the matter with Rakkhal? And er – er, how are the ladies of your family?"

Kailas Babu was spotlessly neat in his dress on all occasions, though his supply of clothes was sorely limited. Every day he used to air his shirts and vests and coats and trousers carefully, and put them out in the sun, along with his bed-quilt, his pillowcase, and the small carpet on which he always sat. After airing them he would shake them, and brush them, and put them carefully away. His little bits of furniture made his small room decent, and hinted that there was more in reserve if needed. Very often, for want of a servant, he would shut up his house for a while. Then he would iron out his shirts and linen with his own hands, and do other little menial tasks. After this he would open his door and receive his friends again.

Though Kailas Babu, as I have said, had lost all his landed property, he had still some family heirlooms left. There was a silver cruet for sprinkling scented water, a filigree box for otto-of-roses, a small gold salver, a costly ancient shawl, and the old-fashioned ceremonial dress and ancestral turban. These he had rescued with the greatest difficulty from the money-lenders' clutches. On every suitable occasion he would bring them out in state, and thus try to save the world-famed dignity of the Babus of Nayanjore. At heart the most modest of men, in his daily speech he regarded it as a sacred duty, owed to his rank, to give free play to his family pride. His friends would encourage this trait in his character with kindly good-humour, and it gave them great amusement.

The neighbourhood soon learnt to call him their Thakur Dada. They would flock to his house and sit with him for hours together. To prevent his incurring any expense, one or other of his friends would bring him tobacco and say: "Thakur Dada, this morning some tobacco was sent to me from Gaya. Do take it and see how you like it."

Thakur Dada would take it and say it was excellent. He would then go on to tell of a certain exquisite tobacco which they once smoked in the old days of Nayanjore at the cost of a guinea an ounce.

"I wonder," he used to say, "if any one would like to try it now. I have some left, and can get it at once."

Every one knew that, if they asked for it, then somehow or other the key of the cupboard would be missing; or else Ganesh, his old family servant, had put it away somewhere.

"You never can be sure," he would add, "where things go to when servants are about. Now, this Ganesh of mine, – I can't tell you what a fool he is, but I haven't the heart to dismiss him."

Ganesh, for the credit of the family, was quite ready to bear all the blame without a word.

One of the company usually said at this point: "Never mind, Thakur Dada. Please don't trouble to look for it. This tobacco we're smoking will do quite well. The other would be too strong."

Then Thakur Dada would be relieved and settle down again, and the talk would go on.

When his guests got up to go away, Thakur Dada would accompany them to the door and say to them on the door-step: "Oh, by the way, when are you all coming to dine with me?"

One or other of us would answer: "Not just yet, Thakur Dada, not just yet. We'll fix a day later."

"Quite right," he would answer. "Quite right. We had much better wait till the rains come. It's too hot now. And a grand rich dinner such as I should want to give you would upset us in weather like this."

But when the rains did come, every one was very careful not to remind him of his promise. If the subject was brought up, some friend would suggest gently that it was very inconvenient to get about when the rains were so severe, and therefore it would be much better to wait till they were over. Thus the game went on.

Thakur Dada's poor lodging was much too small for his position, and we used to condole with him about it. His friends would assure him they quite understood his difficulties: it was next to impossible to get a decent house in Calcutta. Indeed, they had all been looking out for years for a house to suit him.

But, I need hardly add, no friend had been foolish enough to find one. Thakur Dada used to say, with a sigh of resignation: "Well, well, I suppose I shall have to put up with this house after all." Then he would add with a genial smile: "But, you know, I could never bear to be away from my friends. I must be near you. That really compensates for everything."

Somehow I felt all this very deeply indeed. I suppose the real reason was, that when a man is young, stupidity appears to him the worst of crimes. Kailas Babu was not really stupid. In ordinary business matters every one was ready to consult him. But with regard to Nayanjore his utterances were certainly void of common sense. Because, out of amused affection for him, no one contradicted his impossible statements, he refused to keep them in bounds. When people recounted in his hearing the glorious history of Nayanjore with absurd exaggerations, he would accept all they said with the utmost gravity, and never doubted, even in his dreams, that any one could disbelieve it.

II

When I sit down and try to analyse the thoughts and feelings that I had towards Kailas Babu, I see that there was a still deeper reason for my dislike. I will now explain.

Though I am the son of a rich man, and might have wasted time at college, my industry was such that I took my M.A. degree in Calcutta University when quite young. My moral character was flawless. In addition, my outward appearance was so handsome, that if I were to call myself beautiful, it might be thought a mark of self-estimation, but could not be considered an untruth.

There could be no question that among the young men of Bengal I was regarded by parents generally as a very eligible match. I was myself quite clear on the point and had determined to obtain my full value in the marriage market. When I pictured my choice, I had before my mind's eye a wealthy father's only daughter, extremely beautiful and highly educated. Proposals came pouring in to me from far and near; large sums in cash were offered. I weighed these offers with rigid impartiality in the delicate scales of my own estimation. But there was no one fit to be my partner. I became convinced, with the poet Bhabavuti, that,

In this world's endless time and boundless space one *may* be born at last to match my sovereign grace.

But in this puny modern age, and this contracted space of modern Bengal, it was doubtful if the peerless creature existed as yet.

Meanwhile my praises were sung in many tunes, and in different metres, by designing parents.

Whether I was pleased with their daughters or not, this worship which they offered was never unpleasing. I used to regard it as my proper due, because I was so good. We are told that when the gods withhold their boons from mortals they still expect their worshippers to pay them fervent honour and are angry if it is withheld. I had that divine expectance strongly developed in myself.

I have already mentioned that Thakur Dada had an only grand-daughter. I had seen her many times, but had never mistaken her for beautiful. No thought had ever entered my mind that she would be a possible partner for myself. All the same, it seemed quite certain to me that some day or other Kailas Babu would offer her, with all due worship, as an oblation at my shrine. Indeed – this was the inner secret of my dislike – I was thoroughly annoyed that he had not done so already.

I heard that Thakur Dada had told his friends that the Babus of Nayanjore never craved a boon. Even if the girl remained unmarried, he would not break the family tradition. It was this arrogance of his that made me angry. My indignation smouldered for some time. But I remained perfectly silent and bore it with the utmost patience, because I was so good.

As lightning accompanies thunder, so in my character a flash of humour was mingled with the mutterings of my wrath.

It was, of course, impossible for me to punish the old man merely to give vent to my rage; and for a long time I did nothing at all. But suddenly one day such an amusing plan came into my head, that I could not resist the temptation of carrying it into effect.

I have already said that many of Kailas Babu's friends used to flatter the old man's vanity to the full. One, who was a retired Government servant, had told him that whenever he saw the Chota Lât Sahib he always asked for the latest news about the Babus of Nayanjore, and the Chota Lât had been heard to say that in all Bengal the only really respectable families were those of the Maharaja of Cossipore and the Babus of Nayanjore. When this monstrous falsehood was told to Kailas Babu he was extremely gratified and often repeated the story. And wherever after that he met this Government servant in company he would ask, along with other questions:

"Oh! er – by the way, how is the Chota Lât Sahib? Quite well, did you say? Ah, yes, I am so delighted to hear it! And the dear Mem Sahib, is she quite well too? Ah, yes! and the little children – are they quite well also? Ah, yes! that's very good news! Be sure and give them my compliments when you see them."

Kailas Babu would constantly express his intention of going some day and paying a visit to the Lord Sahib. But it may be taken for granted that many Chota Lâts and Burra Lâts also would come and go, and much water would pass down the Hoogly, before the family coach of Nayanjore would be furbished up to pay a visit to Government House.

One day I took Kailas Babu aside and told him in a whisper: "Thakur Dada, I was at the Levee yesterday, and the Chota Lât Sahib happened to mention the Babus of Nayanjore. I told him that Kailas Babu had come to town. Do you know, he was terribly hurt because you hadn't called. He told me he was going to put etiquette on one side and pay you a private visit himself this very afternoon."

Anybody else could have seen through this plot of mine in a moment. And, if it had been directed against another person, Kailas Babu would have understood the joke. But after all that he had heard from his friend the Government servant, and after all his own exaggerations, a visit from the Lieutenant-Governor seemed the most natural thing in the world. He became highly nervous and excited at my news. Each detail of the coming visit exercised him greatly, – most of all his own ignorance of English. How on earth was that difficulty to be met? I told him there was no difficulty at all: it was aristocratic not to know English: and, besides, the Lieutenant-Governor always brought an interpreter with him, and he had expressly mentioned that this visit was to be private.

About midday, when most of our neighbours are at work, and the rest are asleep, a carriage and pair stopped before the lodging of Kailas Babu. Two flunkeys in livery came up the stairs, and announced in a loud voice, "The Chota Lât Sahib has arrived!" Kailas Babu was ready, waiting for him, in his old-fashioned ceremonial robes and ancestral turban, and Ganesh was by his side, dressed in his master's best suit of clothes for the occasion.

When the Chota Lât Sahib was announced, Kailas Babu ran panting and puffing and trembling to the door, and led in a friend of mine, in disguise, with repeated salaams, bowing low at each step and walking backward as best he could. He had his old family shawl spread over a hard wooden chair and he asked the Lât Sahib to be seated. He then made a high-flown speech in Urdu, the ancient Court language of the Sahibs, and presented on the golden salver a string of gold *mohurs*, the last relics of his broken fortune. The old family servant Ganesh, with an expression of awe bordering on terror, stood behind with the scent-sprinkler, drenching the Lât Sahib, and touched him gingerly from time to time with the otto-of-roses from the filigree box.

Kailas Babu repeatedly expressed his regret at not being able to receive His Honour Bahadur with all the ancestral magnificence of his own family estate at Nayanjore. There he could have welcomed him properly with due ceremonial. But in Calcutta he was a mere stranger and sojourner, – in fact a fish out of water.

My friend, with his tall silk hat on, very gravely nodded. I need hardly say that according to English custom the hat ought to have been removed inside the room. But my friend did not dare to take it off for fear of detection: and Kailas Babu and his old servant Ganesh were sublimely unconscious of the breach of etiquette.

After a ten minutes' interview, which consisted chiefly of nodding the head, my friend rose to his feet to depart. The two flunkeys in livery, as had been planned beforehand, carried off in state the string of gold *mohurs*, the gold salver, the old ancestral shawl, the silver scent-sprinkler, and the otto-of-roses filigree box; they placed them ceremoniously in the carriage. Kailas Babu regarded this as the usual habit of Chota Lât Sahibs.

I was watching all the while from the next room. My sides were aching with suppressed laughter. When I could hold myself in no longer, I rushed into a further room, suddenly to discover, in a corner, a young girl sobbing as if her heart would break. When she saw my uproarious laughter she stood upright in passion, flashing the lightning of her big dark eyes in mine, and said with a tear-choked voice: "Tell me! What harm has my grandfather done to you? Why have you come to deceive him? Why have you come here? Why – –"

She could say no more. She covered her face with her hands and broke into sobs.

My laughter vanished in a moment. It had never occurred to me that there was anything but a supremely funny joke in this act of mine, and here I discovered that I had given the cruellest pain to this tenderest little heart. All the ugliness of my cruelty rose up to condemn me. I slunk out of the room in silence, like a kicked dog.

Hitherto I had only looked upon Kusum, the grand-
daughter of Kailas Babu, as a somewhat worthless commodity
in the marriage market, waiting in vain to attract a husband.
But now I found, with a shock of surprise, that in the corner of
that room a human heart was beating.

The whole night through I had very little sleep. My mind
was in a tumult. On the next day, very early in the morning,
I took all those stolen goods back to Kailas Babu's lodgings,
wishing to hand them over in secret to the servant Ganesh. I
waited outside the door, and, not finding any one, went upstairs
to Kailas Babu's room. I heard from the passage Kusum asking
her grandfather in the most winning voice: "Dada, dearest, do
tell me all that the Chota Lât Sahib said to you yesterday. Don't
leave out a single word. I am dying to hear it all over again."

And Dada needed no encouragement. His face beamed
over with pride as he related all manner of praises which the
Lât Sahib had been good enough to utter concerning the
ancient families of Nayanjore. The girl was seated before him,
looking up into his face, and listening with rapt attention. She
was determined, out of love for the old man, to play her part
to the full.

My heart was deeply touched, and tears came to my eyes. I
stood there in silence in the passage, while Thakur Dada finished
all his embellishments of the Chota Lât Sahib's wonderful visit.
When he left the room at last, I took the stolen goods and laid
them at the feet of the girl and came away without a word.

Later in the day I called again to see Kailas Babu himself.
According to our ugly modern custom, I had been in the habit
of making no greeting at all to this old man when I came into
the room. But on this day I made a low bow and touched his
feet. I am convinced the old man thought that the coming
of the Chota Lât Sahib to his house was the cause of my new
politeness. He was highly gratified by it, and an air of benign
serenity shone from his eyes. His friends had looked in, and
he had already begun to tell again at full length the story of
the Lieutenant-Governor's visit with still further adornments

of a most fantastic kind. The interview was already becoming an epic, both in quality and in length.

When the other visitors had taken their leave, I made my proposal to the old man in a humble manner. I told him that, "though I could never for a moment hope to be worthy of marriage connection with such an illustrious family, yet – etc. etc."

When I made clear my proposal of marriage, the old man embraced me and broke out in a tumult of joy: "I am a poor man, and could never have expected such great good fortune."

That was the first and last time in his life that Kailas Babu confessed to being poor. It was also the first and last time in his life that he forgot, if only for a single moment, the ancestral dignity that belongs to the Babus of Nayanjore.

Master Mashai

I

Adhar Babu lives upon the interest of the capital left him by his father. Only the brokers, negotiating loans, come to his drawing room and smoke the silver-chased hookah, and the clerks from the attorney's office discuss the terms of some mortgage or the amount of the stamp fees. He is so careful with his money that even the most dogged efforts of the boys from the local football club fail to make any impression on his pocket.

At the time this story opens a new guest came into his household. After a long period of despair, his wife, Nanibala, bore him a son.

The child resembled his mother, – large eyes, well-formed nose, and fair complexion. Ratikanta, Adharlal's protege, gave verdict, – "He is worthy of this noble house." They named him Venugopal.

Never before had Adharlal's wife expressed any opinion differing from her husband's on household expenses. There had been a hot discussion now and then about the propriety of some necessary item and up to this time she had merely acknowledged defeat with silent contempt. But now Adharlal could no longer maintain his supremacy. He had to give way little by little when things for his son were in question.

II

As Venugopal grew up, his father gradually became accustomed to spending money on him. He obtained an old teacher, who had a considerable repute for his learning and also for his success in dragging impassable boys through their examinations. But such a training does not lead to the cultivation of amiability. This man tried his best to win the boy's heart, but the little that was left in him of the natural milk of human kindness had turned sour, and the child repulsed his advances from the very beginning. The mother, in consequence, objected to him strongly, and complained that the very sight of him made her boy ill. So the teacher left.

Just then, Haralal made his appearance with a dirty dress and a torn pair of old canvas shoes. Haralal's mother, who was a widow, had kept him with great difficulty at a District school out of the scanty earnings which she made by cooking in strange houses and husking rice. He managed to pass the Matriculation and determined to go to College. As a result of his half-starved condition, his pinched face tapered to a point in an unnatural manner, – like Cape Comorin in the map of India; and the only broad portion of it was his forehead, which resembled the ranges of the Himalayas.

The servant asked Haralal what he wanted, and he answered timidly that he wished to see the master.

The servant answered sharply: "You can't see him." Haralal was hesitating, at a loss what to do next, when Venugopal, who had finished his game in the garden, suddenly came to the door. The servant shouted at Haralal: "Get away." Quite unaccountably Venugopal grew excited and cried: "No, he shan't get away." And he dragged the stranger to his father.

Adharlal had just risen from his mid-day sleep and was sitting quietly on the upper verandah in his cane chair, rocking his legs. Ratikanta was enjoying his hookah, seated in a chair next to him. He asked Haralal how far he had got in his reading. The young man bent his head and answered that he had passed the Matriculation. Ratikanta looked stern and expressed surprise that he should be so backward for his age. Haralal kept silence. It was Ratikanta's special pleasure to torture his patron's dependants, whether actual or potential.

Suddenly it struck Adharlal that he would be able to employ this youth as a tutor for his son on next to nothing. He agreed, there and then, to take him at a salary of five rupees a month with board and lodging free.

III

This time the post of tutor remained occupied longer than before. From the very beginning of their acquaintance Haralal and his pupil became great friends. Never before did Haralal have such an opportunity of loving any young human creature. His mother had been so poor and dependent, that he had never had the privilege of playing with the children where she was employed at work. He had not hitherto suspected the hidden stores of love which lay all the while accumulating in his own heart.

Venu, also, was glad to find a companion in Haralal. He was the only boy in the house. His two younger sisters were looked down upon, as unworthy of being his playmates. So his new tutor became his only companion, patiently bearing the undivided weight of the tyranny of his child friend.

IV

Venu was now eleven. Haralal had passed his Intermediate, winning a scholarship. He was working hard for his B.A. degree. After College lectures were over, he would take Venu out into the public park and tell him stories about the heroes from Greek History and Victor Hugo's romances. The child used to get quite impatient to run to Haralal, after school hours, in spite of his mother's attempts to keep him by her side.

This displeased Nanibala. She thought that it was a deep-laid plot of Haralal's to captivate her boy, in order to prolong his own appointment. One day she talked to him from behind the purdah: "It is your duty to teach my son only for an hour or two in the morning and evening. But why are you always with him? The child has nearly forgotten his own parents. You must understand that a man of your position is no fit companion for a boy belonging to this house."

Haralal's voice choked a little as he answered that for the future he would merely be Venu's teacher and would keep away from him at other times.

It was Haralal's usual practice to begin his College study early before dawn. The child would come to him directly after he had washed himself. There was a small pool in the garden and they used to feed the fish in it with puffed rice. Venu was also engaged in building a miniature garden-house, at the corner of the garden, with its liliputian gates and hedges and gravel paths. When the sun became too hot they would go back into the house, and Venu would have his morning lesson from Haralal.

On the day in question Venu had risen earlier than usual, because he wished to hear the end of the story which Haralal had begun the evening before. But he found his teacher absent. When asked about him, the door-servant said that he had gone out. At lesson time Venu remained unnaturally quiet. He never even asked Haralal why he had gone out, but went on mechanically with his lessons. When the child was with his mother taking his breakfast, she asked him what had happened to make him so gloomy, and why he was not eating his food. Venu gave no answer. After his meal his mother caressed him and questioned him repeatedly. Venu burst out crying and said, – "Master Mashai." His mother asked Venu, – "What about Master Mashai?" But Venu found it difficult to name the offence which his teacher had committed.

His mother said to Venu: "Has your Master Mashai been saying anything to you against *me?*"

Venu could not understand the question and went away.

V

There was a theft in Adhar Babu's house. The police were called in to investigate. Even Haralal's trunks were searched. Ratikanta said with meaning: "The man who steals anything, does not keep his thefts in his own box."

Adharlal called his son's tutor and said to him: "It will not be convenient for me to keep any of you in my own house. From to-day you will have to take up your quarters outside, only coming in to teach my son at the proper time."

Ratikanta said sagely, drawing at his hookah: "That is a good proposal, – good for both parties."

Haralal did not utter a word, but he sent a letter saying that it would be no longer possible for him to remain as tutor to Venu.

When Venu came back from school, he found his tutor's room empty. Even that broken steel trunk of his was absent. The rope was stretched across the corner, but there were no clothes or towel hanging on it. Only on the table, which formerly was strewn with books and papers, stood a bowl containing some gold-fish with a label on which was written the word "Venu" in Haralal's hand-writing. The boy ran up at once to his father and asked him what had happened. His father told him that Haralal had resigned his post. Venu went to his room and flung himself down and began to cry. Adharlal did not know what to do with him.

The next day, when Haralal was sitting on his wooden bedstead in the Hostel, debating with himself whether he should attend his college lectures, suddenly he saw Adhar Babu's servant coming into his room followed by Venu. Venu at once ran up to him and threw his arms round his neck asking him to come back to the house.

Haralal could not explain why it was absolutely impossible for him to go back, but the memory of those clinging arms and that pathetic request used to choke his breath with emotion long after.

VI

Haralal found out, after this, that his mind was in an unsettled state, and that he had but a small chance of winning the scholarship, even if he could pass the examination. At the same time, he knew that, without the scholarship, he could not continue his studies. So he tried to get employment in some office.

Fortunately for him, an English Manager of a big merchant firm took a fancy to him at first sight. After only a brief exchange of words the Manager asked him if he had any experience, and could he bring any testimonial. Haralal could only answer "No"; nevertheless a post was offered him of twenty rupees a month and fifteen rupees were allowed him in advance to help him to come properly dressed to the office.

The Manager made Haralal work extremely hard. He had to stay on after office hours and sometimes go to his master's house late in the evening. But, in this way, he learnt his work quicker than others, and his fellow clerks became jealous of him and tried to injure him, but without effect. He rented a small house in a narrow lane and brought his mother to live with him as soon as his salary was raised to forty rupees a month. Thus happiness came back to his mother after weary years of waiting.

Haralal's mother used to express a desire to see Venugopal, of whom she had heard so much. She wished to prepare some dishes with her own hand and to ask him to come just once to dine with her son. Haralal avoided the subject by saying that his house was not big enough to invite him for that purpose.

VII

The news reached Haralal that Venu's mother had died. He could not wait a moment, but went at once to Adharlal's house to see Venu. After that they began to see each other frequently.

But times had changed. Venu, stroking his budding moustache, had grown quite a young man of fashion. Friends, befitting his present condition, were numerous. That old dilapidated study chair and ink-stained desk had vanished, and the room now seemed to be bursting with pride at its new acquisitions, – its looking-glasses, oleographs, and other furniture. Venu had entered college, but showed no haste in crossing the boundary of the Intermediate examination.

Haralal remembered his mother's request to invite Venu to dinner. After great hesitation, he did so. Venugopal, with his handsome face, at once won the mother's heart. But as soon as ever the meal was over he became impatient to go, and looking at his gold watch he explained that he had pressing engagements elsewhere. Then he jumped into his carriage, which was waiting at the door, and drove away. Haralal with a sigh said to himself that he would never invite him again.

VIII

One day, on returning from office, Haralal noticed the presence of a man in the dark room on the ground floor of his house. Possibly he would have passed him by, had not the heavy scent of some foreign perfume attracted his attention. Haralal asked who was there, and the answer came:

"It is I, Master Mashai."

"What is the matter, Venu?" said Haralal. "When did you arrive?"

"I came hours ago," said Venu. "I did not know that you returned so late."

They went upstairs together and Haralal lighted the lamp and asked Venu whether all was well. Venu replied that his college classes were becoming a fearful bore, and his father did not realize how dreadfully hard it was for him to go on in the same class, year after year, with students much younger than himself. Haralal asked him what he wished to do. Venu then told him that he wanted to go to England and become a barrister. He gave an instance of a student, much less advanced than himself, who was getting ready to go. Haralal asked him if he had received his father's permission. Venu replied that his father would not hear a word of it until he had passed the Intermediate, and that was an impossibility in his present frame of mind. Haralal suggested that he himself should go and try to talk over his father.

"No," said Venu, "I can never allow that!"

Haralal asked Venu to stay for dinner and while they were waiting he gently placed his hand on Venu's shoulder and said:

"Venu, you should not quarrel with your father, or leave home."

Venu jumped up angrily and said that if he was not welcome, he could go elsewhere. Haralal caught him by the hand and implored him not to go away without taking his food. But Venu snatched away his hand and was just leaving the room when Haralal's mother brought the food in on a tray. On seeing Venu about to leave she pressed him to remain and he did so with bad grace.

While he was eating the sound of a carriage stopping at the door was heard. First a servant entered the room with creaking shoes and then Adhar Babu himself. Venu's face became pale. The mother left the room as soon as she saw strangers enter. Adhar Babu called out to Haralal in a voice thick with anger:

"Ratikanta gave me full warning, but I could not believe that you had such devilish cunning hidden in you. So, you think you're going to live upon Venu? This is sheer kidnapping, and I shall prosecute you in the Police Court."

Venu silently followed his father and went out of the house.

IX

The firm to which Haralal belonged began to buy up large quantities of rice and dhal from the country districts. To pay for this, Haralal had to take the cash every Saturday morning by the early train and disburse it. There were special centres where the brokers and middlemen would come with their receipts and accounts for settlement. Some discussion had taken place in the office about Haralal being entrusted with this work, without any security, but the Manager undertook all the responsibility and said that a security was not needed. This special work used to go on from the middle of December to the middle of April. Haralal would get back from it very late at night.

One day, after his return, he was told by his mother that Venu had called and that she had persuaded him to take his dinner at their house. This happened more than once. The mother said that it was because Venu missed his own mother, and the tears came into her eyes as she spoke about it.

One day Venu waited for Haralal to return and had a long talk with him.

"Master Mashai!" he said. "Father has become so cantankerous of late that I cannot live with him any longer. And, besides, I know that he is getting ready to marry again. Ratikanta is seeking a suitable match, and they are always conspiring about it. There used to be a time when my father would get anxious, if I were absent from home even for a few hours. Now, if I am away for more than a week, he takes no notice, – indeed he is greatly relieved. If this marriage takes place, I feel that I cannot live in the house any longer. You must show me a way out of this. I want to become independent."

Haralal felt deeply pained, but he did not know how to help his former pupil. Venu said that he was determined to go to England and become a barrister. Somehow or other he must get the passage money out of his father: he could borrow it on a note of hand and his father would have to pay when the creditors filed a suit. With this borrowed money he would get away, and when he was in England his father was certain to remit his expenses.

"But who is there," Haralal asked, "who would advance you the money?"

"You!" said Venu.

"I!" exclaimed Haralal in amazement.

"Yes," said Venu, "I've seen the servant bringing heaps of money here in bags."

"The servant and the money belong to someone else."

Haralal explained why the money came to his house at night, like birds to their nest, to be scattered next morning.

"But can't the Manager advance the sum?" Venu asked.

"He may do so," said Haralal, "if your father stands security."

The discussion ended at this point.

X

One Friday night a carriage and pair stopped before Haralal's lodging house. When Venu was announced Haralal was counting money in his bedroom, seated on the floor. Venu entered the room dressed in a strange manner. He had discarded his Bengali dress and was wearing a Parsee coat and trousers and had a cap on his head. Rings were prominent on almost all the fingers of both hands, and a thick gold chain was hanging round his neck: there was a gold-watch in his pocket, and diamond studs could be seen peeping from his shirt sleeves. Haralal at once asked him what was the matter and why he was wearing that dress.

"My father's marriage," said Venu, "comes off to-morrow. He tried hard to keep it from me, but I found it out. I asked him to allow me to go to our garden-house at Barrackpur for a few days, and he was only too glad to get rid of me so easily. I am going there, and I wish to God I had never to come back."

Haralal looked pointedly at the rings on his fingers. Venu explained that they had belonged to his mother. Haralal then asked him if he had already had his dinner. He answered, "Yes, haven't you had yours?"

"No," said Haralal, "I cannot leave this room until I have all the money safely locked up in this iron chest."

"Go and take your dinner," said Venu, "while I keep guard here: your mother will be waiting for you."

For a moment Haralal hesitated, and then he went out and had his dinner. In a short time he came back with his mother and the three of them sat among the bags of money talking together. When it was about midnight, Venu took out his watch and looked at it and jumped up saying that he would miss his train. Then he asked Haralal to keep all his rings and his watch and chain until he asked for them again. Haralal put them all together in a leather bag and laid it in the iron safe. Venu went out.

The canvas bags containing the currency notes had already been placed in the safe: only the loose coins remained to be counted over and put away with the rest.

XI

Haralal lay down on the floor of the same room, with the key under his pillow, and went to sleep. He dreamt that Venu's mother was loudly reproaching him from behind the curtain. Her words were indistinct, but rays of different colours from the jewels on her body kept piercing the curtain like needles and violently vibrating. Haralal struggled to call Venu, but his voice seemed to forsake him. At last, with a noise, the curtain fell down. Haralal started up from his sleep and found darkness piled up round about him. A sudden gust of wind had flung open the window and put out the light. Haralal's whole body was wet with perspiration. He relighted the lamp and saw, by the clock, that it was four in the morning. There was no time to sleep again; for he had to get ready to start.

After Haralal had washed his face and hands his mother called from her own room, – "Baba, why are you up so soon?"

It was the habit of Haralal to see his mother's face the first thing in the morning in order to bring a blessing upon the day. His mother said to him: "I was dreaming that you were going out to bring back a bride for yourself." Haralal went to his own bedroom and began to take out the bags containing the silver and the currency notes.

Suddenly his heart stopped beating. Three of the bags appeared to be empty. He knocked them against the iron safe, but this only proved his fear to be true. He opened them and shook them with all his might. Two letters from Venu dropped out from one of the bags. One was addressed to his father and one to Haralal.

Haralal tore open his own letter and began reading. The words seemed to run into one another. He trimmed the lamp, but felt as if he could not understand what he read. Yet the purport of the letter was clear. Venu had taken three thousand rupees, in currency notes, and had started for England. The steamer was to sail before day-break that very morning. The letter ended with the words: "I am explaining everything in a letter to my father. He will pay off the debt; and then, again, my mother's ornaments, which I have left in your care, will more than cover the amount I have taken."

Haralal locked up his room and hired a carriage and went with all haste to the jetty. But he did not know even the name of the steamer which Venu had taken. He ran the whole length of the wharves from Prinsep's Ghat to Metiaburuj. He found that two steamers had started on their voyage to England early that morning. It was impossible for him to know which of them carried Venu, or how to reach him.

When Haralal got home, the sun was strong and the whole of Calcutta was awake. Everything before his eyes seemed blurred. He felt as if he were pushing against a fearful obstacle which was bodiless and without pity. His mother came on the verandah to ask him anxiously where he had gone. With a dry laugh he said to her, – "To bring home a bride for myself," and then he fainted away.

On opening his eyes after a while, Haralal asked his mother to leave him. Entering his room he shut the door from the inside while his mother remained seated on the floor of the verandah in the fierce glare of the sun. She kept calling to him fitfully, almost mechanically, – "Baba, Baba!"

The servant came from the Manager's office and knocked at the door, saying that they would miss the train if they did not start out at once. Haralal called from inside, "It will not be possible for me to start this morning."

"Then where are we to go, Sir?"

"I will tell you later on."

The servant went downstairs with a gesture of impatience.

Suddenly Haralal thought of the ornaments which Venu had left behind. Up till now he had completely forgotten about them, but with the thought came instant relief. He took the leather bag containing them, and also Venu's letter to his father, and left the house.

Before he reached Adharlal's house he could hear the bands playing for the wedding, yet on entering he could feel that there had been some disturbance. Haralal was told that there had been a theft the night before and one or two servants were suspected. Adhar Babu was sitting in the upper verandah flushed with anger and Ratikanta was smoking his hookah. Haralal said to Adhar Babu, "I have something private to tell you." Adharlal flared up, "I have no time now!" He was afraid that Haralal had come to borrow money or to ask his help. Ratikanta suggested that if there was any delicacy in making the request in his presence he would leave the place. Adharlal told him angrily to sit where he was. Then Haralal handed over the bag which Venu had left behind. Adharlal asked what was inside it and Haralal opened it and gave the contents into his hands.

Then Adhar Babu said with a sneer: "It's a paying business that you two have started – you and your former pupil! You were certain that the stolen property would be traced, and so you come along with it to me to claim a reward!"

Haralal presented the letter which Venu had written to his father. This only made Adharlal all the more furious.

"What's all this?" he shouted, "I'll call for the police! My son has not yet come of age, – and *you* have smuggled him out of the country! I'll bet my soul you've lent him a few hundred rupees, and then taken a note of hand for three thousand! But I am not going to be bound by *this*!"

"I never advanced him any money at all," said Haralal.

"Then how did he find it?" said Adharlal, "Do you mean to tell me he broke open your safe and stole it?"

Haralal stood silent.

Ratikanta sarcastically remarked: "I don't believe this fellow ever set hands on as much as three thousand rupees in his life."

When Haralal left the house he seemed to have lost the power of dreading anything, or even of being anxious. His mind seemed to refuse to work. Directly he entered the lane he saw a carriage waiting before his own lodging. For a moment he felt certain that it was Venu's. It was impossible to believe that his calamity could be so hopelessly final.

Haralal went up quickly, but found an English assistant from the firm sitting inside the carriage. The man came out when he saw Haralal and took him by the hand and asked him: "Why didn't you go out by train this morning?" The servant had told the Manager his suspicions and he had sent this man to find out.

Haralal answered: "Notes to the amount of three thousand rupees are missing."

The man asked how that could have happened.

Haralal remained silent.

The man said to Haralal: "Let us go upstairs together and see where you keep your money." They went up to the room and counted the money and made a thorough search of the house.

When the mother saw this she could not contain herself any longer. She came out before the stranger and said: "Baba, what has happened?" He answered in broken Hindustani that some money had been stolen.

"Stolen!" the mother cried, "Why! How could it be stolen? Who could do such a dastardly thing?" Haralal said to her: "Mother, don't say a word."

The man collected the remainder of the money and told Haralal to come with him to the Manager. The mother barred the way and said:

"Sir, where are you taking my son? I have brought him up, starving and straining to do honest work. My son would never touch money belonging to others."

The Englishman, not knowing Bengali, said, "Achcha! Achcha!" Haralal told his mother not to be anxious; he would explain it all to the Manager and soon be back again. The mother entreated him, with a distressed voice,

"Baba, you haven't taken a morsel of food all morning." Haralal stepped into the carriage and drove away, and the mother sank to the ground in the anguish of her heart.

The Manager said to Haralal: "Tell me the truth. What did happen?"

Haralal said to him, "I haven't taken any money."

"I fully believe it," said the Manager, "but surely you know who has taken it."

Haralal looked on the ground and remained silent.

"Somebody," said the Manager, "must have taken it away with your connivance."

"Nobody," replied Haralal, "could take it away with my knowledge without taking first my life."

"Look here, Haralal," said the Manager, "I trusted you completely. I took no security. I employed you in a post of great responsibility. Every one in the office was against me for doing so. The three thousand rupees is a small matter, but the shame of all this to me is a great matter. I will do one thing. I will give you the whole day to bring back this money. If you do so, I shall say nothing about it and I will keep you on in your post."

It was now eleven o'clock. Haralal with bent head went out of the office. The clerks began to discuss the affair with exultation.

"What can I *do*? What can I *do*?" Haralal repeated to himself, as he walked along like one dazed, the sun's heat pouring down upon him. At last his mind ceased to think at all about what could be done, but the mechanical walk went on without ceasing.

This city of Calcutta, which offered its shelter to thousands and thousands of men had become like a steel trap. He could see no way out. The whole body of people were conspiring to surround and hold him captive – this most insignificant of men, whom no one knew. Nobody had any special grudge against him, yet everybody was his enemy. The crowd passed by, brushing against him: the clerks of the offices were eating their lunch on the road side from their plates made of leaves: a tired wayfarer on the Maidan, under the shade of a tree, was lying with one hand beneath his head and one leg upraised over the other: The up-country women, crowded into hackney carriages, were wending their way to the temple: a chuprassie came up with a letter and asked him the address on the envelope, – so the afternoon went by.

Then came the time when the offices were all about to close. Carriages started off in all directions, carrying people back to their homes. The clerks, packed tightly on the seats of the trams, looked at the theatre advertisements as they returned to their lodgings. From to-day, Haralal had neither his work in the office, nor release from work in the evening. He had no need to hurry to catch the tram to take him to his home. All the busy occupations of the city – the buildings – the horses and carriages – the incessant traffic – seemed, now at one time, to swell into dreadful reality, and at another time, to subside into the shadowy unreal.

Haralal had taken neither food, nor rest, nor shelter all that day.

The street lamps were lighted from one road to another and it seemed to him that a watchful darkness, like some demon, was keeping its eyes wide open to guard every movement of its victim. Haralal did not even have the energy to enquire how late it was. The veins on his forehead throbbed, and he felt as if his head would burst. Through the paroxysms of pain, which alternated with the apathy of dejection, only one thought came again and again to his mind; among the innumerable multitudes in that vast city, only one name found its way through his dry throat, – "Mother!"

He said to himself, "At the deep of night, when no one is awake to capture me – me, who am the least of all men, – I will silently creep to my mother's arms and fall asleep, and may I never wake again!"

Haralal's one trouble was lest some police officer should molest him in the presence of his mother, and this kept him back from going home. When it became impossible for him at last to bear the weight of his own body, he hailed a carriage. The driver asked him where he wanted to go. He said: "Nowhere, I want to drive across the Maidan to get the fresh air." The man at first did not believe him and was about to drive on, when Haralal put a rupee into his hand as an advance payment. Thereupon the driver crossed, and then re-crossed, the Maidan from one side to the other, traversing the different roads.

Haralal laid his throbbing head on the side of the open window of the carriage and closed his eyes. Slowly all the pain abated. His body became cool. A deep and intense peace filled his heart and a supreme deliverance seemed to embrace him on every side. It was *not* true, – the day's despair which threatened him with its grip of utter helplessness. It was *not* true, it was false. He knew now that it was only an empty fear of the mind. Deliverance was in the infinite sky and there was no end to peace. No king or emperor in the world had the power to keep captive this nonentity, this Haralal. In the sky, surrounding his emancipated heart on every side, he felt the presence of his mother, that one poor woman. She seemed to grow and grow till she filled the infinity of darkness. All the roads and buildings and shops of Calcutta gradually became enveloped by her. In her presence vanished all the aching pains and thoughts and consciousness of Haralal. It burst, – that bubble filled with the hot vapour of pain. And now there was neither darkness nor light, but only one tense fulness.

The Cathedral clock struck one. The driver called out impatiently: "Babu, my horse can't go on any longer. Where do you want to go?"

There came no answer.

The driver came down and shook Haralal and asked him again where he wanted to go.

There came no answer.

And the answer was never received from Haralal, where he wanted to go.

The Child's Return

I

Raicharan was twelve years old when he came as a servant to his master's house. He belonged to the same caste as his master and was given his master's little son to nurse. As time went on the boy left Raicharan's arms to go to school. From school he went on to college, and after college he entered the judicial service. Always, until he married, Raicharan was his sole attendant.

But when a mistress came into the house, Raicharan found two masters instead of one. All his former influence passed to the new mistress. This was compensated by a fresh arrival. Anukul had a son born to him and Raicharan by his unsparing attentions soon got a complete hold over the child. He used to toss him up in his arms, call to him in absurd baby language, put his face close to the baby's and draw it away again with a laugh.

Presently the child was able to crawl and cross the doorway. When Raicharan went to catch him, he would scream with mischievous laughter and make for safety. Raicharan was amazed at the profound skill and exact judgment the baby showed when pursued. He would say to his mistress with a look of awe and mystery: "Your son will be a judge some day."

New wonders came in their turn. When the baby began to toddle, that was to Raicharan an epoch in human history. When he called his father Ba-ba and his mother Ma-ma and Raicharan Chan-na, then Raicharan's ecstasy knew no bounds. He went out to tell the news to all the world.

After a while Raicharan was asked to show his ingenuity in other ways. He had, for instance, to play the part of a horse, holding the reins between his teeth and prancing with his feet. He had also to wrestle with his little charge; and if he could not, by a wrestler's trick, fall on his back defeated at the end a great outcry was certain.

About this time Anukul was transferred to a district on the banks of the Padma. On his way through Calcutta he bought his son a little go-cart. He bought him also a yellow satin waistcoat, a gold-laced cap, and some gold bracelets and anklets. Raicharan was wont to take these out and put them on his little charge, with ceremonial pride, whenever they went for a walk.

Then came the rainy season and day after day the rain poured down in torrents. The hungry river, like an enormous serpent, swallowed down terraces, villages, cornfields, and covered with its flood the tall grasses and wild casuarinas on the sandbanks. From time to time there was a deep thud as the river-banks crumbled. The unceasing roar of the main current could be heard from far away. Masses of foam, carried swiftly past, proved to the eye the swiftness of the stream.

One afternoon the rain cleared. It was cloudy, but cool and bright. Raicharan's little despot did not want to stay in on such a fine afternoon. His lordship climbed into the go-cart. Raicharan, between the shafts, dragged him slowly along till he reached the rice-fields on the banks of the river. There was no one in the fields and no boat on the stream. Across the water, on the farther side, the clouds were rifted in the west. The silent ceremonial of the setting sun was revealed in all its glowing splendour. In the midst of that stillness the child, all of a sudden, pointed with his finger in front of him and cried: "Chan-na! Pitty fow."

Close by on a mud-flat stood a large *Kadamba* tree in full flower. My lord, the baby, looked at it with greedy eyes and Raicharan knew his meaning. Only a short time before he had made, out of these very flower balls, a small go-cart; and the child had been so entirely happy dragging it about with a string, that for the whole day Raicharan was not asked to put on the reins at all. He was promoted from a horse into a groom.

But Raicharan had no wish that evening to go splashing knee-deep through the mud to reach the flowers. So he quickly pointed his finger in the opposite direction, calling out: "Look, baby, look! Look at the bird." And with all sorts of curious noises he pushed the go-cart rapidly away from the tree.

But a child, destined to be a judge, cannot be put off so easily. And besides, there was at the time nothing to attract his eyes. And you cannot keep up for ever the pretence of an imaginary bird.

The little Master's mind was made up, and Raicharan was at his wits' end. "Very well, baby," he said at last, "you sit still in the cart, and I'll go and get you the pretty flower. Only mind you don't go near the water."

As he said this, he made his legs bare to the knee, and waded through the oozing mud towards the tree.

The moment Raicharan had gone, his little Master's thoughts went off at racing speed to the forbidden water. The baby saw the river rushing by, splashing and gurgling as it went. It seemed as though the disobedient wavelets themselves were running away from some greater Raicharan with the laughter of a thousand children. At the sight of their mischief, the heart of the human child grew excited and restless. He got down stealthily from the go-cart and toddled off towards the river. On his way he picked up a small stick and leant over the bank of the stream pretending to fish. The mischievous fairies of the river with their mysterious voices seemed inviting him into their play-house.

Raicharan had plucked a handful of flowers from the tree and was carrying them back in the end of his cloth, with his face wreathed in smiles. But when he reached the go-cart there was no one there. He looked on all sides and there was no one there. He looked back at the cart and there was no one there.

In that first terrible moment his blood froze within him. Before his eyes the whole universe swam round like a dark mist. From the depth of his broken heart he gave one piercing cry: "Master, Master, little Master."

But no voice answered "Chan-na." No child laughed mischievously back: no scream of baby delight welcomed his return. Only the river ran on with its splashing, gurgling noise as before, – as though it knew nothing at all and had no time to attend to such a tiny human event as the death of a child.

As the evening passed by Raicharan's mistress became very anxious. She sent men out on all sides to search. They went with lanterns in their hands and reached at last the banks of the Padma. There they found Raicharan rushing up and down the fields, like a stormy wind, shouting the cry of despair: "Master, Master, little Master!"

When they got Raicharan home at last, he fell prostrate at the feet of his mistress. They shook him, and questioned him, and asked him repeatedly where he had left the child; but all he could say was that he knew nothing.

Though every one held the opinion that the Padma had swallowed the child, there was a lurking doubt left in the mind. For a band of gipsies had been noticed outside the village that afternoon, and some suspicion rested on them. The mother went so far in her wild grief as to think it possible that Raicharan himself had stolen the child. She called him aside with piteous entreaty and said: "Raicharan, give me back my baby. Give me back my child. Take from me any money you ask, but give me back my child!"

Raicharan only beat his forehead in reply. His mistress ordered him out of the house.

Anukul tried to reason his wife out of this wholly unjust suspicion: "Why on earth," he said, "should he commit such a crime as that?"

The mother only replied: "The baby had gold ornaments on his body. Who knows?"

It was impossible to reason with her after that.

II

Raicharan went back to his own village. Up to this time he had had no son, and there was no hope that any child would now be born to him. But it came about before the end of a year that his wife gave birth to a son and died.

An overwhelming resentment at first grew up in Raicharan's heart at the sight of this new baby. At the back of his mind was resentful suspicion that it had come as a usurper in place of the little Master. He also thought it would be a grave offence to be happy with a son of his own after what had happened to his master's little child. Indeed, if it had not been for a widowed sister, who mothered the new baby, it would not have lived long.

But a change gradually came over Raicharan's mind. A wonderful thing happened. This new baby in turn began to crawl about, and cross the doorway with mischief in its face. It also showed an amusing cleverness in making its escape to safety. Its voice, its sounds of laughter and tears, its gestures, were those of the little Master. On some days, when Raicharan listened to its crying, his heart suddenly began thumping wildly against his ribs, and it seemed to him that his former little Master was crying somewhere in the unknown land of death because he had lost his Chan-na.

Phailna (for that was the name Raicharan's sister gave to the new baby) soon began to talk. It learnt to say Ba-ba and Ma-ma with a baby accent. When Raicharan heard those familiar sounds the mystery suddenly became clear. The little Master could not cast off the spell of his Chan-na and therefore he had been reborn in his own house.

The three arguments in favour of this were, to Raicharan, altogether beyond dispute:

The new baby was born soon after his little master's death.

His wife could never have accumulated such merit as to give birth to a son in middle age.

The new baby walked with a toddle and called out Ba-ba and Ma-ma. – There was no sign lacking which marked out the future judge.

Then suddenly Raicharan remembered that terrible accusation of the mother. "Ah," he said to himself with amazement, "the mother's heart was right. She knew I had stolen her child."

When once he had come to this conclusion, he was filled with remorse for his past neglect. He now gave himself over, body and soul, to the new baby and became its devoted attendant. He began to bring it up as if it were the son of a rich man. He bought a go-cart, a yellow satin waistcoat, and a gold-embroidered cap. He melted down the ornaments of his dead wife and made gold bangles and anklets. He refused to let the little child play with any one of the neighbourhood and became himself its sole companion day and night. As the baby grew up to boyhood, he was so petted and spoilt and clad in such finery that the village children would call him "Your Lordship," and jeer at him; and older people regarded Raicharan as unaccountably crazy about the child.

At last the time came for the boy to go to school. Raicharan sold his small piece of land and went to Calcutta. There he got employment with great difficulty as a servant and sent Phailna to school. He spared no pains to give him the best education, the best clothes, the best food. Meanwhile, he himself lived on a mere handful of rice and would say in secret: "Ah, my little Master, my dear little Master, you loved me so much that you came back to my house! You shall never suffer from any neglect of mine."

Twelve years passed away in this manner. The boy was able to read and write well. He was bright and healthy and good-looking. He paid a great deal of attention to his personal appearance and was specially careful in parting his hair. He was inclined to extravagance and finery and spent money freely. He could never quite look on Raicharan as a father, because, though fatherly in affection, he had the manner of a servant. A further fault was this, that Raicharan kept secret from every one that he himself was the father of the child.

The students of the hostel, where Phailna was a boarder, were greatly amused by Raicharan's country manners, and I have to confess that behind his father's back Phailna joined in their fun. But, in the bottom of their hearts, all the students loved the innocent and tender-hearted old man, and Phailna was very fond of him also. But, as I have said before, he loved him with a kind of condescension.

Raicharan grew older and older, and his employer was continually finding fault with him for his incompetent work. He had been starving himself for the boy's sake, so he had grown physically weak and no longer up to his daily task. He would forget things and his mind became dull and stupid. But his employer expected a full servant's work out of him and would not brook excuses. The money that Raicharan had brought with him from the sale of his land was exhausted. The boy was continually grumbling about his clothes and asking for more money.

III

Raicharan made up his mind. He gave up the situation where he was working as a servant, and left some money with Phailna and said: "I have some business to do at home in my village, and shall be back soon."

He went off at once to Baraset where Anukul was magistrate. Anukul's wife was still broken down with grief. She had had no other child.

One day Anukul was resting after a long and weary day in court. His wife was buying, at an exorbitant price, a herb from a mendicant quack, which was said to ensure the birth of a child. A voice of greeting was heard in the courtyard. Anukul went out to see who was there. It was Raicharan. Anukul's heart was softened when he saw his old servant. He asked him many questions and offered to take him back into service.

Raicharan smiled faintly and said in reply: "I want to make obeisance to my mistress."

Anukul went with Raicharan into the house, where the mistress did not receive him as warmly as his old master. Raicharan took no notice of this, but folded his hands and said: "It was not the Padma that stole your baby. It was I."

Anukul exclaimed: "Great God! Eh! What! Where is he?"

Raicharan replied: "He is with me. I will bring him the day after to-morrow."

It was Sunday. There was no magistrate's court sitting. Both husband and wife were looking expectantly along the road, waiting from early morning for Raicharan's appearance. At ten o'clock he came leading Phailna by the hand.

Anukul's wife, without a question, took the boy into her lap and was wild with excitement, sometimes laughing, sometimes weeping, touching him, kissing his hair and his forehead, and gazing into his face with hungry, eager eyes. The boy was very good-looking and dressed like a gentleman's son. The heart of Anukul brimmed over with a sudden rush of affection.

Nevertheless the magistrate in him asked: "Have you any proofs?"

Raicharan said: "How could there be any proof of such a deed? God alone knows that I stole your boy, and no one else in the world."

When Anukul saw how eagerly his wife was clinging to the boy, he realised the futility of asking for proofs. It would be wiser to believe. And then, – where could an old man like Raicharan get such a boy from? And why should his faithful servant deceive him for nothing?

"But," he added severely, "Raicharan, you must not stay here."

"Where shall I go, Master?" said Raicharan, in a choking voice, folding his hands. "I am old. Who will take in an old man as a servant?"

The mistress said: "Let him stay. My child will be pleased. I forgive him."

But Anukul's magisterial conscience would not allow him. "No," he said, "he cannot be forgiven for what he has done."

Raicharan bowed to the ground and clasped Anukul's feet. "Master," he cried, "let me stay. It was not I who did it. It was God."

Anukul's conscience was more shocked than ever when Raicharan tried to put the blame on God's shoulders.

"No," he said, "I could not allow it. I cannot trust you any more. You have done an act of treachery."

Raicharan rose to his feet and said: "It was not I who did it."

"Who was it then?" asked Anukul.

Raicharan replied: "It was my fate."

But no educated man could take this for an excuse. Anukul remained obdurate.

When Phailna saw that he was the wealthy magistrate's son, and not Raicharan's, he was angry at first, thinking that he had been cheated all this time of his birthright. But seeing Raicharan in distress, he generously said to his father: "Father, forgive him. Even if you don't let him live with us, let him have a small monthly pension."

After hearing this, Raicharan did not utter another word. He looked for the last time on the face of his son. He made obeisance to his old master and mistress. Then he went out and was mingled with the numberless people of the world.

At the end of the month Anukul sent him some money to his village. But the money came back. There was no one there of the name of Raicharan.

The Home-coming

Phatik Chakravorti was ringleader among the boys of the village. A new mischief got into his head. There was a heavy log lying on the mud-flat of the river waiting to be shaped into a mast for a boat. He decided that they should all work together to shift the log by main force from its place and roll it away. The owner of the log would be angry and surprised, and they would all enjoy the fun. Every one seconded the proposal, and it was carried unanimously.

But just as the fun was about to begin, Mākhan, Phatik's younger brother, sauntered up and sat down on the log in front of them all without a word. The boys were puzzled for a moment. He was pushed, rather timidly, by one of the boys and told to get up; but he remained quite unconcerned. He appeared like a young philosopher meditating on the futility of games. Phatik was furious. "Mākhan," he cried, "if you don't get down this minute I'll thrash you!"

Mākhan only moved to a more comfortable position.

Now, if Phatik was to keep his regal dignity before the public, it was clear he ought to carry out his threat. But his courage failed him at the crisis. His fertile brain, however, rapidly seized upon a new manœuvre which would discomfit his brother and afford his followers an added amusement. He gave the word of command to roll the log and Mākhan over together. Mākhan heard the order and made it a point of honour to stick on. But he overlooked the fact, like those who attempt earthly fame in other matters, that there was peril in it.

The boys began to heave at the log with all their might, calling out, "One, two, three, go!" At the word "go" the log went; and with it went Mākhan's philosophy, glory and all.

The other boys shouted themselves hoarse with delight. But Phatik was a little frightened. He knew what was coming. And, sure enough, Mākhan rose from Mother Earth blind as Fate and screaming like the Furies. He rushed at Phatik and scratched his face and beat him and kicked him, and then went crying home. The first act of the drama was over.

Phatik wiped his face, and sat down on the edge of a sunken barge by the river bank, and began to chew a piece of grass. A boat came up to the landing and a middle-aged man, with grey hair and dark moustache, stepped on shore. He saw the boy sitting there doing nothing and asked him where the Chakravortis lived. Phatik went on chewing the grass and said: "Over there," but it was quite impossible to tell where he pointed. The stranger asked him again. He swung his legs to and fro on the side of the barge and said: "Go and find out," and continued to chew the grass as before.

But now a servant came down from the house and told Phatik his mother wanted him. Phatik refused to move. But the servant was the master on this occasion. He took Phatik up roughly and carried him, kicking and struggling in impotent rage.

When Phatik came into the house, his mother saw him. She called out angrily: "So you have been hitting Mākhan again?"

Phatik answered indignantly: "No, I haven't! Who told you that?"

His mother shouted: "Don't tell lies! You have."

Phatik said sullenly: "I tell you, I haven't. You ask Mākhan!" But Mākhan thought it best to stick to his previous statement. He said: "Yes, mother. Phatik did hit me."

Phatik's patience was already exhausted. He could not bear this injustice. He rushed at Mākhan and hammered him with blows: "Take that," he cried, "and that, and that, for telling lies."

His mother took Mākhan's side in a moment, and pulled Phatik away, beating him with her hands. When Phatik pushed her aside, she shouted out: "What! you little villain! Would you hit your own mother?"

It was just at this critical juncture that the grey-haired stranger arrived. He asked what was the matter. Phatik looked sheepish and ashamed.

But when his mother stepped back and looked at the stranger, her anger was changed to surprise. For she recognized her brother and cried: "Why, Dada! Where have you come from?"

As she said these words, she bowed to the ground and touched his feet. Her brother had gone away soon after she had married; and he had started business in Bombay. His sister had lost her husband while he was there. Bishamber had now come back to Calcutta and had at once made enquiries about his sister. He had then hastened to see her as soon as he found out where she was.

The next few days were full of rejoicing. The brother asked after the education of the two boys. He was told by his sister that Phatik was a perpetual nuisance. He was lazy, disobedient, and wild. But Mākhan was as good as gold, as quiet as a lamb, and very fond of reading. Bishamber kindly offered to take Phatik off his sister's hands and educate him with his own children in Calcutta. The widowed mother readily agreed. When his uncle asked Phatik if he would like to go to Calcutta with him, his joy knew no bounds and he said: "Oh, yes, uncle!" in a way that made it quite clear that he meant it.

It was an immense relief to the mother to get rid of Phatik. She had a prejudice against the boy, and no love was lost between the two brothers. She was in daily fear that he would either drown Mākhan some day in the river, or break his head in a fight, or run him into some danger. At the same time she was a little distressed to see Phatik's extreme eagerness to get away.

Phatik, as soon as all was settled, kept asking his uncle every minute when they were to start. He was on pins and needles all day long with excitement and lay awake most of the night. He bequeathed to Mākhan, in perpetuity, his fishing-rod, his big kite, and his marbles. Indeed, at this time of departure, his generosity towards Mākhan was unbounded.

When they reached Calcutta, Phatik made the acquaintance of his aunt for the first time. She was by no means pleased with this unnecessary addition to her family. She found her own three boys quite enough to manage without taking any one else. And to bring a village lad of fourteen into their midst was terribly upsetting. Bishamber should really have thought twice before committing such an indiscretion.

In this world of human affairs there is no worse nuisance than a boy at the age of fourteen. He is neither ornamental nor useful. It is impossible to shower affection on him as on a little boy; and he is always getting in the way. If he talks with a childish lisp he is called a baby, and if he answers in a grown-up way he is called impertinent. In fact any talk at all from him is resented. Then he is at the unattractive, growing age. He grows out of his clothes with indecent haste; his voice grows hoarse and breaks and quavers; his face grows suddenly angular and unsightly. It is easy to excuse the shortcomings of early childhood, but it is hard to tolerate even unavoidable lapses in a boy of fourteen. The lad himself becomes painfully self-conscious. When he talks with elderly people he is either unduly forward, or else so unduly shy that he appears ashamed of his very existence.

Yet it is at this very age when, in his heart of hearts, a young lad most craves for recognition and love; and he becomes the devoted slave of any one who shows him consideration. But none dare openly love him, for that would be regarded as undue indulgence and therefore bad for the boy. So, what with scolding and chiding, he becomes very much like a stray dog that has lost his master.

For a boy of fourteen his own home is the only Paradise. To live in a strange house with strange people is little short of torture, while the height of bliss is to receive the kind looks of women and never to be slighted by them.

It was anguish to Phatik to be the unwelcome guest in his aunt's house, despised by this elderly woman and slighted on every occasion. If ever she asked him to do anything for her, he would be so overjoyed that he would overdo it; and then she would tell him not to be so stupid, but to get on with his lessons.

The cramped atmosphere of neglect oppressed Phatik so much that he felt that he could hardly breathe. He wanted to go out into the open country and fill his lungs with fresh air. But there was no open country to go to. Surrounded on all sides by Calcutta houses and walls, he would dream night after night of his village home and long to be back there. He remembered the glorious meadow where he used to fly his kite all day long; the broad river-banks where he would wander about the live-long day singing and shouting for joy; the narrow brook where he could go and dive and swim at any time he liked. He thought of his band of boy companions over whom he was despot; and, above all, the memory of that tyrant mother of his, who had such a prejudice against him, occupied him day and night. A kind of physical love like that of animals, a longing to be in the presence of the one who is loved, an inexpressible wistfulness during absence, a silent cry of the inmost heart for the mother, like the lowing of a calf in the twilight, – this love, which was almost an animal instinct, agitated the shy, nervous, lean, uncouth and ugly boy. No one could understand it, but it preyed upon his mind continually.

There was no more backward boy in the whole school than Phatik. He gaped and remained silent when the teacher asked him a question, and like an overladen ass patiently suffered all the blows that came down on his back. When other boys were out at play, he stood wistfully by the window and gazed at the roofs of the distant houses. And if by chance he espied children playing on the open terrace of any roof, his heart would ache with longing.

One day he summoned up all his courage and asked his uncle: "Uncle, when can I go home?"

His uncle answered: "Wait till the holidays come."

But the holidays would not come till October and there was a long time still to wait.

One day Phatik lost his lesson book. Even with the help of books he had found it very difficult indeed to prepare his lesson. Now it was impossible. Day after day the teacher would cane him unmercifully. His condition became so abjectly miserable that even his cousins were ashamed to own him. They began to jeer and insult him more than the other boys. He went to his aunt at last and told her that he had lost his book.

His aunt pursed her lips in contempt and said: "You great clumsy, country lout! How can I afford, with all my family, to buy you new books five times a month?"

That night, on his way back from school, Phatik had a bad headache with a fit of shivering. He felt he was going to have an attack of malarial fever. His one great fear was that he would be a nuisance to his aunt.

The next morning Phatik was nowhere to be seen. All searches in the neighbourhood proved futile. The rain had been pouring in torrents all night, and those who went out in search of the boy got drenched through to the skin. At last Bishamber asked help from the police.

At the end of the day a police van stopped at the door before the house. It was still raining and the streets were all flooded. Two constables brought out Phatik in their arms and placed him before Bishamber. He was wet through from head to foot, muddy all over, his face and eyes flushed red with fever and his limbs trembling. Bishamber carried him in his arms and took him into the inner apartments. When his wife saw him she exclaimed: "What a heap of trouble this boy has given us! Hadn't you better send him home?"

Phatik heard her words and sobbed out loud: "Uncle, I was just going home; but they dragged me back again."

The fever rose very high, and all that night the boy was delirious. Bishamber brought in a doctor. Phatik opened his eyes, flushed with fever, and looked up to the ceiling and said vacantly: "Uncle, have the holidays come yet?"

Bishamber wiped the tears from his own eyes and took Phatik's lean and burning hands in his own and sat by him through the night. The boy began again to mutter. At last his voice became excited: "Mother!" he cried, "don't beat me like that – Mother! I *am* telling the truth!"

The next day Phatik became conscious for a short time. He turned his eyes about the room, as if expecting some one to come. At last, with an air of disappointment, his head sank back on the pillow. He turned his face to the wall with a deep sigh.

Bishamber knew his thoughts and bending down his head whispered: "Phatik, I have sent for your mother."

The day went by. The doctor said in a troubled voice that the boy's condition was very critical.

Phatik began to cry out: "By the mark – three fathoms. By the mark – four fathoms. By the mark – – ." He had heard the sailor on the river-steamer calling out the mark on the plumb-line. Now he was himself plumbing an unfathomable sea.

Later in the day Phatik's mother burst into the room, like a whirlwind, and began to toss from side to side and moan and cry in a loud voice.

Bishamber tried to calm her agitation, but she flung herself on the bed, and cried: "Phatik, my darling, my darling."

Phatik stopped his restless movements for a moment. His hands ceased beating up and down. He said: "Eh?"

The mother cried again: "Phatik, my darling, my darling."

Phatik very slowly turned his head and without seeing anybody said: "Mother, the holidays have come."

The Skeleton

In the room next to the one in which we boys used to sleep, there hung a human skeleton. In the night it would rattle in the breeze which played about its bones. In the day these bones were rattled by us. We were taking lessons in osteology from a student in the Campbell Medical School, for our guardians were determined to make us masters of all the sciences. How far they succeeded we need not tell those who know us; and it is better hidden from those who do not.

Many years have passed since then. In the meantime the skeleton has vanished from the room, and the science of osteology from our brains, leaving no trace behind.

The other day, our house was crowded with guests, and I had to pass the night in the same old room. In these now unfamiliar surroundings, sleep refused to come, and, as I tossed from side to side, I heard all the hours of the night chimed, one after another, by the church clock near by. At length the lamp in the corner of the room, after some minutes of choking and spluttering, went out altogether. One or two bereavements had recently happened in the family, so the going out of the lamp naturally led me to thoughts of death. In the great arena of nature, I thought, the light of a lamp losing itself in eternal darkness, and the going out of the light of our little human lives, by day or by night, were much the same thing.

My train of thought recalled to my mind the skeleton. While I was trying to imagine what the body which had clothed it could have been like, it suddenly seemed to me that something was walking round and round my bed, groping along the walls of the room. I could hear its rapid breathing. It seemed as if it was searching for something which it could not find, and pacing round the room with ever-hastier steps. I felt quite sure that this was a mere fancy of my sleepless, excited brain; and that the throbbing of the veins in my temples was really the sound which seemed like running footsteps. Nevertheless, a cold shiver ran all over me. To help to get rid of this hallucination, I called out aloud: 'Who is there?' The footsteps seemed to stop at my bedside, and the reply came: 'It is I. I have come to look for that skeleton of mine.'

It seemed absurd to show any fear before the creature of my own imagination; so, clutching my pillow a little more tightly, I said in a casual sort of way: 'A nice business for this time of night! Of what use will that skeleton be to you now?'

The reply seemed to come almost from my mosquito-curtain itself. 'What a question! In that skeleton were the bones that encircled my heart; the youthful charm of my six-and-twenty years bloomed about it. Should I not desire to see it once more?'

'Of course,' said I, 'a perfectly reasonable desire. Well, go on with your search, while I try to get a little sleep.'

Said the voice: 'But I fancy you are lonely. All right; I'll sit down a while, and we will have a little chat. Years ago I used to sit by men and talk to them. But during the last thirty-five years I have only moaned in the wind in the burning-places of the dead. I would talk once more with a man as in the old times.'

I felt that some one sat down just near my curtain. Resigning myself to the situation, I replied with as much cordiality as I could summon: 'That will be very nice indeed. Let us talk of something cheerful.'

'The funniest thing I can think of is my own life-story. Let me tell you that.'

The church clock chimed the hour of two.

'When I was in the land of the living, and young, I feared one thing like death itself, and that was my husband. My feelings can be likened only to those of a fish caught with a hook. For it was as if a stranger had snatched me away with the sharpest of hooks from the peaceful calm of my childhood's home – and from him I had no means of escape. My husband died two months after my marriage, and my friends and relations moaned pathetically on my behalf. My husband's father, after scrutinising my face with great care, said to my mother-in-law: "Do you not see, she has the evil eye?" – Well, are you listening? I hope you are enjoying the story?'

'Very much indeed!' said I. 'The beginning is extremely humorous.'

'Let me proceed then. I came back to my father's house in great glee. People tried to conceal it from me, but I knew well that I was endowed with a rare and radiant beauty. What is your opinion?'

'Very likely,' I murmured. 'But you must remember that I never saw you.'

'What! Not seen me? What about that skeleton of mine? Ha! ha! ha! Never mind. I was only joking. How can I ever make you believe that those two cavernous hollows contained the brightest of dark, languishing eyes? And that the smile which was revealed by those ruby lips had no resemblance whatever to the grinning teeth which you used to see? The mere attempt to convey to you some idea of the grace, the charm, the soft, firm, dimpled curves, which in the fulness of youth were growing and blossoming over those dry old bones makes me smile; it also makes me angry. The most eminent doctors of my time could not have dreamed of the bones of that body of mine as materials for teaching osteology. Do you know, one young doctor that I knew of, actually compared me to a golden *champak* blossom. It meant that to him the rest of humankind was fit only to illustrate the science of physiology, that I was a flower of beauty. Does any one think of the skeleton of a *champak*flower?

'When I walked, I felt that, like a diamond scattering splendour, my every movement set waves of beauty radiating on every side. I used to spend hours gazing on my hands – hands which could gracefully have reined the liveliest of male creatures.

'But that stark and staring old skeleton of mine has borne false-witness to you against me, while I was unable to refute the shameless libel. That is why of all men I hate you most! I feel I would like once for all to banish sleep from your eyes with a vision of that warm rosy loveliness of mine, to sweep out with it all the wretched osteological stuff of which your brain is full.'

'I could have sworn by your body,' cried I, 'if you had it still, that no vestige of osteology has remained in my head, and that the only thing that it is now full of is a radiant vision of perfect loveliness, glowing against the black background of night. I cannot say more than that.'

'I had no girl-companions,' went on the voice. 'My only brother had made up his mind not to marry. In the zenana I was alone. Alone I used to sit in the garden under the shade of the trees, and dream that the whole world was in love with me; that the stars with sleepless gaze were drinking in my beauty; that the wind was languishing in sighs as on some pretext or other it brushed past me; and that the lawn on which my feet rested, had it been conscious, would have lost consciousness again at their touch. It seemed to me that all the young men in the world were as blades of grass at my feet; and my heart, I know not why, used to grow sad.

'When my brother's friend, Shekhar, had passed out of the Medical College, he became our family doctor. I had already often seen him from behind a curtain. My brother was a strange man, and did not care to look on the world with open eyes. It was not empty enough for his taste; so he gradually moved away from it, until he was quite lost in an obscure corner. Shekhar was his one friend, so he was the only young man I could ever get to see. And when I held my evening court in my garden, then the host of imaginary young men whom I had at my feet were each one a Shekhar. – Are you listening? What are you thinking of?'

I sighed as I replied: 'I was wishing I was Shekhar!'

'Wait a bit. Hear the whole story first. One day, in the rains, I was feverish. The doctor came to see me. That was our first meeting. I was reclining opposite the window, so that the blush of the evening sky might temper the pallor of my complexion. When the doctor, coming in, looked up into my face, I put myself into his place, and gazed at myself in imagination. I saw in the glorious evening light that delicate wan face laid like a drooping flower against the soft white pillow, with the unrestrained curls playing over the forehead, and the bashfully lowered eyelids casting a pathetic shade over the whole countenance.

'The doctor, in a tone bashfully low, asked my brother: "Might I feel her pulse?"

'I put out a tired, well-rounded wrist from beneath the coverlet. "Ah!" thought I, as I looked on it, "if only there had been a sapphire bracelet." I have never before seen a doctor so awkward about feeling a patient's pulse. His fingers trembled as they felt my wrist. He measured the heat of my fever, I gauged the pulse of his heart. – Don't you believe me?'

'Very easily,' said I; 'the human heart-beat tells its tale.'

'After I had been taken ill and restored to health several times, I found that the number of the courtiers who attended my imaginary evening reception began to dwindle till they were reduced to only one! And at last in my little world there remained only one doctor and one patient.

'In these evenings I used to dress myself secretly in a canary-coloured *sari*; twine about the braided knot into which I did my hair a garland of white jasmine blossoms; and with a little mirror in my hand betake myself to my usual seat under the trees.

'Well! Are you perhaps thinking that the sight of one's own beauty would soon grow wearisome? Ah no! for I did not see myself with my own eyes. I was then one and also two. I used to see myself as though I were the doctor; I gazed, I was charmed, I fell madly in love. But, in spite of all the caresses I lavished on myself, a sigh would wander about my heart, moaning like the evening breeze.

'Anyhow, from that time I was never alone. When I walked I watched with downcast eyes the play of my dainty little toes on the earth, and wondered what the doctor would have felt had he been there to see. At mid-day the sky would be filled with the glare of the sun, without a sound, save now and then the distant cry of a passing kite. Outside our garden-walls the hawker would pass with his musical cry of "Bangles for sale, crystal bangles." And I, spreading a snow-white sheet on the lawn, would lie on it with my head on my arm. With studied carelessness the other arm would rest lightly on the soft sheet, and I would imagine to myself that some one had caught sight of the wonderful pose of my hand, that some one had clasped it in both of his and imprinted a kiss on its rosy palm, and was slowly walking away. – What if I ended the story here? How would it do?'

'Not half a bad ending,' I replied thoughtfully. 'It would no doubt remain a little incomplete, but I could easily spend the rest of the night putting in the finishing touches.'

'But that would make the story too serious. Where would the laugh come in? Where would be the skeleton with its grinning teeth?

'So let me go on. As soon as the doctor had got a little practice, he took a room on the ground-floor of our house for a consulting-chamber. I used then sometimes to ask him jokingly about medicines and poisons, and how much of this drug or that would kill a man. The subject was congenial and he would wax eloquent. These talks familiarised me with the idea of death; and so love and death were the only two things that filled my little world. My story is now nearly ended – there is not much left.'

'Not much of the night is left either,' I muttered.

'After a time I noticed that the doctor had grown strangely absent-minded, and it seemed as if he were ashamed of something which he was trying to keep from me. One day he came in, somewhat smartly dressed, and borrowed my brother's carriage for the evening.

'My curiosity became too much for me, and I went up to my brother for information. After some talk beside the point, I at last asked him: "By the way, Dada, where is the doctor going this evening in your carriage?"

'My brother briefly replied: "To his death."

'"Oh, do tell me," I importuned. "Where is he really going?"

'"To be married," he said, a little more explicitly.

'"Oh, indeed!" said I, as I laughed long and loudly.

'I gradually learnt that the bride was an heiress, who would bring the doctor a large sum of money. But why did he insult me by hiding all this from me? Had I ever begged and prayed him not to marry, because it would break my heart? Men are not to be trusted. I have known only one man in all my life, and in a moment I made this discovery.

'When the doctor came in after his work and was ready to start, I said to him, rippling with laughter the while: "Well, doctor, so you are to be married to-night?"

'My gaiety not only made the doctor lose countenance; it thoroughly irritated him.

'"How is it," I went on, "that there is no illumination, no band of music?"

'With a sigh he replied: "Is marriage then such a joyful occasion?"

'I burst out into renewed laughter. "No, no," said I, "this will never do. Who ever heard of a wedding without lights and music?"

'I bothered my brother about it so much that he at once ordered all the trappings of a gay wedding.

'All the time I kept on gaily talking of the bride, of what would happen, of what I would do when the bride came home. "And, doctor," I asked, "will you still go on feeling pulses?" Ha! ha! ha! Though the inner workings of people's, especially men's, minds are not visible, still I can take my oath that these words were piercing the doctor's bosom like deadly darts.

'The marriage was to be celebrated late at night. Before starting, the doctor and my brother were having a glass of wine together on the terrace, as was their daily habit. The moon had just risen.

'I went up smiling, and said: "Have you forgotten your wedding, doctor? It is time to start."

'I must here tell you one little thing. I had meanwhile gone down to the dispensary and got a little powder, which at a convenient opportunity I had dropped unobserved into the doctor's glass.

'The doctor, draining his glass at a gulp, in a voice thick with emotion, and with a look that pierced me to the heart, said: "Then I must go."

'The music struck up. I went into my room and dressed myself in my bridal-robes of silk and gold. I took out my jewellery and ornaments from the safe and put them all on; I put the red mark of wifehood on the parting in my hair. And then under the tree in the garden I prepared my bed.

'It was a beautiful night. The gentle south wind was kissing away the weariness of the world. The scent of jasmine and bela filled the garden with rejoicing.

'When the sound of the music began to grow fainter and fainter; the light of the moon to get dimmer and dimmer; the world with its lifelong associations of home and kin to fade away from my perceptions like some illusion; – then I closed my eyes, and smiled.

'I fancied that when people came and found me they would see that smile of mine lingering on my lips like a trace of rose-coloured wine, that when I thus slowly entered my eternal bridal-chamber I should carry with me this smile, illuminating my face. But alas for the bridal-chamber! Alas for the bridal-robes of silk and gold! When I woke at the sound of a rattling within me, I found three urchins learning osteology from my skeleton. Where in my bosom my joys and griefs used to throb, and the petals of youth to open one by one, there the master with his pointer was busy naming my bones. And as to that last smile, which I had so carefully rehearsed, did you see any sign of that?

'Well, well, how did you like the story?'

'It has been delightful,' said I.

At this point the first crow began to caw. 'Are you there?' I asked. There was no reply.

The morning light entered the room.

The Auspicious Vision

Kantichandra was young; yet after his wife's death he sought no second partner, and gave his mind to the hunting of beasts and birds. His body was long and slender, hard and agile; his sight keen; his aim unerring. He dressed like a countryman, and took with him Hira Singh the wrestler, Chakkanlal, Khan Saheb the musician, Mian Saheb, and many others. He had no lack of idle followers.

In the month of *Agrahayan* Kanti had gone out shooting near the swamp of Nydighi with a few sporting companions. They were in boats, and an army of servants, in boats also, filled the bathing-*ghats*. The village women found it well-nigh impossible to bathe or to draw water. All day long, land and water trembled to the firing of the guns; and every evening musicians killed the chance of sleep.

One morning as Kanti was seated in his boat cleaning a favourite gun, he suddenly started at what he thought was the cry of wild duck. Looking up, he saw a village maiden, coming to the water's edge, with two white ducklings clasped to her breast. The little stream was almost stagnant. Many weeds choked the current. The girl put the birds into the water, and watched them anxiously. Evidently the presence of the sportsmen was the cause of her care and not the wildness of the ducks.

The girl's beauty had a rare freshness - as if she had just come from Vishwakarma's workshop. It was difficult to guess her age. Her figure was almost a woman's, but her face was so childish that clearly the world had left no impression there. She seemed not to know herself that she had reached the threshold of youth.

Kanti's gun-cleaning stopped for a while. He was fascinated. He had not expected to see such a face in such a spot. And yet its beauty suited its surroundings better than it would have suited a palace. A bud is lovelier on the bough than in a golden vase. That day the blossoming reeds glittered in the autumn dew and morning sun, and the fresh, simple face set in the midst was like a picture of festival to Kanti's enchanted mind. Kalidos has forgotten to sing how Siva's Mountain-Queen herself sometimes has come to the young Ganges, with just such ducklings in her breast. As he gazed, the maiden started in terror, and hurriedly took back the ducks into her bosom with a half-articulate cry of pain. In another moment, she had left the river-bank and disappeared into the bamboo thicket hard by. Looking round, Kanti saw one of his men pointing an unloaded gun at the ducks. He at once went up to him, wrenched away his gun, and bestowed on his cheek a prodigious slap. The astonished humourist finished his joke on the floor. Kanti went on cleaning his gun.

But curiosity drove Kanti to the thicket wherein he had seen the girl disappear. Pushing his way through, he found himself in the yard of a well-to-do householder. On one side was a row of conical thatched barns, on the other a clean cow-shed, at the end of which grew a *zizyph* bush. Under the bush was seated the girl he had seen that morning, sobbing over a wounded dove, into whose yellow beak she was trying to wring a little water from the moist corner of her garment. A grey cat, its fore-paws on her knee, was looking eagerly at the bird, and every now and then, when it got too forward, she kept it in its place by a warning tap on the nose.

This little picture, set in the peaceful mid-day surroundings of the householder's yard, instantly impressed itself on Kanti's sensitive heart. The checkered light and shade, flickering beneath the delicate foliage of the *zizyph*, played on the girl's lap. Not far off a cow was chewing the cud, and lazily keeping off the flies with slow movements of its head and tail. The north wind whispered softly in the rustling bamboo thickets. And she who at dawn on the river-bank had looked like the Forest Queen, now in the silence of noon showed the eager pity of the Divine Housewife. Kanti, coming in upon her with his gun, had a sense of intrusion. He felt like a thief caught red-handed. He longed to explain that it was not he who had hurt the dove. As he wondered how he should begin, there came a call of 'Sudha!' from the house. The girl jumped up. 'Sudha!' came the voice again. She took up her dove, and ran within. 'Sudha,' thought Kanti, 'what an appropriate name!'

Kanti returned to the boat, handed his gun to his men, and went over to the front door of the house. He found a middle-aged Brahmin, with a peaceful, clean-shaven face, seated on a bench outside, and reading a devotional book. Kanti saw in his kindly, thoughtful face something of the tenderness which shone in the face of the maiden.

Kanti saluted him, and said: 'May I ask for some water, sir? I am very thirsty.' The elder man welcomed him with eager hospitality, and, offering him a seat on the bench, went inside and fetched with his own hands a little brass plate of sugar wafers and a bell-metal vessel full of water.

After Kanti had eaten and drunk, the Brahmin begged him to introduce himself. Kanti gave his own name, his father's name, and the address of his home, and then said in the usual way: 'If I can be of any service, sir, I shall deem myself fortunate.'

'I require no service, my son,' said Nabin Banerji; 'I have only one care at present.'

'What is that, sir?' said Kanti.

'It is my daughter, Sudha, who is growing up' (Kanti smiled as he thought of her babyish face), 'and for whom I have not yet been able to find a worthy bridegroom. If I could only see her well married, all my debt to this world would be paid. But there is no suitable bridegroom here, and I cannot leave my charge of Gopinath here, to search for a husband elsewhere.'

'If you would see me in my boat, sir, we would have a talk about the marriage of your daughter.' So saying, Kanti repeated his salute and went back. He then sent some of his men into the village to inquire, and in answer heard nothing but praise of the beauty and virtues of the Brahmin's daughter.

When next day the old man came to the boat on his promised visit, Kanti bent low in salutation, and begged the hand of his daughter for himself. The Brahmin was so much overcome by this undreamed-of piece of good fortune - for Kanti not only belonged to a well-known Brahmin family, but was also a landed proprietor of wealth and position - that at first he could hardly utter a word in reply. He thought there must have been some mistake, and at length mechanically repeated: 'You desire to marry my daughter?'

'If you will deign to give her to me,' said Kanti.

'You mean Sudha?' he asked again.

'Yes,' was the reply.

'But will you not first see and speak to her - - ?'

Kanti, pretending he had not seen her already, said: 'Oh, that we shall do at the moment of the Auspicious Vision.'

In a voice husky with emotion the old man said: 'My Sudha is indeed a good girl, well skilled in all the household arts. As you are so generously taking her on trust, may she never cause you a moment's regret. This is my blessing!'

The brick-built mansion of the Mazumdars had been borrowed for the wedding ceremony, which was fixed for next *Magh*, as Kanti did not wish to delay. In due time the bridegroom arrived on his elephant, with drums and music and with a torchlight procession, and the ceremony began.

When the bridal couple were covered with the scarlet screen for the rite of the Auspicious Vision, Kanti looked up at his bride. In that bashful, downcast face, crowned with the wedding coronet and bedecked with sandal paste, he could scarcely recognise the village maiden of his fancy, and in the fulness of his emotion a mist seemed to becloud his eyes.

At the gathering of women in the bridal chamber, after the wedding ceremony was over, an old village dame insisted that Kanti himself should take off his wife's bridal veil. As he did so he started back. It was not the same girl.

Something rose from within his breast and pierced into his brain. The light of the lamps seemed to grow dim, and darkness to tarnish the face of the bride herself.

At first he felt angry with his father-in-law. The old scoundrel had shown him one girl, and married him to another. But on calmer reflection he remembered that the old man had not shown him any daughter at all - that it was all his own fault. He thought it best not to show his arrant folly to the world, and took his place again with apparent calmness.

He could swallow the powder; he could not get rid of its taste. He could not bear the merry-makings of the festive throng. He was in a blaze of anger with himself as well as with everybody else.

Suddenly he felt the bride, seated by his side, give a little start and a suppressed scream; a leveret, scampering into the room, had brushed across her feet. Close upon it followed the girl he had seen before. She caught up the leveret into her arms, and began to caress it with an affectionate murmuring. 'Oh, the mad girl!' cried the women as they made signs to her to leave the room. She heeded them not, however, but came and unconcernedly sat in front of the wedded pair, looking into their faces with a childish curiosity. When a maidservant came and took her by the arm to lead her away, Kanti hurriedly interposed, saying, 'Let her be.'

'What is your name?' he then went on to ask her.

The girl swayed backwards and forwards but gave no reply. All the women in the room began to titter.

Kanti put another question: 'Have those ducklings of yours grown up?'

The girl stared at him as unconcernedly as before.

The bewildered Kanti screwed up courage for another effort, and asked tenderly after the wounded dove, but with no avail. The increasing laughter in the room betokened an amusing joke.

At last Kanti learned that the girl was deaf and dumb, the companion of all the animals and birds of the locality. It was but by chance that she rose the other day when the name of Sudha was called.

Kanti now received a second shock. A black screen lifted from before his eyes. With a sigh of intense relief, as of escape from calamity, he looked once more into the face of his bride. Then came the true Auspicious Vision. The light from his heart and from the smokeless lamps fell on her gracious face; and he saw it in its true radiance, knowing that Nabin's blessing would find fulfilment.

The Trust Property

I

Brindaban Kundu came to his father in a rage and said: 'I am off this moment.'

'Ungrateful wretch!' sneered the father, Jaganath Kundu. 'When you have paid me back all that I have spent on your food and clothing, it will be time enough to give yourself these airs.'

Such food and clothing as was customary in Jaganath's household could not have cost very much. Our *rishis* of old managed to feed and clothe themselves on an incredibly small outlay. Jaganath's behaviour showed that his ideal in these respects was equally high. That he could not fully live up to it was due partly to the bad influence of the degenerate society around him, and partly to certain unreasonable demands of Nature in her attempt to keep body and soul together.

So long as Brindaban was single, things went smoothly enough, but after his marriage he began to depart from the high and rarefied standard cherished by his sire. It was clear that the son's ideas of comfort were moving away from the spiritual to the material, and imitating the ways of the world.

He was unwilling to put up with the discomforts of heat and cold, thirst and hunger. His minimum of food and clothing rose apace.

Frequent were the quarrels between the father and the son. At last Brindaban's wife became seriously ill and a *kabiraj* was called in. But when the doctor prescribed a costly medicine for his patient, Jaganath took it as a proof of sheer incompetence, and turned him out immediately. At first Brindaban besought his father to allow the treatment to continue; then he quarrelled with him about it, but to no purpose. When his wife died, he abused his father and called him a murderer.

'Nonsense!' said the father. 'Don't people die even after swallowing all kinds of drugs? If costly medicines could save life, how is it that kings and emperors are not immortal? You don't expect your wife to die with more pomp and ceremony than did your mother and your grandmother before her, do you?'

Brindaban might really have derived a great consolation from these words, had he not been overwhelmed with grief and incapable of proper thinking. Neither his mother nor his grandmother had taken any medicine before making their exit from this world, and this was the time-honoured custom of the family. But, alas, the younger generation was unwilling to die according to ancient custom. The English had newly come to the country at the time we speak of. Even in those remote days, the good old folks were horrified at the unorthodox ways of the new generation, and sat speechless, trying to draw comfort from their *hookas*.

Be that as it may, the modern Brindaban said to his old fogy of a father: 'I am off.'

The father instantly agreed, and wished publicly that, should he ever give his son one single pice in future, the gods might reckon his act as shedding the holy blood of cows. Brindaban in his turn similarly wished that, should he ever accept anything from his father, his act might be held as bad as matricide.

The people of the village looked upon this small revolution as a great relief after a long period of monotony. And when Jaganath disinherited his only son, every one did his best to console him. All were unanimous in the opinion that to quarrel with a father for the sake of a wife was possible only in these degenerate days. And the reason they gave was sound too. 'When your wife dies,' they said, 'you can find a second one without delay. But when your father dies, you can't get another to replace him for love or money.' Their logic no doubt was perfect, but we suspect that the utter hopelessness of getting another father did not trouble the misguided son very much. On the contrary, he looked upon it as a mercy.

Nor did separation from Brindaban weigh heavily on the mind of his father. In the first place, his absence from home reduced the household expenses. Then, again, the father was freed from a great anxiety. The fear of being poisoned by his son and heir had always haunted him. When he ate his scanty fare, he could never banish the thought of poison from his mind. This fear had abated somewhat after the death of his daughter-in-law, and, now that the son was gone, it disappeared altogether.

But there was one tender spot in the old man's heart. Brindaban had taken away with him his four-year-old son, Gokul Chandra. Now, the expense of keeping the child was comparatively small, and so Jaganath's affection for him was without a drawback. Still, when Brindaban took him away, his grief, sincere as it was, was mingled at first with calculation as to how much he would save a month by the absence of the two, how much the sum would come to in the year, and what would be the capital to bring it in as interest.

But the empty house, without Gokul Chandra in it to make mischief, became more and more difficult for the old man to live in. There was no one now to play tricks upon him when he was engaged in his *puja*, no one to snatch away his food and eat it, no one to run away with his inkpot, when he was writing up his accounts. His daily routine of life, now uninterrupted, became an intolerable burden to him. He bethought him that this unworried peace was endurable only in the world to come. When he caught sight of the holes made in his quilt by his grandchild, and the pen-and-ink sketches executed by the same artist on his rush-mat, his heart was heavy with grief. Once upon a time he had reproached the boy bitterly because he had torn his *dhoti* into pieces within the short space of two years; now tears stood in Jaganath's eyes as he gazed upon the dirty remnants lying in the bedroom. He carefully put them away in his safe, and registered a vow that, should Gokul ever come back again, he should not be reprimanded even if he destroyed one *dhoti* a year.

But Gokul did not return, and poor Jaganath aged rapidly. His empty home seemed emptier every day.

No longer could the old man stay peacefully at home. Even in the middle of the day, when all respectable folks in the village enjoyed their after-dinner siesta, Jaganath might be seen roaming over the village, *hooka* in hand. The boys, at sight of him, would give up their play, and, retiring in a body to a safe distance, chant verses composed by a local poet, praising the old gentleman's economical habits. No one ventured to say his real name, lest he should have to go without his meal that day – and so people gave him names after their own fancy. Elderly people called him Jaganash, but the reason why the younger generation preferred to call him a vampire was hard to guess. It may be that the bloodless, dried-up skin of the old man had some physical resemblance to the vampire's.

II

One afternoon, when Jaganath was rambling as usual through the village lanes shaded by mango topes, he saw a boy, apparently a stranger, assuming the captaincy of the village boys and explaining to them the scheme of some new prank. Won by the force of his character and the startling novelty of his ideas, the boys had all sworn allegiance to him. Unlike the others, he did not run away from the old man as he approached, but came quite close to him and began to shake his own *chadar*. The result was that a live lizard sprang out of it on to the old man's body, ran down his back and off towards the jungle. Sudden fright made the poor man shiver from head to foot, to the great amusement of the other boys, who shouted with glee. Before Jaganath had gone far, cursing and swearing, the *gamcha* on his shoulder suddenly disappeared, and the next moment it was seen on the head of the new boy, transformed into a turban.

The novel attentions of this manikin came as a great relief to Jaganath. It was long since any boy had taken such freedom with him. After a good deal of coaxing and many fair promises, he at last persuaded the boy to come to him, and this was the conversation which followed:

'What's your name, my boy?'

'Nitai Pal.'

'Where's your home?'

'Won't tell.'

'Who's your father?'

'Won't tell.'

'Why won't you?'

'Because I have run away from home.'

'What made you do it?'

'My father wanted to send me to school.'

It occurred to Jaganath that it would be useless extravagance to send such a boy to school, and his father must have been an unpractical fool not to have thought so.

'Well, well,' said Jaganath, 'how would you like to come and stay with me?'

'Don't mind,' said the boy, and forthwith he installed himself in Jaganath's house. He felt as little hesitation as though it were the shadow of a tree by the wayside. And not only that. He began to proclaim his wishes as regards his food and clothing with such coolness that you would have thought he had paid his reckoning in full beforehand; and, when anything went wrong, he did not scruple to quarrel with the old man. It had been easy enough for Jaganath to get the better of his own child; but, now, where another man's child was concerned, he had to acknowledge defeat.

III

The people of the village marvelled when Nitai Pal was unexpectedly made so much of by Jaganath. They felt sure that the old man's end was near, and the prospect of his bequeathing all his property to this unknown brat made their hearts sore. Furious with envy, they determined to do the boy an injury, but the old man took care of him as though he was a rib in his breast.

At times, the boy threatened that he would go away, and the old man used to say to him temptingly: 'I will leave you all the property I possess.' Young as he was, the boy fully understood the grandeur of this promise.

The village people then began to make inquiries after the father of the boy. Their hearts melted with compassion for the agonised parents, and they declared that the son must be a rascal to cause them so much suffering. They heaped abuses on his head, but the heat with which they did it betrayed envy rather than a sense of justice.

One day the old man learned from a wayfarer that one Damodar Pal was seeking his lost son, and was even now coming towards the village. Nitai, when he heard this, became very restless and was ready to run away, leaving his future wealth to take care of itself. Jaganath reassured him, saying: 'I mean to hide you where nobody can find you – not even the village people themselves.'

This whetted the curiosity of the boy and he said: 'Oh, where? Do show me.'

'People will know, if I show you now. Wait till it is night,' said Jaganath.

The hope of discovering the mysterious hiding-place delighted Nitai. He planned to himself how, as soon as his father had gone away without him, he would have a bet with his comrades, and play hide-and-seek. Nobody would be able to find him. Wouldn't it be fun? His father, too, would ransack the whole village, and not find him – that would be rare fun also.

At noon, Jaganath shut the boy up in his house, and disappeared for some time. When he came home again, Nitai worried him with questions.

No sooner was it dark than Nitai said: 'Grandfather, shall we go now?'

'It isn't night yet,' replied Jaganath.

A little while later the boy exclaimed: 'It is night now, grandfather; come let's go.'

'The village people haven't gone to bed yet,' whispered Jaganath.

Nitai waited but a moment, and said: 'They have gone to bed now, grandfather; I am sure they have. Let's start now.'

The night advanced. Sleep began to weigh heavily on the eyelids of the poor boy, and it was a hard struggle for him to keep awake. At midnight, Jaganath caught hold of the boy's arm, and left the house, groping through the dark lanes of the sleeping village. Not a sound disturbed the stillness, except the occasional howl of a dog, when all the other dogs far and near would join in chorus, or perhaps the flapping of a night-bird, scared by the sound of human footsteps at that unusual hour. Nitai trembled with fear, and held Jaganath fast by the arm.

Across many a field they went, and at last came to a jungle, where stood a dilapidated temple without a god in it. 'What, here!' exclaimed Nitai in a tone of disappointment. It was nothing like what he had imagined. There was not much mystery about it. Often, since running away from home, he had passed nights in deserted temples like this. It was not a bad place for playing hide-and-seek; still it was quite possible that his comrades might track him there.

From the middle of the floor inside, Jaganath removed a slab of stone, and an underground room with a lamp burning in it was revealed to the astonished eyes of the boy. Fear and curiosity assailed his little heart. Jaganath descended by a ladder and Nitai followed him.

Looking around, the boy saw that there were brass *ghurras* on all sides of him. In the middle lay spread an *assan*, and in front of it were arranged vermilion, sandal paste, flowers, and other articles of *puja*. To satisfy his curiosity the boy dipped his hand into some of the *ghurras*, and drew out their contents. They were rupees and gold *mohurs*.

Jaganath, addressing the boy, said: 'I told you, Nitai, that I would give you all my money. I have not got much, – these *ghurras* are all that I possess. These I will make over to you to-day.'

The boy jumped with delight. 'All?' he exclaimed; 'you won't take back a rupee, will you?'

'If I do,' said the old man in solemn tones, 'may my hand be attacked with leprosy. But there is one condition. If ever my grandson, Gokul Chandra, or his son, or his grandson, or his great-grandson or any of his progeny should happen to pass this way, then you must make over to him, or to them, every rupee and every *mohur* here.'

The boy thought that the old man was raving. 'Very well,' he replied.

'Then sit on this *assan*,' said Jaganath.

'What for?'

'Because *puja* will be done to you.'

'But why?' said the boy, taken aback.

'This is the rule.'

The boy squatted on the *assan* as he was told. Jaganath smeared his forehead with sandal paste, put a mark of vermilion between his eyebrows, flung a garland of flowers round his neck, and began to recite *mantras*.

To sit there like a god, and hear *mantras* recited made poor Nitai feel very uneasy. 'Grandfather,' he whispered.

But Jaganath did not reply, and went on muttering his incantations.

Finally, with great difficulty he dragged each *ghurra* before the boy and made him repeat the following vow after him:

'I do solemnly promise that I will make over all this treasure to Gokul Chandra Kundu, the son of Brindaban Kundu, the grandson of Jaganath Kundu, or to the son or to the grandson or to the great-grandson of the said Gokul Chandra Kundu, or to any other progeny of his who may be the rightful heir.'

The boy repeated this over and over again, until he felt stupefied, and his tongue began to grow stiff in his mouth. When the ceremony was over, the air of the cave was laden with the smoke of the earthen lamp and the breath-poison of the two. The boy felt that the roof of his mouth had become dry as dust, and his hands and feet were burning. He was nearly suffocated.

The lamp became dimmer and dimmer, and then went out altogether. In the total darkness that followed, Nitai could hear the old man climbing up the ladder. 'Grandfather, where are you going to?' said he, greatly distressed.

'I am going now,' replied Jaganath; 'you remain here. No one will be able to find you. Remember the name Gokul Chandra, the son of Brindaban, and the grandson of Jaganath.'

He then withdrew the ladder. In a stifled, agonised voice the boy implored: 'I want to go back to father.'

Jaganath replaced the slab. He then knelt down and placed his ear on the stone. Nitai's voice was heard once more – 'Father' – and then came a sound of some heavy object falling with a bump – and then – everything was still.

Having thus placed his wealth in the hands of a *yak*, Jaganath began to cover up the stone with earth. Then he piled broken bricks and loose mortar over it. On the top of all he planted turfs of grass and jungle weeds. The night was almost spent, but he could not tear himself away from the spot. Now and again he placed his ear to the ground, and tried to listen. It seemed to him that from far far below – from the abysmal depth of the earth's interior – came a wailing. It seemed to him that the night-sky was flooded with that one sound, that the sleeping humanity of all the world was awake, and was sitting on its beds, trying to listen.

The old man in his frenzy kept on heaping earth higher and higher. He wanted somehow to stifle that sound, but still he fancied he could hear 'Father.'

He struck the spot with all his might and said: 'Be quiet – people might hear you.' But still he imagined he heard 'Father.'

The sun lighted up the eastern horizon. Jaganath then left the temple, and came into the open fields.

There, too, somebody called out 'Father.' Startled at the sound, he turned back and saw his son at his heels.

'Father,' said Brindaban, 'I hear my boy is hiding himself in your house. I must have him back.'

With eyes dilated and distorted mouth, the old man leaned forward and exclaimed: 'Your boy?'

'Yes, my boy Gokul. He is Nitai Pal now, and I myself go by the name of Damodar Pal. Your *fame* has spread so widely in the neighbourhood, that we were obliged to cover up our origin, lest people should have refused to pronounce our names.'

Slowly the old man lifted both his arms above his head. His fingers began to twitch convulsively, as though he was trying to catch hold of some imaginary object in the air. He then fell on the ground.

When he came to his senses again, he dragged his son towards the ruined temple. When they were both inside it, he said: 'Do you hear any wailing sound?'

'No, I don't,' said Brindaban.

'Just listen very carefully. Do you hear anybody calling out "Father"?'

'No.'

This seemed to relieve him greatly.

From that day forward, he used to go about asking people: 'Do you hear any wailing sound?' They laughed at the raving dotard.

About four years later, Jaganath lay on his death-bed. When the light of this world was gradually fading away from his eyes, and his breathing became more and more difficult, he suddenly sat up in a state of delirium. Throwing both his hands in the air he seemed to grope about for something, muttering: 'Nitai, who has removed my ladder?'

Unable to find the ladder to climb out of his terrible dungeon, where there was no light to see and no air to breathe, he fell on his bed once more, and disappeared into that region where no one has ever been found out in the world's eternal game of hide-and-seek.

Raja and Rani

Bipin Kisore was born 'with a golden spoon in his mouth'; hence he knew how to squander money twice as well as how to earn it. The natural result was that he could not live long in the house where he was born.

He was a delicate young man of comely appearance, an adept in music, a fool in business, and unfit for life's handicap. He rolled along life's road like the wheel of Jagannath's car. He could not long command his wonted style of magnificent living.

Luckily, however, Raja Chittaranjan, having got back his property from the Court of Wards, was intent upon organising an Amateur Theatre Party. Captivated by the prepossessing looks of Bipin Kisore and his musical endowments, the Raja gladly 'admitted him of his crew.'

Chittaranjan was a B.A. He was not given to any excesses. Though the son of a rich man, he used to dine and sleep at appointed hours and even at appointed places. And he suddenly became enamoured of Bipin like one unto drink. Often did meals cool and nights grow old while he listened to Bipin and discussed with him the merits of operatic compositions. The Dewan remarked that the only blemish in the otherwise perfect character of his master was his inordinate fondness for Bipin Kisore.

Rani Basanta Kumari raved at her husband, and said that he was wasting himself on a luckless baboon. The sooner she could do away with him, the easier she would feel.

The Raja was much pleased in his heart at this seeming jealousy of his youthful wife. He smiled, and thought that women-folk know only one man upon the earth – him whom they love; and never think of other men's deserts. That there may be many whose merits deserve regard, is not recorded in the scriptures of women. The only good man and the only object of a woman's favours is he who has blabbered into her ears the matrimonial incantations. A little moment behind the usual hour of her husband's meals is a world of anxiety to her, but she never cares a brass button if her husband's dependents have a mouthful or not. This inconsiderate partiality of the softer sex might be cavilled at, but to Chittaranjan it did not seem unpleasant. Thus, he would often indulge in hyperbolic laudations of Bipin in his wife's presence, just to provoke a display of her delightful fulminations.

But what was sport to the 'royal' couple, was death to poor Bipin. The servants of the house, as is their wont, took their cue from the Rani's apathetic and wilful neglect of the wretched hanger-on, and grew more apathetic and wilful still. They contrived to forget to look after his comforts, to Bipin's infinite chagrin and untold sufferings.

Once the Rani rebuked the servant Pute, and said: 'You are always shirking work; what do you do all through the day?' 'Pray, madam, the whole day is taken up in serving Bipin Babu under the Maharaja's orders,' stammered the poor valet.

The Rani retorted: 'Your Bipin Babu is a great Nawab, eh?' This was enough for Pute. He took the hint. From the very next day he left Bipin Babu's orts as they were, and at times forgot to cover the food for him. With unpractised hands Bipin often scoured his own dishes and not unfrequently went without meals. But it was not in him to whine and report to the Raja. It was not in him to lower himself by petty squabblings with menials. He did not mind it; he took everything in good part.

And thus while the Raja's favours grew, the Rani's disfavour intensified, and at last knew no bounds.

Now the opera of *Subhadraharan* was ready after due rehearsal. The stage was fitted up in the palace court-yard. The Raja acted the part of 'Krishna,' and Bipin that of 'Arjuna.' Oh, how sweetly he sang! how beautiful he looked! The audience applauded in transports of joy.

The play over, the Raja came to the Rani and asked her how she liked it. The Rani replied: 'Indeed, Bipin acted the part of "Arjuna" gloriously! He does look like the scion of a noble family. His voice is rare!' The Raja said jocosely: 'And how do I look? Am I not fair? Have I not a sweet voice?' 'Oh, yours is different case!' added the Rani, and again fell to dilating on the histrionic abilities of Bipin Kisore.

The tables were now turned. He who used to praise, now began to deprecate. The Raja, who was never weary of indulging in high-sounding panegyrics of Bipin before his consort, now suddenly fell reflecting that, after all, unthinking people made too much of Bipin's actual merits. What was extraordinary about his appearance or voice? A short while before he himself was one of those unthinking men, but in a sudden and mysterious way he developed symptoms of thoughtfulness!

From the day following, every good arrangement was made for Bipin's meals. The Rani told the Raja: 'It is undoubtedly wrong to lodge Bipin Babu with the petty officers of the Raj in the Kachari; for all he now is, he was once a man of means.' The Raja ejaculated curtly: 'Ha!' and turned the subject. The Rani proposed that there might be another performance on the occasion of the first-rice ceremony of the 'royal' weanling. The Raja heard and heard her not.

Once on being reprimanded by the Raja for not properly laying his cloth, the servant Pute replied: 'What can I do? According to the Rani's behests I have to look after Bipin Babu and wait on him the livelong day.' This angered the Raja, and he exclaimed, highly nettled: 'Pshaw! Bipin Babu is a veritable

Nawab, I see! Can't he cleanse his own dishes himself?' The servant, as before, took his cue, and Bipin lapsed back into his former wretchedness.

The Rani liked Bipin's songs – they were sweet – there was no gainsaying it. When her husband sat with Bipin to the wonted discourses of sweet music of an evening, she would listen from behind the screen in an adjoining room. Not long afterwards, the Raja began again his old habit of dining and sleeping at regular hours. The music came to an end. Bipin's evening services were no more needed.

Raja Chittaranjan used to look after his *zemindari* affairs at noon. One day he came earlier to the zenana, and found his consort reading something. On his asking her what she read, the Rani was a little taken aback, but promptly replied: 'I am conning over a few songs from Bipin Babu's song-book. We have not had any music since you tired abruptly of your musical hobby.' Poor woman! it was she who had herself made no end of efforts to eradicate the hobby from her husband's mind.

On the morrow the Raja dismissed Bipin – without a thought as to how and where the poor fellow would get a morsel henceforth!

Nor was this the only matter of regret to Bipin. He had been bound to the Raja by the dearest and most sincere tie of attachment. He served him more for affection than for pay. He was fonder of his friend than of the wages he received. Even after deep cogitation, Bipin could not ascertain the cause of the Raja's sudden estrangement. "Tis Fate! all is Fate!' Bipin said to himself. And then, silently and bravely, he heaved a deep sigh, picked up his old guitar, put it up in the case, paid the last two coins in his pocket as a farewell *bakshish* to Pute, and walked out into the wide wide world where he had not a soul to call his friend.

The Riddle Solved

I

Krishna Gopal Sircar, zemindar of Jhikrakota, made over his estates to his eldest son, and retired to Kasi, as befits a good Hindu, to spend the evening of his life in religious devotion. All the poor and the destitute of the neighbourhood were in tears at the parting. Every one declared that such piety and benevolence were rare in these degenerate days.

His son, Bipin Bihari, was a young man well educated after the modern fashion, and had taken the degree of Bachelor of Arts. He sported a pair of spectacles, wore a beard, and seldom mixed with others. His private life was unsullied. He did not smoke, and never touched cards. He was a man of stern disposition, though he looked soft and pliable. This trait of his character soon came home to his tenantry in diverse ways. Unlike his father, he would on no account allow the remission of one single pice out of the rents justly due to him. In no circumstances would he grant any tenant one single day's grace in paying up.

On taking over the management of the property, Bipin Bihari discovered that his father had allowed a large number of Brahmins to hold land entirely rent-free, and a larger number at rents much below the prevailing rates. His father was incapable of resisting the importunate solicitation of others – such was the weakness of his character.

Bipin Bihari said this could never be. He could not abandon the income of half his property – and he reasoned with himself thus: *Firstly*, the persons who were in actual enjoyment of the concessions and getting fat at his expense were a lot of worthless people, and wholly undeserving of charity. Charity bestowed on such objects only encouraged idleness. *Secondly*, living nowadays had become much costlier than in the days of his ancestors. Wants had increased apace. For a gentleman to keep up his position had become four times as expensive as in days past. So he could not afford to scatter gifts right and left as his father had done. On the contrary, it was his bounden duty to call back as many of them as he possibly could.

So Bipin Bihari lost no time in carrying into effect what he conceived to be his duty. He was a man of strict principles.

What had gone out of his grasp, returned to him little by little. Only a very small portion of his father's grants did he allow to remain undisturbed, and he took good care to arrange that even those should not be deemed permanent.

The wails of the tenants reached Krishna Gopal at Benares through the post. Some even made a journey to that place to represent their grievances to him in person. Krishna Gopal wrote to his son intimating his displeasure. Bipin Bihari replied, pointing out that the times had changed. In former days, he said, the *zemindar* was compensated for the gifts he made by the many customary presents he received from his tenantry. Recent statutes had made all such impositions illegal. The *zemindar* had now to rest content with just the stipulated rent, and nothing more. 'Unless,' he continued, 'we keep a strict watch over the payment of our just dues, what will be left to us? Since the tenants won't give us anything extra now, how can we allow them concessions? Our relations must henceforth be strictly commercial. We shall be ruined if we go on making gifts and endowments, and the preservation of our property and the keeping up of our position will be rendered very difficult.'

Krishna Gopal became uneasy at finding that times should have changed so much. 'Well, well,' he murmured to himself, 'the younger generation knows best, I suppose. Our old-fashioned methods won't do now. If I interfere, my son might refuse to manage the property, and insist on my going back. No, thank you – I would rather not. I prefer to devote the few days that are left me to the service of my God.'

II

So things went on. Bipin Bihari put his affairs in order after much litigation in the Courts, and by less constitutional methods outside. Most of the tenants submitted to his will out of fear. Only a fellow called Asimuddin, son of Mirza Bibi, remained refractory.

Bipin's displeasure was keenest against this man. He could quite understand his father having granted rent-free lands to Brahmins, but why this Mohammedan should be holding so much land, some free and some at rents lower than the prevailing rates, was a riddle to him. And what was he? The son of a low Mohammedan widow, giving himself airs and defying the whole world, simply because he had learnt to read and write a little at the village school. To Bipin it was intolerable.

He made inquiries of his clerks about Asimuddin's holdings. All that they could tell him was that Babu Krishna Gopal himself had made these grants to the family many years back, but they had no idea as to what his motive might have been. They imagined, however, that perhaps the widow won the compassion of the kind-hearted *zemindar*, by representing to him her woe and misery.

To Bipin these favours seemed to be utterly undeserved. He had not seen the pitiable condition of these people in days gone by. Their comparative ease at the present day and their arrogance drove him to the conclusion that they had impudently swindled his tender-hearted father out of a part of his lawful income.

Asimuddin was a stiff-necked sort of a fellow, too. He vowed that he would lay down his life sooner than give up an inch of his land. Then came open hostilities.

The poor old widow tried her best to pacify her son. 'It is no good fighting with the *zemindar*,' she would often say to him. 'His kindness has kept us alive so long; let us depend upon him still, though he may curtail his favours. Surrender to him part of the lands as he desires.'

'Oh, mother!' protested Asimuddin. 'What do you know of these matters, pray?'

One by one, Asimuddin lost the cases instituted against him. The more he lost, the more his obstinacy increased. For the sake of his all, he staked all that was his.

One afternoon, Mirza Bibi collected some fruits and vegetables from her little garden, and unknown to her son went and sought an interview with Bipin Babu. She looked at him with a tenderness maternal in its intensity, and spoke: 'May Allah bless you, my son. Do not destroy Asim – it wouldn't be right of you. To your charge I commit him. Take him as though he were one whom it is your duty to support – as though he were a ne'er-do-well younger brother of yours. Vast is your wealth – don't grudge him a small particle of it, my son.'

This assumption of familiarity on the part of the garrulous old woman annoyed Bipin not a little. 'What do you know of these things, my good woman?' he condescended to say. 'If you have any representations to make, send your son to me.'

Being assured for the second time that she knew nothing about these affairs, Mirza Bibi returned home, wiping her eyes with her apron all the way, and offering her silent prayers to Allah.

III

The litigation dragged its weary length from the Criminal to the Civil Courts, and thence to the High Court, where at last Asimuddin met with a partial success. Eighteen months passed in this way. But he was a ruined man now – plunged in debts up to his very ears. His creditors took this opportunity to execute the decrees they had obtained against him. A date was fixed for putting up to auction every stick and stone that he had left.

It was Monday. The village market had assembled by the side of a tiny river, now swollen by the rains. Buying and selling were going on, partly on the bank and partly in the boats moored there. The hubbub was great. Among the commodities for sale jack-fruits preponderated, it being the month of *Asadh*. *Hilsa* fish were seen in large quantities also. The sky was cloudy. Many of the stall-holders, apprehending a downpour, had stretched a piece of cloth overhead, across bamboo poles put up for the purpose.

Asimuddin had come too – but he had not a copper with him. No shopkeepers allowed him credit nowadays. He therefore had brought a brass *thali* and a *dao* with him. These he would pawn, and then buy what he needed.

Towards evening, Bipin Babu was out for a walk attended by two or three retainers armed with *lathis*. Attracted by the noise, he directed his steps towards the market. On his arrival, he stopped awhile before the stall of Dwari, the oilman, and made kindly inquiries about his business. All on a sudden, Asimuddin raised his *dao* and ran towards Bipin Babu, roaring like a tiger. The market people caught hold of him half-way, and quickly disarmed him. He was forthwith given in custody to the police. Business in the market then went on as usual.

We cannot say that Bipin Babu was not inwardly pleased at this incident. It is intolerable that the creature we are hunting down should turn and show fight. 'The *badmash*,' Bipin chuckled; 'I have got him at last.'

The ladies of Bipin Babu's house, when they heard the news, exclaimed with horror: 'Oh, the ruffian! What a mercy they seized him in time!' They found consolation in the prospect of the man being punished as he richly deserved.

In another part of the village the same evening the widow's humble cottage, devoid of bread and bereft of her son, became darker than death. Others dismissed the incident of the afternoon from their minds, sat down to their meals, retired to bed and went to sleep, but to the widow the event loomed larger than anything else in this wide world. But, alas, who was there to combat it? Only a bundle of wearied bones and a helpless mother's heart trembling with fear.

IV

Three days have passed in the meanwhile. To-morrow the case would come up for trial before a Deputy Magistrate. Bipin Babu would have to be examined as a witness. Never before this did a *zemindar* of Jhikrakota appear in the witness-box, but Bipin did not mind.

The next day at the appointed hour, Bipin Babu arrived at the Court in a palanquin in great state. He wore a turban on his head, and a watch-chain dangled on his breast. The Deputy Magistrate invited him to a seat on the daïs, beside his own. The Court-room was crowded to suffocation. So great a sensation had not been witnessed in this Court for many years.

When the time for the case to be called drew near, a *chaprassi* came and whispered something in Bipin Babu's ear. He got up very agitated and walked out, begging the Deputy Magistrate to excuse him for a few minutes.

Outside he saw his old father a little way off, standing under a *banian* tree, barefooted and wrapped in a piece of *namabali*. A string of beads was in his hand. His slender form shone with a gentle lustre, and tranquil compassion seemed to radiate from his forehead.

Bipin, hampered by his close-fitting trousers and his flowing *chapkan*, touched his father's feet with his forehead. As he did this his turban came off and kissed his nose, and his watch, popping out of his pocket, swung to and fro in the air. Bipin hurriedly straightened his turban, and begged his father to come to his pleader's house close by.

'No, thank you,' Krishna Gopal replied, 'I will tell you here what I have got to say.'

A curious crowd had gathered by this time. Bipin's attendants pushed them back.

Then Krishna Gopal said: 'You must do what you can to get Asim acquitted, and restore him the lands that you have taken away from him.'

'Is it for this, father,' said Bipin, very much surprised, 'that you have come all the way from Benares? Would you tell me why you have made these people the objects of your special favour?'

'What would you gain by knowing it, my boy?'

But Bipin persisted. 'It is only this, father,' he went on; 'I have revoked many a grant because I thought the tenants were not deserving. There were many Brahmins among them, but of them you never said a word. Why are you so keen about these Mohammedans now? After all that has happened, if I drop this case against Asim, and give him back his lands, what shall I say to people?'

Krishna Gopal kept silence for some moments. Then, passing the beads through his shaky fingers with rapidity, he spoke with a tremulous voice: 'Should it be necessary to explain your conduct to people, you may tell them that Asimuddin is my son – and your brother.'

'What?' exclaimed Bipin in painful surprise. 'From a Musalman's womb?'

'Even so, my son,' was the calm reply.

Bipin stood there for some time in mute astonishment. Then he found words to say: 'Come home, father; we will talk about it afterwards.'

'No, my son,' replied the old man, 'having once relinquished the world to serve my God, I cannot go home again. I return hence. Now I leave you to do what your sense of duty may suggest.' He then blessed his son, and, checking his tears with difficulty, walked off with tottering steps.

Bipin was dumbfounded, not knowing what to say nor what to do. 'So, such was the piety of the older generation,' he said to himself. He reflected with pride how much better he was than his father in point of education and morality. This was the result, he concluded, of not having a principle to guide one's actions.

Returning to the Court, he saw Asimuddin outside between two constables, awaiting his trial. He looked emaciated and worn out. His lips were pale and dry, and his eyes unnaturally bright. A dirty piece of cloth worn to shreds covered him. 'This my brother!' Bipin shuddered at the thought.

The Deputy Magistrate and Bipin were friends, and the case ended in a fiasco. In a few days Asimuddin was restored to his former condition. Why all this happened, he could not understand. The village people were greatly surprised also.

However, the news of Krishna Gopal's arrival just before the trial soon got abroad. People began to exchange meaning glances. The pleaders in their shrewdness guessed the whole affair. One of them, Ram Taran Babu, was beholden to Krishna Gopal for his education and his start in life. Somehow or other he had always suspected that the virtue and piety of his benefactor were shams. Now he was fully convinced that, if a searching inquiry were made, all 'pious' men might be found out. 'Let them tell their beads as much as they like,' he thought with glee, 'everybody in this world is just as bad as myself. The only difference between a good and a bad man is that the good practise dissimulation while the bad don't.' The revelation that Krishna Gopal's far-famed piety, benevolence, and magnanimity were nothing but a cloak of hypocrisy, settled a difficulty that had oppressed Ram Taran Babu for many years. By what process of reasoning, we do not know, the burden of gratitude was greatly lifted off his mind. It was a vast relief to him!

The Elder Sister

I

Having described at length the misdeeds of an unfortunate woman's wicked, tyrannical husband, Tara, the woman's neighbour in the village, very shortly declared her verdict: 'Fire be to such a husband's mouth.'

At this Joygopal Babu's wife felt much hurt; it did not become womankind to wish, in any circumstances whatever, a worse species of fire than that of a cigar in a husband's mouth.

When, therefore, she mildly disapproved the verdict, hard-hearted Tara cried with redoubled vehemence: "Twere better to be a widow seven births over than the wife of such a husband,' and saying this she broke up the meeting and left.

Sasi said within herself: 'I can't imagine any offence in a husband that could so harden the heart against him.' Even as she turned the matter over in her mind, all the tenderness of her loving soul gushed forth towards her own husband now abroad. Throwing herself with outstretched arms on that part of the bed whereon her husband was wont to lie, she kissed the empty pillow, caught the smell of her husband's head, and, shutting the door, brought out from a wooden box an old and almost faded photograph with some letters in his handwriting, and sat gazing upon them. Thus she passed the hushed noontide alone in her room, musing of old memories and shedding tears of sadness.

It was no new yoke this between Sasikala and Joygopal. They had been married at an early age and had children. Their long companionship had made the days go by in an easy, commonplace sort of way. On neither side had there been any symptoms of excessive passion. They had lived together nearly sixteen years without a break, when her husband was suddenly called away from home on business, and then a great impulse of love awoke in Sasi's soul. As separation strained the tie, love's knot grew tighter, and the passion, whose existence Sasi had not felt, now made her throb with pain.

So it happened that after so many long years, and at such an age, and being the mother of children, Sasi, on this spring noon, in her lonely chamber, lying on the bed of separation, began to dream the sweet dream of a bride in her budding youth. That love of which hitherto she had been unconscious suddenly aroused her with its murmuring music. She wandered a long way up the stream, and saw many a golden mansion and many a grove on either bank; but no foothold could she find now amid the vanished hopes of happiness. She began to say to herself that, when next she met her husband, life should not be insipid nor should the spring come in vain. How very often, in idle disputation or some petty quarrel, had she teased her husband! With all the singleness of a penitent heart she vowed that she would never show impatience again, never oppose her husband's wishes, bear all his commands, and with a tender heart submit to whatever he wished of good or ill; for the husband was all-in-all, the husband was the dearest object of love, the husband was divine.

Sasikala was the only and much-petted daughter of her parents. For this reason, though he had only a small property of his own, Joygopal had no anxieties about the future. His father-in-law had enough to support them in a village with royal state.

And then in his old age a son was born untimely to Sasikala's father. To tell the truth, Sasi was very sore in her mind at this unlooked-for, improper, and unjust action of her parents; nor was Joygopal particularly pleased.

The parents' love centred in this son of their advanced years, and when the newly arrived, diminutive, sleepy brother-in-law seized with his two weak tiny fists all the hopes and expectations of Joygopal, Joygopal found a place in a tea-garden in Assam.

His friends urged him to look for employment hard-by, but whether out of a general feeling of resentment, or knowing the chances of rapid rise in a tea-garden, Joygopal would not pay heed to anybody. He sent his wife and children to his father-in-law's, and left for Assam. It was the first separation between husband and wife in their married life.

This incident made Sasikala very angry with her baby brother. The soreness which may not pass the lips is felt the more keenly within. When the little fellow sucked and slept at his ease, his big sister found a hundred reasons, such as the rice is cold, the boys are too late for school, to worry herself and others, day and night, with her petulant humours.

But in a short time the child's mother died. Before her death, she committed her infant son to her daughter's care.

Then did the motherless child easily conquer his sister's heart. With loud whoops he would fling himself upon her, and with right good-will try to get her mouth, nose, eyes within his own tiny mouth; he would seize her hair within his little fists and refuse to give it up; awaking before the dawn, he would roll over to her side and thrill her with his soft touch, and babble like a noisy brook; later on, he would call her *jiji* and *jijima*, and in hours of work and rest, by doing forbidden things, eating forbidden food, going to forbidden places, would set up a regular tyranny over her; then Sasi could resist no longer. She surrendered herself completely to this wayward little tyrant. Since the child had no mother, his influence over her became the greater.

II

The child was named Nilmani. When he was two years old his father fell seriously ill. A letter reached Joygopal asking him to come as quickly as possible. When after much trouble he got leave and arrived, Kaliprasanna's last hour had come.

Before he died Kaliprasanna entrusted Joygopal with the charge of his son, and left a quarter of his estate to his daughter.

So Joygopal gave up his appointment, and came home to look after his property.

After a long time husband and wife met again. When a material body breaks it may be put together again. But when two human beings are divided, after a long separation, they never re-unite at the same place, and to the same time; for the mind is a living thing, and moment by moment it grows and changes.

In Sasi reunion stirred a new emotion. The numbness of age-long habit in their old marriage was entirely removed by the longing born of separation, and she seemed to win her husband much more closely than before. Had she not vowed in her mind that whatever days might come, and how long soever they might be, she would never let the brightness of this glowing love for her husband be dimmed.

Of this reunion, however, Joygopal felt differently. When they were constantly together before he had been bound to his wife by his interests and idiosyncrasies. His wife was then a living truth in his life, and there would have been a great rent in the web of his daily habit if she were left out. Consequently Joygopal found himself in deep waters at first when he went abroad. But in time this breach in habit was patched up by a new habit.

And this was not all. Formerly his days went by in the most indolent and careless fashion. For the last two years, the stimulus of bettering his condition had stirred so powerfully in his breast that he had nothing else in his thoughts. As compared with the intensity of this new passion, his old life seemed like an unsubstantial shadow. The greatest changes in a woman's nature are wrought by love; in a man's, by ambition.

Joygopal, when he returned after two years, found his wife not quite the same as of old. To her life his infant brother-in-law had added a new breadth. This part of her life was wholly unfamiliar to him – here he had no communion with his wife. His wife tried hard to share her love for the child with him, but it cannot be said that she succeeded. Sasi would come with the child in her arms, and hold him before her husband with a smiling face – Nilmani would clasp Sasi's neck, and hide his face on her shoulder, and admit no obligation of kindred. Sasi wished that her little brother might show Joygopal all the arts he had learnt to capture a man's mind. But Joygopal was not very keen about it. How could the child show any enthusiasm? Joygopal could not at all understand what there was in the heavy-pated, grave-faced, dusky child that so much love should be wasted on him.

Women quickly understand the ways of love. Sasi at once understood that Joygopal did not care for Nilmani. Henceforth she used to screen her brother with the greatest care – to keep him away from the unloving, repelling look of her husband. Thus the child came to be the treasure of her secret care, the object of her isolated love.

Joygopal was greatly annoyed when Nilmani cried; so Sasi would quickly press the child to her breast, and with her whole heart and soul try to soothe him. And when Nilmani's cry happened to disturb Joygopal's sleep at night, and Joygopal with an expression of displeasure, and in a tortured spirit, growled at the child, Sasi felt humbled and fluttered like a guilty thing. Then she would take up the child in her lap, retire to a distance, and in a voice of pleading love, with such endearments as 'my gold, my treasure, my jewel,' lull him to sleep.

Children will fall out for a hundred things. Formerly in such cases, Sasi would punish her children, and side with her brother, for he was motherless. Now the law changed with the judge. Nilmani had often to bear heavy punishment without fault and without inquiry. This wrong went like a dagger to Sasi's heart; so she would take her punished brother into her room, and with sweets and toys, and by caressing and kissing him, solace as much as she could his stricken heart.

Thus the more Sasi loved Nilmani, the more Joygopal was annoyed with him. On the other hand, the more Joygopal showed his contempt for Nilmani, the more would Sasi bathe the child with the nectar of her love.

And when the fellow Joygopal behaved harshly to his wife, Sasi would minister to him silently, meekly, and with loving-kindness. But inwardly they hurt each other, moment by moment, about Nilmani.

The hidden clash of a silent conflict like this is far harder to bear than an open quarrel.

III

Nilmani's head was the largest part of him. It seemed as if the Creator had blown through a slender stick a big bubble at its top. The doctors feared sometimes that the child might be as frail and as quickly evanescent as a bubble. For a long time he could neither speak nor walk. Looking at his sad grave face, you might think that his parents had unburdened all the sad weight of their advanced years upon the head of this little child.

With his sister's care and nursing, Nilmani passed the period of danger, and arrived at his sixth year.

In the month of Kartik, on the *bhaiphoto* day, Sasi had dressed Nilmani up as a little Babu, in coat and *chadar* and red-bordered *dhoti*, and was giving him the 'brother's mark,' when her outspoken neighbour Tara came in and, for one reason or another, began a quarrel.

"Tis no use,' cried she, 'giving the "brother's mark" with so much show and ruining the brother in secret.'

At this Sasi was thunderstruck with astonishment, rage, and pain. Tara repeated the rumour that Sasi and her husband had conspired together to put the minor Nilmani's property up for sale for arrears of rent, and to purchase it in the name of her husband's cousin. When Sasi heard this, she uttered a curse that those who could spread such a foul lie might be stricken with leprosy in the mouth. And then she went weeping to her husband, and told him of the gossip. Joygopal said: 'Nobody can be trusted in these days. Upen is my aunt's son, and I felt quite safe in leaving him in charge of the property. He could not have allowed the *taluk* Hasilpur to fall into arrears and purchase it himself in secret, if I had had the least inkling about it.'

'Won't you sue then?' asked Sasi in astonishment.

'Sue one's cousin!' said Joygopal. 'Besides, it would be useless, a simple waste of money.'

It was Sasi's supreme duty to trust her husband's word, but Sasi could not. At last her happy home, the domesticity of her love seemed hateful to her. That home life which had once seemed her supreme refuge was nothing more than a cruel snare of self-interest, which had surrounded them, brother and sister, on all sides. She was a woman, single-handed, and she knew not how she could save the helpless Nilmani. The more she thought, the more her heart filled with terror, loathing, and an infinite love for her imperilled little brother. She thought that, if she only knew how, she would appear before the *Lat Saheb*, nay, write to the Maharani herself, to save her brother's property. The Maharani would surely not allow Nilmani's *taluk* of Hasilpur, with an income of seven hundred and fifty-eight rupees a year, to be sold.

When Sasi was thus thinking of bringing her husband's cousin to book by appealing to the Maharani herself, Nilmani was suddenly seized with fever and convulsions.

Joygopal called in the village doctor. When Sasi asked for a better doctor, Joygopal said: 'Why, Matilal isn't a bad sort.'

Sasi fell at his feet, and charged him with an oath on her own head; whereupon Joygopal said: 'Well, I shall send for the doctor from town.'

Sasi lay with Nilmani in her lap, nor would Nilmani let

her out of his sight for a minute; he clung to her lest by some pretence she should escape; even while he slept he would not loosen his hold of her dress.

Thus the whole day passed, and Joygopal came after nightfall to say that the doctor was not at home; he had gone to see a patient at a distance. He added that he himself had to leave that very day on account of a lawsuit, and that he had told Matilal, who would regularly call to see the patient.

At night Nilmani wandered in his sleep. As soon as the morning dawned, Sasi, without the least scruple, took a boat with her sick brother, and went straight to the doctor's house. The doctor was at home – he had not left the town. He quickly found lodgings for her, and having installed her under the care of an elderly widow, undertook the treatment of the boy.

The next day Joygopal arrived. Blazing with fury, he ordered his wife to return home with him at once.

'Even if you cut me to pieces, I won't return,' replied his wife. 'You all want to kill my Nilmani, who has no father, no mother, none other than me, but I will save him.'

'Then you remain here, and don't come back to my house,' cried Joygopal indignantly.

Sasi at length fired up. '*Your* house! Why, 'tis my brother's!'

'All right, we'll see,' said Joygopal. The neighbours made a great stir over this incident. 'If you want to quarrel with your husband,' said Tara, 'do so at home. What is the good of leaving your house? After all, Joygopal is your husband.'

By spending all the money she had with her, and selling her ornaments, Sasi saved her brother from the jaws of death. Then she heard that the big property which they had in Dwarigram, where their dwelling-house stood, the income of which was more than Rs. 1500 a year, had been transferred by Joygopal into his own name with the help of the Jemindar. And now the whole property belonged to them, not to her brother.

When he had recovered from his illness, Nilmani would cry plaintively: 'Let us go home, sister.' His heart was pining for his nephews and nieces, his companions. So he repeatedly said:

'Let us go home, sister, to that old house of ours.' At this Sasi wept. Where was their home?

But it was no good crying. Her brother had no one else besides herself in the world. Sasi thought of this, wiped her tears, and, entering the Zenana of the Deputy Magistrate, Tarini Babu, appealed to his wife. The Deputy Magistrate knew Joygopal. That a woman should forsake her home, and engage in a dispute with her husband regarding matters of property, greatly incensed him against Sasi. However, Tarini Babu kept Sasi diverted, and instantly wrote to Joygopal. Joygopal put his wife and brother-in-law into a boat by force, and brought them home.

Husband and wife, after a second separation, met again for the second time! The decree of Prajapati!

Having got back his old companions after a long absence, Nilmani was perfectly happy. Seeing his unsuspecting joy, Sasi felt as if her heart would break.

IV

The Magistrate was touring in the Mofussil during the cold weather and pitched his tent within the village to shoot. The Saheb met Nilmani on the village *maidan*. The other boys gave him a wide berth, varying Chanakya's couplet a little, and adding the Saheb to the list of 'the clawed, the toothed, and the horned beasts.' But grave-natured Nilmani in imperturbable curiosity serenely gazed at the Saheb.

The Saheb was amused and came up and asked in Bengali: 'You read at the *pathsala*?'

The boy silently nodded. 'What *pustaks* do you read?' asked the Saheb.

As Nilmani did not understand the word *pustak*, he silently fixed his gaze on the Magistrate's face. Nilmani told his sister the story of his meeting the Magistrate with great enthusiasm.

At noon, Joygopal, dressed in trousers, chapkan, and pagri, went to pay his salams to the Saheb. A crowd of suitors, chaprasies, and constables stood about him. Fearing the heat, the Saheb had seated himself at a court-table outside the tent, in the open shade, and placing Joygopal in a chair, questioned him about the state of the village. Having taken the seat of honour in open view of the community, Joygopal swelled inwardly, and thought it would be a good thing if any of the Chakrabartis or Nandis came and saw him there.

At this moment, a woman, closely veiled, and accompanied by Nilmani, came straight up to the Magistrate. She said: 'Saheb, into your hands I resign my helpless brother. Save him.' The Saheb, seeing the large-headed, solemn boy, whose acquaintance he had already made, and thinking that the woman must be of a respectable family, at once stood up and said: 'Please enter the tent.'

The woman said: 'What I have to say I will say here.'

Joygopal writhed and turned pale. The curious villagers thought it capital fun, and pressed closer. But the moment the Saheb lifted his cane they scampered off.

Holding her brother by the hand, Sasi narrated the history of the orphan from the beginning. As Joygopal tried to interrupt now and then, the Magistrate thundered with a flushed face, 'Chup rao,' and with the tip of his cane motioned to Joygopal to leave the chair and stand up.

Joygopal, inwardly raging against Sasi, stood speechless. Nilmani nestled up close to his sister, and listened awe-struck.

When Sasi had finished her story, the Magistrate put a few questions to Joygopal, and on hearing his answers, kept silence for a long while, and then addressed Sasi thus: 'My good woman, though this matter may not come up before me, still rest assured I will do all that is needful about it. You can return home with your brother without the least misgiving.'

Sasi said: 'Saheb, so long as he does not get back his own home, I dare not take him there. Unless you keep Nilmani with you, none else will be able to save him.'

'And what would you do?' queried the Saheb.

'I will retire to my husband's house,' said Sasi; 'there is nothing to fear for me.'

The Saheb smiled a little, and, as there was nothing else to do, agreed to take charge of this lean, dusty, grave, sedate, gentle Bengali boy whose neck was ringed with amulets.

When Sasi was about to take her leave, the boy clutched her dress. 'Don't be frightened, *baba*, – come,' said the Saheb. With tears streaming behind her veil, Sasi said: 'Do go, my brother, my darling brother – you will meet your sister again!'

Saying this she embraced him and stroked his head and back, and releasing her dress, hastily withdrew; and just then the Saheb put his left arm round him. The child wailed out: 'Sister, oh, my sister!' Sasi turned round at once, and with outstretched arm made a sign of speechless solace, and with a bursting heart withdrew.

Again in that old, ever-familiar house husband and wife met. The decree of Prajapati!

But this union did not last long. For soon after the villagers learnt one morning that Sasi had died of cholera in the night, and had been instantly cremated.

None uttered a word about it. Only neighbour Tara would sometimes be on the point of bursting out, but people would shut up her mouth, saying, 'Hush!'

At parting, Sasi gave her word to her brother they would meet again. Where that word was kept none can tell.

The River Stairs

I f you wish to hear of days gone by, sit on this step of mine, and lend your ears to the murmur of the rippling water.

The month of *Ashwin* (September) was about to begin. The river was in full flood. Only four of my steps peeped above the surface. The water had crept up to the low-lying parts of the bank, where the *kachu* plant grew dense beneath the branches of the mango grove. At that bend of the river, three old brick-heaps towered above the water around them. The fishing-boats, moored to the trunks of the *bābla* trees on the bank, rocked on the heaving flow-tide at dawn. The path of tall grasses on the sandbank had caught the newly risen sun; they had just begun to flower, and were not yet in full bloom.

The little boats puffed out their tiny sails on the sunlit river. The Brahmin priest had come to bathe with his ritual vessels. The women arrived in twos and threes to draw water. I knew this was the time of Kusum's coming to the bathing-stairs.

But that morning I missed her. Bhuban and Swarno mourned at the *ghāt*. They said that their friend had been led away to her husband's house, which was a place far away from the river, with strange people, strange houses, and strange roads.

In time she almost faded out of my mind. A year passed. The women at the *ghāt* now rarely talked of Kusum. But one evening I was startled by the touch of the long familiar feet. Ah, yes, but those feet were now without anklets, they had lost their old music.

Kusum had become a widow. They said that her husband had worked in some far-off place, and that she had met him only once or twice. A letter brought her the news of his death. A widow at eight years old, she had rubbed out the wife's red mark from her forehead, stripped off her bangles, and come back to her old home by the Ganges. But she found few of her old playmates there. Of them, Bhuban, Swarno, and Amala were married, and gone away; only Sarat remained, and she too, they said, would be wed in December next.

As the Ganges rapidly grows to fulness with the coming of the rains, even so did Kusum day by day grow to the fulness of beauty and youth. But her dull-coloured robe, her pensive face, and quiet manners drew a veil over her youth, and hid it from men's eyes as in a mist. Ten years slipped away, and none seemed to have noticed that Kusum had grown up.

One morning such as this, at the end of a far-off September, a tall, young, fair-skinned Sanyasi, coming I know not whence, took shelter in the Shiva temple, in front of me. His arrival was noised abroad in the village. The women left their pitchers behind, and crowded into the temple to bow to the holy man.

The crowd increased day by day. The Sanyasi's fame rapidly spread among the womenkind. One day he would recite the *Bhágbat*, another day he would expound the *Gita*, or hold forth upon a holy book in the temple. Some sought him for counsel, some for spells, some for medicines.

So months passed away. In April, at the time of the solar eclipse, vast crowds came here to bathe in the Ganges. A fair was held under the *bábla* tree. Many of the pilgrims went to visit the Sanyasi, and among them were a party of women from the village where Kusum had been married.

It was morning. The Sanyasi was counting his beads on my steps, when all of a sudden one of the women pilgrims nudged another, and said: 'Why! He is our Kusum's husband!' Another parted her veil a little in the middle with two fingers and cried out: 'Oh dear me! So it is! He is the younger son of the Chattergu family of our village!' Said a third, who made little parade of her veil: 'Ah! he has got exactly the same brow, nose, and eyes!' Yet another woman, without turning to the Sanyasi, stirred the water with her pitcher, and sighed: 'Alas! That young man is no more; he will not come back. Bad luck to Kusum!'

But, objected one, 'He had not such a big beard'; and another, 'He was not so thin'; or 'He was most probably not so tall.' That settled the question for the time, and the matter spread no further.

One evening, as the full moon arose, Kusum came and sat upon my last step above the water, and cast her shadow upon me.

There was no other at the *ghat* just then. The crickets were chirping about me. The din of brass gongs and bells had ceased in the temple – the last wave of sound grew fainter and fainter, until it merged like the shade of a sound in the dim groves of the farther bank. On the dark water of the Ganges lay a line of glistening moonlight. On the bank above, in bush and hedge, under the porch of the temple, in the base of ruined houses, by the side of the tank, in the palm grove, gathered shadows of fantastic shape. The bats swung from the *chhatim* boughs. Near the houses the loud clamour of the jackals rose and sank into silence.

Slowly the Sanyasi came out of the temple. Descending a few steps of the *ghat* he saw a woman sitting alone, and was about to go back, when suddenly Kusum raised her head, and looked behind her. The veil slipped away from her. The moonlight fell upon her face, as she looked up.

The owl flew away hooting over their heads. Starting at the sound, Kusum came to herself and put the veil back on her head. Then she bowed low at the Sanyasi's feet.

He gave her blessing and asked: 'Who are you?'

She replied: 'I am called Kusum.'

No other word was spoken that night. Kusum went slowly back to her house which was hard by. But the Sanyasi remained sitting on my steps for long hours that night. At last when the moon passed from the east to the west, and the Sanyasi's shadow, shifting from behind, fell in front of him, he rose up and entered the temple.

Henceforth I saw Kusum come daily to bow at his feet. When he expounded the holy books, she stood in a corner listening to him. After finishing his morning service, he used to call her to himself and speak on religion. She could not have understood it all; but, listening attentively in silence, she tried to understand it. As he directed her, so she acted implicitly. She daily served at the temple – ever alert in the god's worship – gathering flowers for the *puja*, and drawing water from the Ganges to wash the temple floor.

The winter was drawing to its close. We had cold winds. But now and then in the evening the warm spring breeze would blow unexpectedly from the south; the sky would lose its chilly aspect; pipes would sound, and music be heard in the village after a long silence. The boatmen would set their boats drifting down the current, stop rowing, and begin to sing the songs of Krishna. This was the season.

Just then I began to miss Kusum. For some time she had given up visiting the temple, the *ghāt*, or the Sanyasi.

What happened next I do not know, but after a while the two met together on my steps one evening.

With downcast looks, Kusum asked: 'Master, did you send for me?'

'Yes, why do I not see you? Why have you grown neglectful of late in serving the gods?'

She kept silent.

'Tell me your thoughts without reserve.'

Half averting her face, she replied: 'I am a sinner, Master, and hence I have failed in the worship.'

The Sanyasi said: 'Kusum, I know there is unrest in your heart.'

She gave a slight start, and, drawing the end of her sári over her face, she sat down on the step at the Sanyasi's feet, and wept.

He moved a little away, and said: 'Tell me what you have in your heart, and I shall show you the way to peace.'

She replied in a tone of unshaken faith, stopping now and then for words: 'If you bid me, I must speak out. But, then, I cannot explain it clearly. You, Master, must have guessed it all. I adored one as a god, I worshipped him, and the bliss of that devotion filled my heart to fulness. But one night I dreamt that the lord of my heart was sitting in a garden somewhere, clasping my right hand in his left, and whispering to me of love. The whole scene did not appear to me at all strange. The dream vanished, but its hold on me remained. Next day when I beheld him he appeared in another light than before. That dream-picture continued to haunt my mind. I fled far from him in fear, and the picture clung to me. Thenceforth my heart has known no peace, – all has grown dark within me!'

While she was wiping her tears and telling this tale, I felt that the Sanyasi was firmly pressing my stone surface with his right foot.

Her speech done, the Sanyasi said:

'You must tell me whom you saw in your dream.'

With folded hands, she entreated: 'I cannot.'

He insisted: 'You must tell me who he was.'

Wringing her hands she asked: 'Must I tell it?'

He replied: 'Yes, you must.'

Then crying, 'You are he, Master!' she fell on her face on my stony bosom, and sobbed.

When she came to herself, and sat up, the Sanyasi said slowly: 'I am leaving this place to-night that you may not see me again. Know that I am a Sanyasi, not belonging to this world. *You* must forget me.'

Kusum replied in a low voice: 'It will be so, Master.'

The Sanyasi said: 'I take my leave.'

Without a word more Kusum bowed to him, and placed the dust of his feet on her head. He left the place.

The moon set; the night grew dark. I heard a splash in the water. The wind raved in the darkness, as if it wanted to blow out all the stars of the sky.

Saved

Gouri was the beautiful, delicately nurtured child of an old and wealthy family. Her husband, Paresh, had recently by his own efforts improved his straitened circumstances. So long as he was poor, Gouri's parents had kept their daughter at home, unwilling to surrender her to privation; so she was no longer young when at last she went to her husband's house. And Paresh never felt quite that she belonged to him. He was an advocate in a small western town, and had no close kinsman with him. All his thought was about his wife, so much so that sometimes he would come home before the rising of the Court. At first Gouri was at a loss to understand why he came back suddenly. Sometimes, too, he would dismiss one of the servants without reason; none of them ever suited him long. Especially if Gouri desired to keep any particular servant because he was useful, that man was sure to be got rid of forthwith. The high-spirited Gouri greatly resented this, but her resentment only made her husband's behaviour still stranger.

At last when Paresh, unable to contain himself any longer, began in secret to cross-question the maid about her, the whole thing reached his wife's ears. She was a woman of few words; but her pride raged within like a wounded lioness at these insults, and this mad suspicion swept like a destroyer's sword between them. Paresh, as soon as he saw that his wife understood his motive, felt no more delicacy about taxing Gouri to her face; and the more his wife treated it with silent contempt, the more did the fire of his jealousy consume him.

Deprived of wedded happiness, the childless Gouri betook herself to the consolations of religion. She sent for Paramananda Swami, the young preacher of the Prayer-House hard by, and, formally acknowledging him as her spiritual preceptor, asked him to expound the *Gita* to her. All the wasted love and affection of her woman's heart was poured out in reverence at the feet of her Guru.

No one had any doubts about the purity of Paramananda's character. All worshipped him. And because Paresh did not dare to hint at any suspicion against him, his jealousy ate its way into his heart like a hidden cancer.

One day some trifling circumstance made the poison overflow. Paresh reviled Paramananda to his wife as a hypocrite, and said: 'Can you swear that you are not in love with this crane that plays the ascetic?'

Gouri sprang up like a snake that has been trodden on, and, maddened by his suspicion, said with bitter irony: 'And what if I am?' At this Paresh forthwith went off to the Court-house, and locked the door on her.

In a white heat of passion at this last outrage, Gouri got the door open somehow, and left the house.

Paramananda was poring over the scriptures in his lonely room in the silence of noon. All at once, like a flash of lightning out of a cloudless sky, Gouri broke in upon his reading.

'You here?' questioned her Guru in surprise.

'Rescue me, O my lord Guru,' said she, 'from the insults of my home life, and allow me to dedicate myself to the service of your feet.'

With a stern rebuke, Paramananda sent Gouri back home. But I wonder whether he ever again took up the snapped thread of his reading.

Paresh, finding the door open, on his return home, asked: 'Who has been here?'

'No one!' his wife replied. '*I* have been to the house of my Guru.'

'Why?' asked Paresh, pale and red by turns.

'Because I wanted to.'

From that day Paresh had a guard kept over the house, and behaved so absurdly that the tale of his jealousy was told all over the town.

The news of the shameful insults that were daily heaped on his disciple disturbed the religious meditations of Paramananda. He felt he ought to leave the place at once; at the same time he could not make up his mind to forsake the tortured woman. Who can say how the poor ascetic got through those terrible days and nights?

At last one day the imprisoned Gouri got a letter. 'My child,' it ran, 'it is true that many holy women have left the world to devote themselves to God. Should it happen that the trials of this world are driving your thoughts away from God, I will with God's help rescue his handmaid for the holy service of his feet. If you desire, you may meet me by the tank in your garden at two o'clock to-morrow afternoon.'

Gouri hid the letter in the loops of her hair. At noon next day when she was undoing her hair before her bath she found that the letter was not there. Could it have fallen on to the bed and got into her husband's hands, she wondered. At first, she felt a kind of fierce pleasure in thinking that it would enrage him; and then she could not bear to think that this letter, worn as a halo of deliverance on her head, might be defiled by the touch of insolent hands.

With swift steps she hurried to her husband's room. He lay groaning on the floor, with eyes rolled back and foaming mouth. She detached the letter from his clenched fist, and sent quickly for a doctor.

The doctor said it was a case of apoplexy. The patient had died before his arrival.

That very day, as it happened, Paresh had an important appointment away from home. Paramananda had found this out, and accordingly had made his appointment with Gouri. To such a depth had he fallen!

When the widowed Gouri caught sight from the window of her Guru stealing like a thief to the side of the pool, she lowered her eyes as at a lightning flash. And in that flash she saw clearly what a fall his had been.

The Guru called: 'Gouri.'

'I am coming,' she replied.

* * *

When Paresh's friends heard of his death, and came to assist in the last rites, they found the dead body of Gouri lying beside that of her husband. She had poisoned herself. All were lost in admiration of the wifely loyalty she had shown in her *sati*, a loyalty rare indeed in these degenerate days.

My fair neighbour

My feelings towards the young widow who lived in the next house to mine were feelings of worship; at least, that is what I told to my friends and myself. Even my nearest intimate, Nabin, knew nothing of the real state of my mind. And I had a sort of pride that I could keep my passion pure by thus concealing it in the inmost recesses of my heart. She was like a dew-drenched *sephali*-blossom, untimely fallen to earth. Too radiant and holy for the flower-decked marriage-bed, she had been dedicated to Heaven.

But passion is like the mountain stream, and refuses to be enclosed in the place of its birth; it must seek an outlet. That is why I tried to give expression to my emotions in poems; but my unwilling pen refused to desecrate the object of my worship.

It happened curiously that just at this time my friend Nabin was afflicted with a madness of verse. It came upon him like an earthquake. It was the poor fellow's first attack, and he was equally unprepared for rhyme and rhythm. Nevertheless he could not refrain, for he succumbed to the fascination, as a widower to his second wife.

So Nabin sought help from me. The subject of his poems was the old, old one, which is ever new: his poems were all addressed to the beloved one. I slapped his back in jest, and asked him: 'Well, old chap, who is she?'

Nabin laughed, as he replied: 'That I have not yet discovered!'

I confess that I found considerable comfort in bringing help to my friend. Like a hen brooding on a duck's egg, I lavished all the warmth of my pent-up passion on Nabin's effusions. So vigorously did I revise and improve his crude productions, that the larger part of each poem became my own.

Then Nabin would say in surprise: 'That is just what I wanted to say, but could not. How on earth do you manage to get hold of all these fine sentiments?'

Poet-like, I would reply: 'They come from my imagination; for, as you know, truth is silent, and it is imagination only which waxes eloquent. Reality represses the flow of feeling like a rock; imagination cuts out a path for itself.'

And the poor puzzled Nabin would say: 'Y-e-s, I see, yes, of course'; and then after some thought would murmur again: 'Yes, yes, you are right!'

As I have already said, in my own love there was a feeling of reverential delicacy which prevented me from putting it into words. But with Nabin as a screen, there was nothing to hinder the flow of my pen; and a true warmth of feeling gushed out into these vicarious poems.

Nabin in his lucid moments would say: 'But these are yours! Let me publish them over your name.'

'Nonsense!' I would reply. 'They are yours, my dear fellow; I have only added a touch or two here and there.'

And Nabin gradually came to believe it.

I will not deny that, with a feeling akin to that of the astronomer gazing into the starry heavens, I did sometimes turn my eyes towards the window of the house next door. It is also true that now and again my furtive glances would be rewarded with a vision. And the least glimpse of the pure light of that countenance would at once still and clarify all that was turbulent and unworthy in my emotions.

But one day I was startled. Could I believe my eyes? It was a hot summer afternoon. One of the fierce and fitful nor'-westers was threatening. Black clouds were massed in the north-west corner of the sky; and against the strange and fearful light of that background my fair neighbour stood, gazing out into empty space. And what a world of forlorn longing did I discover in the far-away look of those lustrous black eyes! Was there then, perchance, still some living volcano within the serene radiance of that moon of mine? Alas! that look of limitless yearning, which was winging its way through the clouds like an eager bird, surely sought – not heaven – but the nest of some human heart!

At the sight of the unutterable passion of that look I could hardly contain myself. I was no longer satisfied with correcting crude poems. My whole being longed to express itself in some worthy action. At last I thought I would devote myself to making widow-remarriage popular in my country. I was prepared not only to speak and write on the subject, but also to spend money on its cause.

Nabin began to argue with me. 'Permanent widowhood,' said he, 'has in it a sense of immense purity and peace; a calm beauty like that of the silent places of the dead shimmering in the wan light of the eleventh moon. Would not the mere possibility of remarriage destroy its divine beauty?'

Now this sort of sentimentality always makes me furious. In time of famine, if a well-fed man speaks scornfully of food, and advises a starving man at point of death to glut his hunger on the fragrance of flowers and the song of birds, what are we to think of him? I said with some heat: 'Look here, Nabin, to the artist a ruin may be a beautiful object; but houses are built not only for the contemplation of artists, but that people may live therein; so they have to be kept in repair in spite of artistic susceptibilities. It is all very well for you to idealise widowhood from your safe distance, but you should remember that within widowhood there is a sensitive human heart, throbbing with pain and desire.'

I had an impression that the conversion of Nabin would be a difficult matter, so perhaps I was more impassioned than I need have been. I was somewhat surprised to find at the conclusion of my little speech that Nabin after a single thoughtful sigh completely agreed with me. The even more convincing peroration which I felt I might have delivered was not needed!

After about a week Nabin came to me, and said that if I would help him he was prepared to lead the way by marrying a widow himself.

I was overjoyed. I embraced him effusively, and promised him any money that might be required for the purpose. Then Nabin told me his story.

I learned that Nabin's loved one was not an imaginary being. It appeared that Nabin, too, had for some time adored a widow from a distance, but had not spoken of his feelings to any living soul. Then the magazines in which Nabin's poems, or rather *my* poems, used to appear had reached the fair one's hands; and the poems had not been ineffective.

Not that Nabin had deliberately intended, as he was careful to explain, to conduct love-making in that way. In fact, said he, he had no idea that the widow knew how to read. He used to post the magazine, without disclosing the sender's name, addressed to the widow's brother. It was only a sort of fancy of his, a concession to his hopeless passion. It was flinging garlands before a deity; it is not the worshipper's affair whether the god knows or not, whether he accepts or ignores the offering.

And Nabin particularly wanted me to understand that he had no definite end in view when on diverse pretexts he sought and made the acquaintance of the widow's brother. Any near relation of the loved one needs must have a special interest for the lover.

Then followed a long story about how an illness of the brother at last brought them together. The presence of the poet himself naturally led to much discussion of the poems; nor was the discussion necessarily restricted to the subject out of which it arose.

After his recent defeat in argument at my hands, Nabin had mustered up courage to propose marriage to the widow. At first he could not gain her consent. But when he had made full use of my eloquent words, supplemented by a tear or two of his own, the fair one capitulated unconditionally. Some money was now wanted by her guardian to make arrangements.

'Take it at once,' said I.

'But,' Nabin went on, 'you know it will be some months before I can appease my father sufficiently for him to continue my allowance. How are we to live in the meantime?' I wrote out the necessary cheque without a word, and then I said: 'Now tell me who she is. You need not look on me as a possible rival, for I swear I will not write poems to her; and even if I do I will not send them to her brother, but to you!'

'Don't be absurd,' said Nabin; 'I have not kept back her name because I feared your rivalry! The fact is, she was very much perturbed at taking this unusual step, and had asked me not to talk about the matter to my friends. But it no longer matters, now that everything has been satisfactorily settled. She lives at No. 19, the house next to yours.'

If my heart had been an iron boiler it would have burst. 'So she has no objection to remarriage?' I simply asked.

'Not at the present moment,' replied Nabin with a smile.

'And was it the poems alone which wrought the magic change?'

'Well, my poems were not so bad, you know,' said Nabin, 'were they?'

I swore mentally.

But at whom was I to swear? At him? At myself? At Providence? All the same, I swore.

Mashi

I

Mashi! 'Try to sleep, Jotin, it is getting late.' 'Never mind if it is. I have not many days left. I was thinking that Mani should go to her father's house. – I forget where he is now.'

'Sitarampur.'

'Oh yes! Sitarampur. Send her there. She should not remain any longer near a sick man. She herself is not strong.'

'Just listen to him! How can she bear to leave you in this state?'

'Does she know what the doctors – – ?'

'But she can see for herself! The other day she cried her eyes out at the merest hint of having to go to her father's house.'

We must explain that in this statement there was a slight distortion of truth, to say the least of it. The actual talk with Mani was as follows: –

'I suppose, my child, you have got some news from your father? I thought I saw your cousin Anath here.'

'Yes! Next Friday will be my little sister's *annaprashan* ceremony. So I'm thinking – – '

'All right, my dear. Send her a gold necklace. It will please your mother.'

'I'm thinking of going myself. I've never seen my little sister, and I want to ever so much.'

'Whatever do you mean? You surely don't think of leaving Jotin alone? Haven't you heard what the doctor says about him?'

'But he said that just now there's no special cause for – –'

'Even if he did, you can see his state.'

'This is the first girl after three brothers, and she's a great favourite. – I have heard that it's going to be a grand affair. If I don't go, mother will be very – –'

'Yes, yes! I don't understand your mother. But I know very well that your father will be angry enough if you leave Jotin just now.'

'You'll have to write a line to him saying that there is no special cause for anxiety, and that even if I go, there will be no – –'

'You're right there; it will certainly be no great loss if you do go. But remember, if I write to your father, I'll tell him plainly what is in my mind.'

'Then you needn't write. I shall ask my husband, and he will surely – –'

'Look here, child, I've borne a good deal from you, but if you do that, I won't stand it for a moment. Your father knows you too well for you to deceive him.'

When Mashi had left her, Mani lay down on her bed in a bad temper.

Her neighbour and friend came and asked what was the matter.

'Look here! What a shame it is! Here's my only sister's *annaprashan* coming, and they don't want to let me go to it!'

'Why! Surely you're never thinking of going, are you, with your husband so ill?'

'I don't do anything for him, and I couldn't if I tried. It's so deadly dull in this house, that I tell you frankly I can't bear it.'

'You are a strange woman!'

'But I can't pretend, as you people do, and look glum lest any one should think ill of me.'

'Well, tell me your plan.'

'I must go. Nobody can prevent me.'

'Isss! What an imperious young woman you are!'

II

Hearing that Mani had wept at the mere thought of going to her father's house, Jotin was so excited that he sat up in bed. Pulling his pillow towards him, he leaned back, and said: 'Mashi, open this window a little, and take that lamp away.'

The still night stood silently at the window like a pilgrim of eternity; and the stars gazed in, witnesses through untold ages of countless death-scenes.

Jotin saw his Mani's face traced on the background of the dark night, and saw those two big dark eyes brimming over with tears, as it were for all eternity.

Mashi felt relieved when she saw him so quiet, thinking he was asleep.

Suddenly he started up, and said: 'Mashi, you all thought that Mani was too frivolous ever to be happy in our house. But you see now – – '

'Yes, I see now, my Baba, I was mistaken – but trial tests a person.'

'Mashi!'

'Do try to sleep, dear!'

'Let me think a little, let me talk. Don't be vexed, Mashi!'

'Very well.'

'Once, when I used to think I could not win Mani's heart, I bore it silently. But you – – '

'No, dear, I won't allow you to say that; I also bore it.'

'Our minds, you know, are not clods of earth which you can possess by merely picking up. I felt that Mani did not know her own mind, and that one day at some great shock – – '

'Yes, Jotin, you are right.'

'Therefore I never took much notice of her waywardness.'

Mashi remained silent, suppressing a sigh. Not once, but often she had seen Jotin spending the night on the verandah wet with the splashing rain, yet not caring to go into his bedroom. Many a day he lay with a throbbing head, longing, she knew, that Mani would come and soothe his brow, while Mani was getting ready to go to the theatre. Yet when Mashi went to fan him, he sent her away petulantly. She alone knew what pain lay hidden in that distress. Again and again she had wanted to say to Jotin: 'Don't pay so much attention to that silly child, my dear; let her learn to want, – to cry for things.' But these things cannot be said, and are apt to be misunderstood. Jotin had in his heart a shrine set up to the goddess Woman, and there Mani had her throne. It was hard for him to imagine that his own fate was to be denied his share of the wine of love poured out by that divinity. Therefore the worship went on, the sacrifice was offered, and the hope of a boon never ceased.

Mashi imagined once more that Jotin was sleeping, when he cried out suddenly:

'I know you thought that I was not happy with Mani, and therefore you were angry with her. But, Mashi, happiness is like those stars. They don't cover all the darkness; there are gaps between. We make mistakes in life and we misunderstand, and yet there remain gaps through which truth shines. I do not know whence comes this gladness that fills my heart to-night.'

Mashi began gently to soothe Jotin's brow, her tears unseen in the dark.

'I was thinking, Mashi, she's so young! What will she do when I am – – ?'

'Young, Jotin? She's old enough. I too was young when I lost the idol of my life, only to find him in my heart for ever.

Was that any loss, do you think? Besides, is happiness absolutely necessary?'

'Mashi, it seems as if just when Mani's heart shows signs of awakening I have to – – '

'Don't you worry about that, Jotin. Isn't it enough if her heart awakes?'

Suddenly Jotin recollected the words of a village minstrel's song which he had heard long before:

O my heart! you woke not when the man of my heart came to my door.

At the sound of his departing steps you woke up.

Oh, you woke up in the dark!

'Mashi, what is the time now?'

'About nine.'

'So early as that! Why, I thought it must be at least two or three o'clock. My midnight, you know, begins at sundown. But why did you want me to sleep, then?'

'Why, you know how late last night you kept awake talking; so to-day you must get to sleep early.'

'Is Mani asleep?'

'Oh no, she's busy making some soup for you.'

'You don't mean to say so, Mashi? Does she – – ?'

'Certainly! Why, she prepares all your food, the busy little woman.'

'I thought perhaps Mani could not – – '

'It doesn't take long for a woman to learn such things. With the need it comes of itself.'

'The fish soup, that I had in the morning, had such a delicate flavour, I thought you had made it.'

'Dear me, no! Surely you don't think Mani would let me do anything for you? Why, she does all your washing herself. She knows you can't bear anything dirty about you. If only you could see your sitting-room, how spick and span she keeps it! If I were to let her haunt your sick-room, she would wear herself out. But that's what she really wants to do.'

'Is Mani's health, then – – ?'

'The doctors think she should not be allowed to visit the sick-room too often. She's too tender-hearted.'

'But, Mashi, how do you prevent her from coming?'

'Because she obeys me implicitly. But still I have constantly to be giving her news of you.'

The stars glistened in the sky like tear-drops. Jotin bowed his head in gratitude to his life that was about to depart, and when Death stretched out his right hand towards him through the darkness, he took it in perfect trust.

Jotin sighed, and, with a slight gesture of impatience, said: 'Mashi, if Mani is still awake, then, could I – if only for a – – ?'

'Very well! I'll go and call her.'

'I won't keep her long, only for five minutes. I have something particular to tell her.'

Mashi, sighing, went out to call Mani. Meanwhile Jotin's pulse began to beat fast. He knew too well that he had never been able to have an intimate talk with Mani. The two instruments were tuned differently and it was not easy to play them in unison. Again and again, Jotin had felt pangs of jealousy on hearing Mani chattering and laughing merrily with her girl companions. Jotin blamed only himself, – why couldn't he talk irrelevant trifles as they did? Not that he could not, for with his men friends he often chatted on all sorts of trivialities. But the small talk that suits men is not suitable for women. You can hold a philosophical discourse in monologue, ignoring your inattentive audience altogether, but small talk requires the co-operation of at least two. The bagpipes can be played singly, but there must be a pair of cymbals. How often in the evenings had Jotin, when sitting on the open verandah with Mani, made some strained attempts at conversation, only to feel the thread snap. And the very silence of the evening felt ashamed. Jotin was certain that Mani longed to get away. He had even wished earnestly that a third person would come. For talking is easy with three, when it is hard for two.

He began to think what he should say when Mani came. But such manufactured talk would not satisfy him. Jotin felt afraid that this five minutes of to-night would be wasted. Yet, for him, there were but few moments left for intimate talk.

III

'What's this, child, you're not going anywhere, are you?'

'Of course, I'm going to Sitarampur.'

'What do you mean? Who is going to take you?'

'Anath.'

'Not to-day, my child, some other day.'

'But the compartment has already been reserved.'

'What does that matter? That loss can easily be borne. Go to-morrow, early in the morning.'

'Mashi, I don't hold by your inauspicious days. What harm if I do go to-day?'

'Jotin wants to have a talk with you.'

'All right! there's still some time. I'll just go and see him.'

'But you mustn't say that you are going.'

'Very well, I won't tell him, but I shan't be able to stay long. To-morrow is my sister's *annaprashan*, and I must go to-day.'

'Oh, my child! I beg you to listen to me this once. Quiet your mind for a while and sit by him. Don't let him see your hurry.'

'What can I do? The train won't wait for me. Anath will be back in ten minutes. I can sit by him till then.'

'No, that won't do. I shall never let you go to him in that frame of mind.... Oh, you wretch! the man you are torturing is soon to leave this world; but I warn you, you will remember this day till the end of your days! That there is a God! that there is a God! you will some day understand!'

'Mashi, you mustn't curse me like that.'

'Oh, my darling boy! my darling! why do you go on living longer? There is no end to this sin, yet I cannot check it!'

Mashi after delaying a little returned to the sick-room, hoping by that time Jotin would be asleep. But Jotin moved in his bed when she entered. Mashi exclaimed:

'Just look what she has done!'

'What's happened? Hasn't Mani come? Why have you been so long, Mashi?'

'I found her weeping bitterly because she had allowed the milk for your soup to get burnt! I tried to console her, saying, "Why, there's more milk to be had!" But that she could be so careless about the preparation of *your* soup made her wild. With great trouble I managed to pacify her and put her to bed. So I haven't brought her to-day. Let her sleep it off.'

Though Jotin was pained when Mani didn't come, yet he felt a certain amount of relief. He had half feared that Mani's bodily presence would do violence to his heart's image of her. Such things had happened before in his life. And the gladness of the idea that Mani was miserable at burning *his* milk filled his heart to overflowing.

'Mashi!'

'What is it, Baba?'

'I feel quite certain that my days are drawing to a close. But I have no regrets. Don't grieve for me.'

'No, dear, I won't grieve. I don't believe that only life is good and not death.'

'Mashi, I tell you truly that death seems sweet.'

Jotin, gazing at the dark sky, felt that it was Mani herself who was coming to him in Death's guise. She had immortal youth and the stars were flowers of blessing, showered upon her dark tresses by the hand of the World-Mother. It seemed as if once more he had his first sight of his bride under the veil of darkness. The immense night became filled with the loving gaze of Mani's dark eyes. Mani, the bride of this house, the little girl, became transformed into a world-image, – her throne on the altar of the stars at the confluence of life and death. Jotin said to himself with clasped hands: 'At last the veil is raised, the covering is rent in this deep darkness. Ah, beautiful one! how often have you wrung my heart, but no longer shall you forsake me!'

IV

'I'm suffering, Mashi, but nothing like you imagine. It seems to me as if my pain were gradually separating itself from my life. Like a laden boat, it was so long being towed behind, but the rope has snapped, and now it floats away with all my burdens. Still I can see it, but it is no longer mine.... But, Mashi, I've not seen Mani even once for the last two days!'

'Jotin, let me give you another pillow.'

'It almost seems to me, Mashi, that Mani also has left me like that laden boat of sorrow which drifts away.'

'Just sip some pomegranate juice, dear! Your throat must be getting dry.'

'I wrote my will yesterday; did I show it to you? I can't recollect.'

'There's no need to show it to me, Jotin.'

'When mother died, I had nothing of my own. You fed me and brought me up. Therefore I was saying – – '

'Nonsense, child! I had only this house and a little property. You earned the rest.'

'But this house – – ?'

'That's nothing. Why, you've added to it so much that it's difficult to find out where my house was!'

'I'm sure Mani's love for you is really – – '

'Yes, yes! I know that, Jotin. Now you try to sleep.'

'Though I have bequeathed all my property to Mani, it is practically yours, Mashi. She will never disobey you.'

'Why are you worrying so much about that, dear?'

'All I have I owe to you. When you see my will don't think for a moment that – – '

'What do you mean, Jotin? Do you think I shall mind for a moment because you give to Mani what belongs to you? Surely I'm not so mean as that?'

'But you also will have – – '

'Look here, Jotin, I shall get angry with you. You want to console me with money!'

'Oh, Mashi, how I wish I could give you something better than money!'

'That you have done, Jotin! – more than enough. Haven't I had you to fill my lonely house? I must have won that great good-fortune in many previous births! You have given me so much that now, if my destiny's due is exhausted, I shall not complain. Yes, yes! Give away everything in Mani's name, – your house, your money, your carriage, and your land – such burdens are too heavy for me!'

'Of course I know you have lost your taste for the enjoyments of life, but Mani is so young that – – '

'No! you mustn't say that. If you want to leave her your property, it is all right, but as for enjoyment – – '

'What harm if she does enjoy herself, Mashi?'

'No, no, it will be impossible. Her throat will become parched, and it will be dust and ashes to her.'

Jotin remained silent. He could not decide whether it was true or not, and whether it was a matter of regret or otherwise, that the world would become distasteful to Mani for want of him. The stars seemed to whisper in his heart:

'Indeed it is true. We have been watching for thousands of years, and know that all these great preparations for enjoyment are but vanity.'

Jotin sighed and said: 'We cannot leave behind us what is really worth giving.'

'It's no trifle you are giving, dearest. I only pray she may have the power to know the value of what is given her.'

'Give me a little more of that pomegranate juice, Mashi, I'm thirsty. Did Mani come to me yesterday, I wonder?'

'Yes, she came, but you were asleep. She sat by your head, fanning you for a long time, and then went away to get your clothes washed.'

'How wonderful! I believe I was dreaming that very moment that Mani was trying to enter my room. The door was slightly open, and she was pushing against it, but it wouldn't open. But, Mashi, you're going too far, – you ought to let her see that I am dying; otherwise my death will be a terrible shock to her.'

'Baba, let me put this shawl over your feet; they are getting cold.'

'No, Mashi, I can't bear anything over me like that.'

'Do you know, Jotin, Mani made this shawl for you? When she ought to have been asleep, she was busy at it. It was finished only yesterday.'

Jotin took the shawl, and touched it tenderly with his hands. It seemed to him that the softness of the wool was Mani's own. Her loving thoughts had been woven night after night with its threads. It was not made merely of wool, but also of her touch. Therefore, when Mashi drew that shawl over his feet, it seemed as if, night after night, Mani had been caressing his tired limbs.

'But, Mashi, I thought Mani didn't know how to knit, – at any rate she never liked it.'

'It doesn't take long to learn a thing. Of course I had to teach her. Then there are a good many mistakes in it.'

'Let there be mistakes; we're not going to send it to the Paris Exhibition. It will keep my feet warm in spite of its mistakes.'

Jotin's mind began to picture Mani at her task, blundering and struggling, and yet patiently going on night after night. How sweetly pathetic it was! And again he went over the shawl with his caressing fingers.

'Mashi, is the doctor downstairs?'

'Yes, he will stay here to-night.'

'But tell him it is useless for him to give me a sleeping draught. It doesn't bring me real rest and only adds to my pain. Let me remain properly awake. Do you know, Mashi, that my wedding took place on the night of the full moon in the month of *Baisakh*? To-morrow will be that day, and the stars of that very night will be shining in the sky. Mani perhaps has forgotten. I want to remind her of it to-day; just call her to me for a minute or two.... Why do you keep silent? I suppose the doctor has told you I am so weak that any excitement will – – but I tell you truly, Mashi, to-night, if I can have only a few minutes' talk with her, there will be no need for any sleeping draughts. Mashi, don't cry like that! I am quite well. To-day my heart is full as it has never been in my life before. That's why I want to see Mani. No, no, Mashi, I can't bear to see you crying! You have been so quiet all these last days. Why are you so troubled to-night?'

'Oh, Jotin, I thought that I had exhausted all my tears, but I find there are plenty left. I can't bear it any longer.'

'Call Mani. I'll remind her of our wedding night, so that to-morrow she may – – '

'I'm going, dear. Shombhu will wait at the door. If you want anything, call him.'

Mashi went to Mani's bedroom and sat down on the floor crying, – 'Oh come, come once, you heartless wretch! Keep his last request who has given you his all! Don't kill him who is already dying!'

Jotin hearing the sound of footsteps started up, saying, 'Mani!'

'I am Shombhu. Did you call me?'

'Ask your mistress to come?'

'Ask whom?'

'Your mistress.'

'She has not yet returned.'

'Returned? From where?'

'From Sitarampur.'

'When did she go?'

'Three days ago.'

For a moment Jotin felt numb all over, and his head began to swim. He slipped down from the pillows, on which he was reclining, and kicked off the woollen shawl that was over his feet.

When Mashi came back after a long time, Jotin did not mention Mani's name, and Mashi thought he had forgotten all about her.

Suddenly Jotin cried out: 'Mashi, did I tell you about the dream I had the other night?'

'Which dream?'

'That in which Mani was pushing the door, and the door wouldn't open more than an inch. She stood outside unable to enter. Now I know that Mani has to stand outside my door till the last.'

Mashi kept silent. She realised that the heaven she had been building for Jotin out of falsehood had toppled down at last. If sorrow comes, it is best to acknowledge it. – When God strikes, we cannot avoid the blow.

'Mashi, the love I have got from you will last through all my births. I have filled this life with it to carry it with me. In the next birth, I am sure you will be born as my daughter, and I shall tend you with all my love.'

'What are you saying, Jotin? Do you mean to say I shall be born again as a woman? Why can't you pray that I should come to your arms as a son?'

'No, no, not a son! You will come to my house in that wonderful beauty which you had when you were young. I can even imagine how I shall dress you.'

'Don't talk so much, Jotin, but try to sleep.'

'I shall name you "Lakshmi."'

'But that is an old-fashioned name, Jotin!'

'Yes, but you are my old-fashioned Mashi. Come to my house again with those beautiful old-fashioned manners.'

'I can't wish that I should come and burden your home with the misfortune of a girl-child!'

'Mashi, you think me weak, and are wanting to save me all trouble.'

'My child, I am a woman, so I have my weakness. Therefore I have tried all my life to save you from all sorts of trouble, – only to fail.'

'Mashi, I have not had time in this life to apply the lessons I have learnt. But they will keep for my next birth. I shall show then what a man is able to do. I have learnt how false it is always to be looking after oneself.'

'Whatever you may say, darling, you have never grasped anything for yourself, but given everything to others.'

'Mashi, I can boast of one thing at any rate. I have never been a tyrant in my happiness, or tried to enforce my claims by violence. Because lies could not content me, I have had to wait long. Perhaps truth will be kind to me at last. – Who is that, Mashi, who is that?'

'Where? There's no one there, Jotin!'

'Mashi, just go and see in the other room. I thought I – – '

'No, dear! I don't see anybody.'

'But it seemed quite clear to me that – – '

'No, Jotin, it's nothing. So keep quiet! The doctor is coming now.'

When the doctor entered, he said:

'Look here, you mustn't stay near the patient so much, you excite him. You go to bed, and my assistant will remain with him.'

'No, Mashi, I can't let you go.'

'All right, Baba! I will sit quietly in that corner.'

'No, no! you must sit by my side. I can't let go your hand, not till the very end. I have been made by your hand, and only from your hand shall God take me.'

'All right,' said the doctor, 'you can remain there. But, Jotin Babu, you must not talk to her. It's time for you to take your medicine.'

'Time for my medicine? Nonsense! The time for that is over. To give medicine now is merely to deceive; besides I am not afraid to die. Mashi, Death is busy with his physic; why do you add another nuisance in the shape of a doctor? Send him away, send him away! It is you alone I need now! No one else, none whatever! No more falsehood!'

'I protest, as a doctor, this excitement is doing you harm.'

'Then go, doctor, don't excite me any more! – Mashi, has he gone?… That's good! Now come and take my head in your lap.'

'All right, dear! Now, Baba, try to sleep!'

'No, Mashi, don't ask me to sleep. If I sleep, I shall never wake. I still need to keep awake a little longer. Don't you hear a sound? Somebody is coming.'

V

'Jotin dear, just open your eyes a little. She has come. Look once and see!'

'Who has come? A dream?'

'Not a dream, darling! Mani has come with her father.'

'Who are you?'

'Can't you see? This is your Mani!'

'Mani? Has that door opened?'

'Yes, Baba, it is wide open.'

'No, Mashi, not that shawl! not *that* shawl! That shawl is a fraud!'

'It is not a shawl, Jotin! It is our Mani, who has flung herself on your feet. Put your hand on her head and bless her. Don't cry like that, Mani! There will be time enough for that. Keep quiet now for a little.

The Supreme Night

I used to go to the same dame's school with Surabala and play at marriage with her. When I paid visits to her house, her mother would pet me, and setting us side by side would say to herself: 'What a lovely pair!'

I was a child then, but I could understand her meaning well enough. The idea became rooted in my mind that I had a special right to Surabala above that of people in general. So it happened that, in the pride of ownership, at times I punished and tormented her; and she, too, fagged for me and bore all my punishments without complaint. The village was wont to praise her beauty; but in the eyes of a young barbarian like me that beauty had no glory; – I knew only that Surabala had been born in her father's house solely to bear my yoke, and that therefore she was the particular object of my neglect.

My father was the land-steward of the Chaudhuris, a family of *zemindars*. It was his plan, as soon as I had learnt to write a good hand, to train me in the work of estate management and secure a rent collectorship for me somewhere. But in my heart I disliked the proposal. Nilratan of our village had run away to Calcutta, had learnt English there, and finally became the *Nazir* of the District Magistrate; *that* was my life's ideal: I was secretly determined to be the Head Clerk of the Judge's Court, even if I could not become the Magistrate's *Nazir*.

I saw that my father always treated these court officers with the greatest respect. I knew from my childhood that they had to be propitiated with gifts of fish, vegetables, and even money. For this reason I had given a seat of high honour in my heart to the court underlings, even to the bailiffs. These are the gods worshipped in our Bengal, – a modern miniature edition of the 330 millions of deities of the Hindu pantheon. For gaining material success, people have more genuine faith in *them* than in the good Ganesh, the giver of success; hence the people now offer to these officers everything that was formerly Ganesh's due.

Fired by the example of Nilratan, I too seized a suitable opportunity and ran away to Calcutta. There I first put up in the house of a village acquaintance, and afterwards got some funds from my father for my education. Thus I carried on my studies regularly.

In addition, I joined political and benevolent societies. I had no doubt whatever that it was urgently necessary for me to give my life suddenly for my country. But I knew not how such a hard task could be carried out. Also no one showed me the way.

But, nevertheless, my enthusiasm did not abate at all. We country lads had not learnt to sneer at everything like the precocious boys of Calcutta, and hence our faith was very strong. The 'leaders' of our associations delivered speeches, and we went begging for subscriptions from door to door in the hot blaze of noon without breaking our fast; or we stood by the roadside distributing hand-bills, or arranged the chairs and benches in the lecture-hall, and, if anybody whispered a word against our leader, we got ready to fight him. For these things the city boys used to laugh at us as provincials.

I had come to Calcutta to be a *Nazir* or a Head Clerk, but I was preparing to become a Mazzini or a Garibaldi.

At this time Surabala's father and my father laid their heads together to unite us in marriage. I had come to Calcutta at the age of fifteen; Surabala was eight years old then. I was now eighteen, and in my father's opinion I was almost past the age of marriage. But it was my secret vow to remain unmarried all my life and to die for my country; so I told my father that I would not marry before I had finished my education.

In two or three months I learnt that Surabala had been married to a pleader named Ram Lochan. I was then busy collecting subscriptions for raising fallen India, and this news did not seem worth my thought.

I had matriculated, and was about to appear at the Intermediate Examination, when my father died. I was not alone in the world, but had to maintain my mother and two sisters. I had therefore to leave college and look out for employment. After a good deal of exertion I secured the post of second master in the matriculation school of a small town in the Noakhali District.

I thought, here is just the work for me! By my advice and inspiration I shall train up every one of my pupils as a general for future India.

I began to work, and then found that the impending examination was a more pressing affair than the future of India. The headmaster got angry whenever I talked of anything outside grammar or algebra. And in a few months my enthusiasm, too, flagged.

I am no genius. In the quiet of the home I may form vast plans; but when I enter the field of work, I have to bear the yoke of the plough on my neck like the Indian bullock, get my tail twisted by my master, break clods all day, patiently and with bowed head, and then at sunset have to be satisfied if I can get any cud to chew. Such a creature has not the spirit to prance and caper.

One of the teachers lived in the school-house, to guard against fires. As I was a bachelor, this work was thrown on me.

I lodged in a thatched shed close to the large cottage in which the school sat.

The school-house stood at some distance from the inhabited portion of the town, and beside a big tank. Around it were betel-nut, cocoa-nut, and *madar* trees, and very near to the school building two large ancient *nim* trees grew close together, and cast a cool shade around.

One thing I have forgotten to mention, and indeed I had not so long considered it worth mentioning. The local Government pleader, Ram Lochan Ray, lived near our school. I also knew that his wife – my early playmate, Surabala – lived with him.

I got acquainted with Ram Lochan Babu. I cannot say whether he knew that I had known Surabala in childhood. I did not think fit to mention the fact at my first introduction to him. Indeed, I did not clearly remember that Surabala had been ever linked with my life in any way.

One holiday I paid a visit to Ram Lochan Babu. The subject of our conversation has gone out of my mind; probably it was the unhappy condition of present-day India. Not that he was very much concerned or heart-broken over the matter; but the subject was such that one could freely pour forth one's sentimental sorrow over it for an hour or two while puffing at one's *hooka*.

While thus engaged, I heard in a side-room the softest possible jingle of bracelets, crackle of dress, and footfall; and I felt certain that two curious eyes were watching me through a small opening of the window.

All at once there flashed upon my memory a pair of eyes, – a pair of large eyes, beaming with trust, simplicity, and girlhood's love, – black pupils, – thick dark eyelashes, – a calm fixed gaze. Suddenly some unseen force squeezed my heart in an iron grip, and it throbbed with intense pain.

I returned to my house, but the pain clung to me. Whether I read, wrote, or did any other work, I could not shake that weight off my heart; a heavy load seemed to be always swinging from my heart-strings.

In the evening, calming myself a little, I began to reflect: 'What ails me?' From within came the question: 'Where is *your* Surabala now?' I replied: 'I gave her up of my free will. Surely I did not expect her to wait for me for ever.'

But something kept saying: '*Then* you could have got her merely for the asking. *Now* you have not the right to look at her even once, do what you will. That Surabala of your boyhood may come very close to you; you may hear the jingle of her bracelets; you may breathe the air embalmed by the essence of her hair, – but there will always be a wall between you two.'

I answered: 'Be it so. What is Surabala to me?'

My heart rejoined: 'To-day Surabala is nobody to you. But what might she not have been to you?'

Ah! that's true. *What* might she not have been to me? Dearest to me of all things, closer to me than the world besides, the sharer of all my life's joys and sorrows, – she might have been. And now, she is so distant, so much of a stranger, that to look on her is forbidden, to talk with her is improper, and to think of her is a sin! – while this Ram Lochan, coming suddenly from nowhere, has muttered a few set religious texts, and in one swoop has carried off Surabala from the rest of mankind!

I have not come to preach a new ethical code, or to revolutionise society; I have no wish to tear asunder domestic ties. I am only expressing the exact working of my mind, though it may not be reasonable. I could not by any means banish from my mind the sense that Surabala, reigning there within shelter of Ram Lochan's home, was mine far more than his. The thought was, I admit, unreasonable and improper, – but it was not unnatural.

Thereafter I could not set my mind to any kind of work. At noon when the boys in my class hummed, when Nature outside simmered in the sun, when the sweet scent of the *nim* blossoms entered the room on the tepid breeze, I then wished, – I know not what I wished for; but this I can say, that I did not wish to pass all my life in correcting the grammar exercises of those future hopes of India.

When school was over, I could not bear to live in my large lonely house; and yet, if any one paid me a visit, it bored me. In the gloaming as I sat by the tank and listened to the meaningless breeze sighing through the betel- and cocoa-nut palms, I used to muse that human society is a web of mistakes; nobody has the sense to do the right thing at the right time, and when the chance is gone we break our hearts over vain longings.

I could have married Surabala and lived happily. But I must be a Garibaldi, – and I ended by becoming the second master of a village school! And pleader Ram Lochan Ray, who had no special call to be Surabala's husband, – to whom, before his marriage, Surabala was no wise different from a hundred other maidens, – has very quietly married her, and is earning lots of money as Government pleader; when his dinner is badly cooked he scolds Surabala, and when he is in good humour he gives her a bangle! He is sleek and fat, tidily dressed, free from every kind of worry; *he* never passes his evenings by the tank gazing at the stars and sighing.

Ram Lochan was called away from our town for a few days by a big case elsewhere. Surabala in her house was as lonely as I was in my school building.

I remember it was a Monday. The sky was overcast with clouds from the morning. It began to drizzle at ten o'clock. At the aspect of the heavens our headmaster closed the school early. All day the black detached clouds began to run about in the sky as if making ready for some grand display. Next day, towards afternoon, the rain descended in torrents, accompanied by storm. As the night advanced the fury of wind and water increased. At first the wind was easterly; gradually it veered, and blew towards the south and south-west.

It was idle to try to sleep on such a night. I remembered that in this terrible weather Surabala was alone in her house. Our school was much more strongly built than her bungalow. Often and often did I plan to invite her to the school-house, while I meant to pass the night alone by the tank. But I could not summon up courage for it.

When it was half-past one in the morning, the roar of the tidal wave was suddenly heard, – the sea was rushing on us! I left my room and ran towards Surabala's house. In the way stood one embankment of our tank, and as I was wading to it the flood already reached my knees. When I mounted the bank, a second wave broke on it. The highest part of the bank was more than seventeen feet above the plain.

As I climbed up the bank, another person reached it from the opposite side. Who she was, every fibre of my body knew at once, and my whole soul was thrilled with the consciousness. I had no doubt that she, too, had recognised me.

On an island some three yards in area stood we two; all else was covered with water.

It was a time of cataclysm; the stars had been blotted out of the sky; all the lights of the earth had been darkened; there would have been no harm if we had held converse *then*. But we could not bring ourselves to utter a word; neither of us made even a formal inquiry after the other's health. Only we stood gazing at the darkness. At our feet swirled the dense, black, wild, roaring torrent of death.

To-day Surabala has come to *my* side, leaving the whole world. To-day she has none besides *me*. In our far-off childhood this Surabala had come from some dark primeval realm of mystery, from a life in another orb, and stood by my side on this luminous peopled earth; and to-day, after a wide span of time, she has left that earth, so full of light and human beings, to stand alone by *my* side amidst this terrible desolate gloom of Nature's death-convulsion. The stream of birth had flung that tender bud before me, and the flood of death had wafted the same flower, now in full bloom, to *me* and to none else. One more wave and we shall be swept away from this extreme point of the earth, torn from the stalks on which we now sit apart, and made one in death.

May that wave never come! May Surabala live long and happily, girt round by husband and children, household and kinsfolk! This one night, standing on the brink of Nature's destruction, I have tasted eternal bliss.

The night wore out, the tempest ceased, the flood abated; without a word spoken, Surabala went back to her house, and I, too, returned to my shed without having uttered a word.

I reflected: True, I have become no *Nazir* or Head Clerk, nor a Garibaldi; I am only the second master of a beggarly school. But one night had for its brief space beamed upon my whole life's course.

That one night, out of all the days and nights of my allotted span, has been the supreme glory of my humble existence.

Once There Was a King

Once upon a time there was a king! When we were children there was no need to know who the king in the fairy story was. It didn't matter whether he was called Shiladitya or Shaliban, whether he lived at Kashi or Kanauj. The thing that made a seven-year-old boy's heart go thump, thump with delight was this one sovereign truth, this reality of all realities: "Once there was a king."

But the readers of this modern age are far more exact and exacting. When they hear such an opening to a story, they are at once critical and suspicious. They apply the searchlight of science to its legendary haze and ask: "Which king?"

The story-tellers have become more precise in their turn. They are no longer content with the old indefinite, "There was a king," but assume instead a look of profound learning and begin: "Once there was a king named Ajatasatru."

The modern reader's curiosity, however, is not so easily satisfied. He blinks at the author through his scientific spectacles and asks again: "Which Ajatasatru?"

When we were young, we understood all sweet things; and we could detect the sweets of a fairy story by an unerring science of our own. We never cared for such useless things as knowledge.

We only cared for truth. And our unsophisticated little hearts knew well where the Crystal Palace of Truth lay and how to reach it. But to-day we are expected to write pages of facts, while the truth is simply this:

"There was a king."

I remember vividly that evening in Calcutta when the fairy story began. The rain and the storm had been incessant. The whole of the city was flooded. The water was knee-deep in our lane. I had a straining hope, which was almost a certainty, that my tutor would be prevented from coming that evening. I sat on the stool in the far corner of the verandah looking down the lane, with a heart beating faster and faster. Every minute I kept my eye on the rain, and when it began to diminish I prayed with all my might: "Please, God, send some more rain till half-past seven is over." For I was quite ready to believe that there was no other need for rain except to protect one helpless boy one evening in one corner of Calcutta from the deadly clutches of his tutor.

If not in answer to my prayer, at any rate according to some grosser law of nature, the rain did not give up.

But, alas, nor did my teacher!

Exactly to the minute, in the bend of the lane, I saw his approaching umbrella. The great bubble of hope burst in my breast, and my heart collapsed. Truly, if there is a punishment to fit the crime after death, then my tutor will be born again as me, and I shall be born as my tutor.

As soon as I saw his umbrella I ran as hard as I could to my mother's room. My mother and my grandmother were sitting opposite one another playing cards by the light of a lamp. I ran into the room, and flung myself on the bed beside my mother, and said:

"Mother, the tutor has come, and I have such a bad headache; couldn't I have no lessons to-day?"

I hope no child of immature age will be allowed to read this story, and I sincerely trust it will not be used in text-books or primers for junior classes. For what I did was dreadfully bad, and I received no punishment whatever. On the contrary, my wickedness was crowned with success.

My mother said to me: "All right," and turning to the servant added: "Tell the tutor that he can go back home."

It was perfectly plain that she didn't think my illness very serious, as she went on with her game as before and took no further notice. And I also, burying my head in the pillow, laughed to my heart's content. We perfectly understood one another, my mother and I.

But every one must know how hard it is for a boy of seven years old to keep up the illusion of illness for a long time. After about a minute I got hold of Grandmother and said: "Grannie, do tell me a story."

I had to ask this many times. Grannie and Mother went on playing cards and took no notice. At last Mother said to me: "Child, don't bother. Wait till we've finished our game." But I persisted: "Grannie, do tell me a story." I told Mother she could finish her game to-morrow, but she must let Grannie tell me a story there and then.

At last Mother threw down the cards and said: "You had better do what he wants. I can't manage him." Perhaps she had it in her mind that she would have no tiresome tutor on the morrow, while I should be obliged to be back at those stupid lessons.

As soon as ever Mother had given way, I rushed at Grannie. I got hold of her hand, and, dancing with delight, dragged her inside my mosquito curtain on to the bed. I clutched hold of the bolster with both hands in my excitement, and jumped up and down with joy, and when I had got a little quieter said: "Now, Grannie, let's have the story!"

Grannie went on: "And the king had a queen."

That was good to begin with. He had only one!

It is usual for kings in fairy stories to be extravagant in queens. And whenever we hear that there are two queens our hearts begin to sink. One is sure to be unhappy. But in Grannie's story that danger was past. He had only one queen.

We next hear that the king had not got any son. At the age of seven I didn't think there was any need to bother if a man had no son. He might only have been in the way.

Nor are we greatly excited when we hear that the king has gone away into the forest to practise austerities in order to get a son. There was only one thing that would have made me go into the forest, and that was to get away from my tutor!

But the king left behind with his queen a small girl, who grew up into a beautiful princess.

Twelve years pass away, and the king goes on practising austerities, and never thinks all this while of his beautiful daughter. The princess has reached the full bloom of her youth. The age of marriage has passed, but the king does not return. And the queen pines away with grief and cries: "Is my golden daughter destined to die unmarried? Ah me, what a fate is mine!"

Then the queen sent men to the king to entreat him earnestly to come back for a single night and take one meal in the palace. And the king consented.

The queen cooked with her own hand, and with the greatest care, sixty-four dishes. She made a seat for him of sandal-wood and arranged the food in plates of gold and cups of silver. The princess stood behind with the peacock-tail fan in her hand. The king, after twelve years' absence, came into the house, and the princess waved the fan, lighting up all the room with her beauty. The king looked in his daughter's face and forgot to take his food.

At last he asked his queen: "Pray, who is this girl whose beauty shines as the gold image of the goddess? Whose daughter is she?"

The queen beat her forehead and cried: "Ah, how evil is my fate! Do you not know your own daughter?"

The king was struck with amazement. He said at last: "My tiny daughter has grown to be a woman."

"What else?" the queen said with a sigh. "Do you not know that twelve years have passed by?"

"But why did you not give her in marriage?" asked the king.

"You were away," the queen said. "And how could I find her a suitable husband?"

The king became vehement with excitement. "The first man I see to-morrow," he said, "when I come out of the palace shall marry her."

The princess went on waving her fan of peacock feathers, and the king finished his meal.

The next morning, as the king came out of his palace, he saw the son of a Brahman gathering sticks in the forest outside the palace gates. His age was about seven or eight.

The King said: "I will marry my daughter to him."

Who can interfere with a king's command? At once the boy was called, and the marriage garlands were exchanged between him and the princess.

At this point I came up close to my wise Grannie and asked her eagerly: "When then?"

In the bottom of my heart there was a devout wish to substitute myself for that fortunate wood-gatherer of seven years old. The night was resonant with the patter of rain. The earthen lamp by my bedside was burning low. My grandmother's voice droned on as she told the story. And all these things served to create in a corner of my credulous heart the belief that I had been gathering sticks in the dawn of some indefinite time in the kingdom of some unknown king, and in a moment garlands had been exchanged between me and the princess, beautiful as the Goddess of Grace. She had a gold band on her hair and gold earrings in her ears. She had a necklace and bracelets of gold, and a golden waist-chain round her waist, and a pair of golden anklets tinkled above her feet.

If my grandmother were an author, how many explanations she would have to offer for this little story! First of all, every one would ask why the king remained twelve years in the forest? Secondly, why should the king's daughter remain unmarried all that while? This would be regarded as absurd.

Even if she could have got so far without a quarrel, still there would have been a great hue and cry about the marriage itself. First, it never happened. Secondly, how could there be a marriage between a princess of the Warrior Caste and a boy of the priestly Brahman Caste? Her readers would have imagined at once that the writer was preaching against our social customs in an underhand way. And they would write letters to the papers.

So I pray with all my heart that my grandmother may be born a grandmother again, and not through some cursed fate take birth as her luckless grandson.

With a throb of joy and delight, I asked Grannie: "What then?"

Grannie went on: Then the princess took her little husband away in great distress, and built a large palace with seven wings, and began to cherish her husband with great care.

I jumped up and down in my bed and clutched at the bolster more tightly than ever and said: "What then?"

Grannie continued: The little boy went to school and learnt many lessons from his teachers, and as he grew up his class-fellows began to ask him: "Who is that beautiful lady living with you in the palace with the seven wings?"

The Brahman's son was eager to know who she was. He could only remember how one day he had been gathering sticks and a great disturbance arose. But all that was so long ago that he had no clear recollection.

Four or five years passed in this way. His companions always asked him: "Who is that beautiful lady in the palace with the seven wings?" And the Brahman's son would come back from school and sadly tell the princess: "My school companions always ask me who is that beautiful lady in the palace with the seven wings, and I can give them no reply. Tell me, oh, tell me, who you are!"

The princess said: "Let it pass to-day. I will tell you some other day." And every day the Brahman's son would ask: "Who are you?" and the princess would reply: "Let it pass to-day. I will tell you some other day." In this manner four or five more years passed away.

At last the Brahman's son became very impatient and said: "If you do not tell me to-day who you are, O beautiful lady, I will leave this palace with the seven wings." Then the princess said: "I will certainly tell you to-morrow."

Next day the Brahman's son, as soon as he came home from school, said: "Now, tell me who you are." The princess said: "To-night I will tell you after supper, when you are in bed."

The Brahman's son said: "Very well"; and he began to count the hours in expectation of the night. And the princess, on her side, spread white flowers over the golden bed, and lighted a gold lamp with fragrant oil, and adorned her hair, and dressed herself in a beautiful robe of blue, and began to count the hours in expectation of the night.

That evening when her husband, the Brahman's son, had finished his meal, too excited almost to eat, and had gone to the golden bed in the bedchamber strewn with flowers, he said to himself: "To-night I shall surely know who this beautiful lady is in the palace with the seven wings."

The princess took for her food that which was left over by her husband, and slowly entered the bedchamber. She had to answer that night the question, who was the beautiful lady that lived in the palace with the seven wings. And as she went up to the bed to tell him she found a serpent had crept out of the flowers and had bitten the Brahman's son. Her boy-husband was lying on the bed of flowers, with face pale in death.

My heart suddenly ceased to throb, and I asked with choking voice: "What then?"

Grannie said: "Then – "

But what is the use of going on any further with the story? It would only lead on to what was more and more impossible. The boy of seven did not know that, if there were some "What then?" after death, no grandmother of a grandmother could tell us all about it.

But the child's faith never admits defeat, and it would snatch at the mantle of death itself to turn him back. It would be outrageous for him to think that such a story of one teacherless evening could so suddenly come to a stop. Therefore the grandmother had to call back her story from the ever-shut chamber of the great End, but she does it so simply: it is merely by floating the dead body on a banana stem on the river, and having some incantations read by a magician. But in that rainy night and in the dim light of a lamp death loses all its horror in the mind of the boy, and seems nothing more than a deep slumber of a single night. When the story ends the tired eyelids are weighed down with sleep. Thus it is that we send the little body of the child floating on the back of sleep over the still water of time, and then in the morning read a few verses of incantation to restore him to the world of life and light.

The Patriot

I am sure that Chitragupta, who keeps strict record at the gate of Death, must have noted down in big letters accusations against me, which had escaped my attention altogether. On the other hand many of my sins, that have passed unnoticed by others, loom large in my own memory. The story of my transgression, that I am going to relate, belongs to the latter kind, and I hope that a frank confession of it, before it is finally entered in the Book of Doom, may lessen its culpability.

It all happened yesterday afternoon, on a day of festival for the Jains in our neighbourhood. I was going out with my wife, Kalika, to tea at the house of my friend Nayanmohan.

My wife's name means literally a 'bud.' It was given by my father-in-law, who is thus solely responsible for any discrepancy between its implication and the reality to which it is attached. There is not the least tremor of hesitancy in my wife's nature; her opinions on most subjects have reached their terminus. Once, when she had been vigorously engaged in picketing against British cloth in Burrabazar, the awe-struck members of her party in a fit of excessive admiration gave her the name, Dhruva-vrata, the woman of unwavering vows.

My name is Girindra, the Lord of the Rocks, so common among my countrymen, whose character generally fails to act up to it. Kalika's admirers simply know me as the husband of my wife and pay no heed to my name. By good luck inherited from my ancestors I have, however, some kind of significance, which is considered to be convenient by her followers at the time of collecting subscriptions.

There is a greater chance of harmony between husband and wife, when they are different in character, like the shower of rain and the dry earth, than when they are of a uniform constitution. I am somewhat slipshod by nature, having no grip over things, while my wife has a tenacity of mind which never allows her to let go the thing which it has in its clutches. This very dissimilarity helps to preserve peace in our household.

But there is one point of difference between us, regarding which no adjustment has yet become possible. Kalika believes that I am unpatriotic.

This is very disconcerting, because according to her, truth is what she proclaims to be true. She has numerous internal evidences of my love for my country; but as it disdains to don the livery of the brand of nationalism, professed by her own party, she fiercely refuses to acknowledge it.

From my younger days, I have continued to be a confirmed book-lover: indeed, I am hopelessly addicted to buying books. Even my enemies would not dare to deny that I read them; and my friends know only too well how fond I am of discussing their contents. This had the effect of eliminating most of my friends, till I have left to me Banbihari, the sole companion of my lonely debates. We have just passed through a period, when our police authorities, on the one hand, have associated the worst form of sedition with the presence of the Gita in our possession; and our patriots, on their side, have found it impossible to reconcile appreciation of foreign literature with devotion to one's Motherland. Our traditional Goddess of culture, Saraswati, because of her white complexion, has come to be regarded with-suspicion by our young nationalists. It was openly declared, when the students shunned their College lectures, that the water of the divine lake, on which Saraswati had her white lotus seat, had no efficacy in extinguishing the fire of ill-fortune that has been raging for centuries round the throne of our Mother, Bharat-Lakshmi. In any case, intellectual culture was considered to be a superfluity in the proper growth of our political life.

In spite of my wife's excellent example and powerful urgings I do not wear Khaddar, - not because there is anything wrong in it, nor because I am too fastidious in the choice of my wardrobe. On the contrary, among those of my traits, which are not in perfect consonance with our own national habits, I cannot include a scrupulous care as to how I dress. Once upon a time, before Kalika had her modern transformation, I used to wear broad-toed shoes from Chinese shops and forgot to have them polished. I had a dread of putting on socks: I preferred Punjabis to English shirts, and overlooked their accidental deficiency in buttons. These habits of mine constantly produced domestic cataclysms, threatening our permanent separation. Kalika declared that she felt ashamed to appear before the public in my company. I readily absolved her from the wifely duty of accompanying me to those parties where my presence would be discordant.

The times have changed, but my evil fortune persists. Kalika still has the habit of repeating: 'I am ashamed to go out with you.' Formerly, I hesitated to adopt the uniform of her set, when she belonged to the pre-nationalist age; and I still feel reluctant to adopt the uniform of the present regime, to which she owns her allegiance.

The fault lies deep in my own nature. I shrink from all conscious display of sectarian marks about my person. This shyness on my part leads to incessant verbal explosions in our domestic world, because of the inherent incapacity of Kalika to accept as final any natural difference, which her partner in life may possess. Her mind is like a mountain stream, that boisterously goes round and round a rock, pushing against it in a vain effort to make it flow with its own current. Her contact with a different point of view from her own seems to exercise an irresistible reflex action upon her nerves, throwing her into involuntary convulsions.

While getting ready to go out yesterday, the tone with which Kalika protested against my non-Khaddar dress was anything but sweet. Unfortunately, I had my inveterate pride of intellect, that forced me into a discussion with my wife. It was unpleasant, and what more, futile.

'Women find it convenient,' I said to her, 'to veil their eyes and walk tied to the leading strings of authority. They feel safe when they deprive their thoughts of all freedom, and confine them in the strict Zenana of conformity. Our ladies today have easily developed their devotion to Khaddar, because it has added to the over-burdened list of our outward criterion's of propriety, which seem to comfort them.'

Kalika replied with almost fanatical fury: 'It will be a great day for my country, when the sanctity of wearing Khaddar is as blindly believed in as a dip in the holy water of the Ganges. Reason crystallised becomes custom. Free thoughts are like ghosts, which find their bodies in convention. Then alone they have their solid work, and no longer float about in a thin atmosphere of vacillation.'

I could see that these were the wise sayings of Nayanmohan, with the quotation marks worn out; Kalika found no difficulty in imagining that they were her own.

The man who invented the proverb, 'The silent silence all antagonist', must have been unmarried. It made my wife all the more furious, when I offered her no answer. 'Your protest against caste', she explained, 'is only confined to your mouth. We, on the contrary, carry it out in practice by imposing a uniformly white cover over all colour distinctions.'

I was about to reply, that my protest against caste did truly have its origin in my mouth, whenever I accepted with relish the excellent food cooked by a Muhammadan. It was certainly oral, but not verbal; and its movements were truly inward. An external cover hides distinctions, but does not remove them.

I am sure my argument deserved utterance, but being a helpless male, I timidly sought safety in a speechless neutrality; for, I knew, from repeated experience, that such discussions, started in our domestic seclusion, are invariably carried by my wife, like soiled linen, to her friendly circle to be ruthlessly beaten and mangled. She has the unpleasant habit of collecting counter-arguments from the mouth of Professor Nayanmohan, exultantly flinging them in my face, and then rushing away from the arena without waiting for my answer.

I was perfectly certain about what was in store for me at the Professor's tea-table. There would be some abstruse dissertation on the relative position in Hindu culture of tradition and free thought, the inherited experience of ages and reason which is volatile, inconclusive, and colourlessly universal. In the meanwhile, the vision floated before my mind's eye of the newly-brought books, redolent of Morocco leather, mysteriously veiled in a brown paper cover, waiting for me by my cushions, with their shy virginity of uncut pages.

All the same, I was compelled to keep my engagement by the dread of words, uttered and unuttered, and gestures suggestive of trouble.

We had travelled only a short distance from our house. Passing by the street-hydrant, we had reached the tiled hut occupied by an up-country shopkeeper, who was giving various forms to indigestibility in his cauldron of boiling mustard oil, when we were obstructed by a fearful uproar.

The Marwaris, proceeding to their temple, carrying their costly paraphernalia of worship, had suddenly stopped at this place. There were angry shouts, mingled with the sound of thrashing, and I thought that the crowd were dealing with some pickpocket, enjoying the vigour of their own indignation, which gave them the delightful freedom to be merciless towards one of their own fellow beings. When, by dint of impatient footing of horn, our motor car reached the centre of the excited crowd, we found that the old municipal sweeper of our district was being beaten. He had just taken his afternoon bath and was carrying a bucket of clean water in his right hand with a broom under his arm. Dressed in a check-patterned vest, with carefully combed hair still wet, he was walking home, holding his seven-year-old grandson by his left hand, when accidentally he came in contact with somebody, or something, which gave rise to this violent outburst. The boy was piteously imploring everybody not to hurt his grandfather; and the old man himself with joined hands uplifted, was asking forgiveness for his unintentional offence. Tears were streaming from his frightened eyes, and blood was smeared across his grey beard.

The sight was intolerable to me. I decided at once to take up the sweeper into my car and thereby demonstrate to the pious party, that I was not of their cult.

Noticing my restlessness, Kalika guessed what was in my mind. Griping my arm, she whispered: 'What are you doing? Don't you see he is a sweeper?'

'He maybe a sweeper,' said I, 'but those people have no right to beat him in this brutal manner.'

'It's his own fault.' Kalika answered, 'Would it have hurt his dignity, if he had avoided the middle of the road?'

'I don't know', I said impatiently. 'Anyhow, I am going to take him into my car.'

'Then I leave your car this moment,' said Kalika angrily. 'I refuse to travel with a sweeper.'

'Can't you see,' I argued, 'that he was just bathed, and his clothes are clean, - in fact, much cleaner than those of the people who are beating him?'

"He's a sweeper!" She said decisively. Then she called to the chauffeur, 'Gangadin, drive on'.

I was defeated. It was my cowardice.

Nayanmohan, I am told, brought out some very profound sociological arguments, at the tea-table, specially dealing with the inevitable inequality imposed upon men by their profession and the natural humiliation which is inherent in the scheme of things. But his words did not reach my ears, and I sat silent all through the evening.

The Parrot's Training

Once upon a time there was a bird. It was ignorant. It sang all right, but never recited scriptures. It hopped pretty frequently, but lacked manners.

Said the Raja to himself: 'Ignorance is costly in the long run. For fools consume as much food as their betters, and yet give nothing in return.'

He called his nephews to his presence and told them that the bird must have a sound schooling.

The pundits were summoned, and at once went to the root of the matter.

They decided that the ignorance of birds was due to their natural habit of living in poor nests. Therefore, according to the pundits, the first thing necessary for this bird's education was a suitable cage.

The pundits had their rewards and went home happy.

A golden cage was built with gorgeous decorations. Crowds came to see it from all parts of the world. 'Culture, captured and caged!' exclaimed some, in a rapture of ecstasy, and burst into tears. Others remarked: 'Even if culture be missed, the cage will remain, to the end, a substantial fact. How fortunate for the bird!'

The goldsmith filled his bag with money and lost no time in sailing homewards.

The pundit sat down to educate the bird. With proper deliberation he took his pinch of snuff, as he said: 'Text-books can never be too many for our purpose!'

The nephews brought together an enormous crowd of scribes. They copied from books, and copied from copies, till the manuscripts were piled up to an unreachable height. Men murmured in amazement: 'Oh, the tower of culture, egregiously high! The end of it lost in the clouds!'

The scribes, with light hearts, hurried home, their pockets heavily laden.

The nephews were furiously busy keeping the cage in proper trim. As their constant scrubbing and polishing went on, the people said with satisfaction: 'This is progress indeed!'

Men were employed in large numbers, and supervisors were still more numerous. These, with their cousins of all different degrees of distance, built a palace for themselves and lived there happily ever after.

Whatever may be its other deficiencies, the world is never in want of fault- finders; and they went about saying that every creature remotely connected with the cage flourished beyond words, excepting only the bird.

When this remark reached the Raja's ears, he summoned his nephews before him and said: 'My dear nephews, what is this that we hear?'

The nephews said in answer: 'Sire, let the testimony of the goldsmiths and the pundits, the scribes and the supervisors, be taken, if the truth is to be known. Food is scarce with the fault-finders, and that is why their tongues have gained in sharpness.'

The explanation was so luminously satisfactory that the Raja decorated each one of his nephews with his own rare jewels.

The Raja at length, being desirous of seeing with his own eyes how his Education Department busied itself with the little bird, made his appearance one day at the great Hall of Learning.

From the gate rose the sounds of conch-shells and gongs, horns, bugles and trumpets, cymbals, drums and kettle-drums, tomtoms, tambourines, flutes, fifes, barrel-organs and bagpipes. The pundits began chanting mantras with their topmost voices, while the goldsmiths, scribes, supervisors, and their numberless cousins of all different degrees of distance, loudly raised a round of cheers.

The nephews smiled and said: 'Sire, what do you think of it all?'

The Raja said: 'It does seem so fearfully like a sound principle of Education!'

Mightily pleased, the Raja was about to remount his elephant, when the fault-finder, from behind some bush, cried out: 'Maharaja, have you seen the bird?'

'Indeed, I have not!' exclaimed the Raja, 'I completely forgot about the bird.'

Turning back, he asked the pundits about the method they followed in instructing the bird. It was shown to him. He was immensely impressed. The method was so stupendous that the bird looked ridiculously unimportant in comparison. The Raja was satisfied that there was no flaw in the arrangements. As for any complaint from the bird itself, that simply could not be expected. Its throat was so completely choked with the leaves from the books that it could neither whistle nor whisper. It sent a thrill through one's body to watch the process.

This time, while remounting his elephant, the Raja ordered his State ear-puller to give a thorough good pull at both the ears of the fault-finder.

The bird thus crawled on, duly and properly, to the safest verge of inanity. In fact, its progress was satisfactory in the extreme. Nevertheless, nature occasionally triumphed over training, and when the morning light peeped into the bird's cage it sometimes fluttered its wings in a reprehensible manner. And, though it is hard to believe, it pitifully pecked at its bars with its feeble beak.

'What impertinence!' growled the kotwal.

The blacksmith, with his forge and hammer, took his place in the Raja's Department of Education. Oh, what resounding blows! The iron chain was soon completed, and the bird's wings were clipped.

The Raja's brothers-in-law looked black, and shook their heads, saying: 'These birds not only lack good sense, but also gratitude!'

With text-book in one hand and baton in the other, the pundits gave the poor bird what may fitly be called lessons!

The kotwal was honoured with a title for his watchfulness, and the blacksmith for his skill in forging chains.

The bird died.

Nobody had the least notion how long ago this had happened. The fault- finder was the first man to spread the rumour.

The Raja called his nephews and asked them. 'My dear nephews, what is this that we hear?'

The nephews said: 'Sire, the bird's education has been completed.'

'Does it hop?' the Raja enquired.

'Never! 'said the nephews.

'Does it fly?'

'No.'

'Bring me the bird,' said the Raja.

The bird was brought to him, guarded by the kotwal and the sepoys and the sowars. The Raja poked its body with his finger. Only its inner stuffing of book-leaves rustled.

Outside the window, the murmur of the spring breeze amongst the newly budded asoka leaves made the April morning wistful.

The Victory

She was the Princess Ajita. And the court poet of King Narayan had never seen her. On the day he recited a new poem to the king he would raise his voice just to that pitch which could be heard by unseen hearers in the screened balcony high above the hall. He sent up his song towards the star-land out of his reach, where, circled with light, the planet who ruled his destiny shone unknown and out of ken.

He would espy some shadow moving behind the veil. A tinkling sound would come to his ear from afar, and would set him dreaming of the ankles whose tiny golden bells sang at each step. Ah, the rosy red tender feet that walked the dust of the earth like God's mercy on the fallen! The poet had placed them on the altar of his heart, where he wove his songs to the tune of those golden bells. Doubt never arose in his mind as to whose shadow it was that moved behind the screen, and whose anklets they were that sang to the time of his beating heart.

Manjari, the maid of the princess, passed by the poet's house on her way to the river, and she never missed a day to have a few words with him on the sly. When she found the road deserted, and the shadow of dusk on the land, she would boldly enter his room, and sit at the corner of his carpet. There was a suspicion of an added care in the choice of the colour of her veil, in the setting of the flower in her hair.

People smiled and whispered at this, and they were not to blame. For Shekhar the poet never took the trouble to hide the fact that these meetings were a pure joy to him.

The meaning of her name was the spray of flowers. One must confess that for an ordinary mortal it was sufficient in its sweetness. But Shekhar made his own addition to this name, and called her the Spray of Spring Flowers. And ordinary mortals shook their heads and said, Ah, me!

In the spring songs that the poet sang the praise of the spray of spring flowers was conspicuously reiterated; and the king winked and smiled at him when he heard it, and the poet smiled in answer.

The king would put him the question: 1s it the business of the bee merely to hum in the court of the spring?'

The poet would answer: 'No, but also to sip the honey of the spray of spring flowers.'

And they all laughed in the king's hall. And it was rumoured that the Princess Ajita also laughed at her maid's accepting the poet's name for her, and Manjari felt glad in her heart.

Thus truth and falsehood mingle in life - and to what God builds man adds his own decoration.

Only those were pure truths which were sung by the poet. The theme was Krishna, the lover god, and Radha, the beloved, the Eternal Man and the Eternal Woman, the sorrow that comes from the beginning of time, and the joy without end. The truth of these songs was tested in his inmost heart by everybody from the beggar to the king himself. The poet's songs were on the lips of all. At the merest glimmer of the moon and the faintest whisper of the summer breeze his songs would break forth in the land from windows and courtyards, from sailing-boats, from shadows of the wayside trees, in number-less voices.

Thus passed the days happily. The poet recited, the king listened, the hearers applauded. Manjari passed and repassed by the poet's room on her way to the river - the shadow flitted behind the screened balcony, and the tiny golden bells tinkled from afar.

Just then set forth from his home in the south a poet on his path of conquest. He came to King Narayan, in the kingdom of Amarapur. He stood before the throne, and uttered averse in praise of the king. He had challenged all the court poets on his way, and his career of victory had been unbroken.

The king received him with honour, and said: 'Poet, I offer you welcome.'

Pundarik, the poet, proudly replied: 'Sire, I ask for war.'

Shekhar, the court poet of the king did not know how the battle of the Muse was to be waged. He had no sleep at night. The mighty figure of the famous Pundarik, his sharp nose curved like a scimitar, and his proud head tilted on one side, haunted the poet's vision in the dark.

With a trembling heart Shekhar entered the arena in the morning. The theatre was filled with the crowd.

The poet greeted his rival with a smile and a bow. Pundarik returned it with a slight toss of his head, and turned his face towards his circle of adoring followers with a meaning smile.

Shekhar cast his glance towards the screened balcony high above, and saluted his lady in his mind, saying: If I am the winner at the combat today, my lady, thy victorious name shall be glorified.'

The trumpet sounded. The great crowd stood up, shouting victory to the king. The king, dressed in an ample robe of white, slowly came into the hall like a floating cloud of autumn, and sat on his throne.

Pundarik stood up, and the vast hall became still. With his head raised high and chest expanded, he began in his thundering voice to recite the praise of King Narayan. His words burst upon the walls of the hall like breakers of the sea, and seemed to rattle against the ribs of the listening crowd. The skill with which he gave varied meanings to the name Narayan, and wove each letter of it through the web of his verses in all manner of combinations, took away the breath of his amazed hearers.

For some minutes after he took his seat his voice continued to vibrate among the numberless pillars of the king's court and in thousands of speechless hearts. The learned professors who had come from distant lands raised their right hands, and cried, Bravo!

The king threw a glance on Shekhar's face, and Shekhar in answer raised for a moment his eyes full of pain towards his master, and then stood up like a stricken deer at bay. His face was pale, his bashfulness was almost that of a woman, his slight youthful figure, delicate in its outline, seemed like a tensely strung vina ready to break out in music at the least touch.

His head was bent, his voice was low, when he began. The first few verses were almost inaudible. Then he slowly raised his head, and his clear sweet voice rose into the sky like a quivering flame of fire. He began with the ancient legend of the kingly line lost in the haze of the past, and brought it down through its long course of heroism and matchless generosity to the present age. He fixed his gaze on the king's face, and all the vast and unexpressed love of the people for the royal house rose like incense in his song, and enwreathed the throne on all sides. These were his last words when, trembling, he took his seat: 'My master, I may be beaten in play of words, but not in my love for thee.'

Tears filled the eyes of the hearers, and the stone walls shook with cries of victory.

Mocking this popular outburst of feeling, with an august shake of his head and a contemptuous sneer, Pundarik stood up, and flung this question to the assembly: 'What is there superior to words? ' In a moment the hall lapsed into silence again.

Then with a marvellous display of learning, he proved that the Word was in the beginning, that the Word was God. He piled up quotations from scriptures, and built a high altar for the Word to be seated above all that there is in heaven and in earth. He repeated that question in his mighty voice: 'What is there superior to words?'

Proudly he looked around him. None dared to accept his challenge, and he slowly took his seat like a lion who had just made a full meal of its victim. The pandits shouted, Bravo! The king remained silent with wonder, and the poet Shekhar felt himself of no account by the side of this stupendous learning. The assembly broke up for that day.

Next day Shekhar began his song. It was of that day when the pipings of love's flute startled for the first time the hushed air of the Vrinda forest. The shepherd women did not know who was the player or whence came the music. Sometimes it seemed to come from the heart of the south, wind, and sometimes from the straying clouds of the hill-tops. It came with a message of tryst from the land of the sunrise, and it floated from the verge of sunset with its sigh of sorrow. The stars seemed to be the stops of the instrument that flooded the dreams of the night with melody. The music seemed to burst all at once from all sides, from fields and groves, from the shady lanes and lonely roads, from the melting blue of the sky, from the shimmering green of the grass. They neither knew its meaning nor could they find words to give utterance to the desire of their hearts. Tears filled their eyes, and their life seemed to long for a death that would be its consummation.

Shekhar forgot his audience, forgot the trial of his strength with a rival. He stood alone amid his thoughts that rustled and quivered round him like leaves in summer breeze, and sang the Song of the Flute. He had in his mind the vision of an image that had taken its shape from a shadow, and the echo of a faint tinkling sound of a distant footstep.

He took his seat. His hearers trembled with the sadness of an indefinable delight, immense and vague, and they forgot to applaud him. As this feeling died away Pundarik stood up before the throne and challenged his rival to define who was this Lover and who was the Beloved. He arrogantly looked around him, he smiled at his followers and then put the question again: 'Who is Krishna, the lover, and who is Radha, the beloved?'

Then he began to analyse the roots of those names - and various interpretations of their meanings. He brought before the bewildered audience all the intricacies of the different schools of metaphysics with consummate skill. Each letter of those names he divided from its fellow, and then pursued them with a relentless logic till they fell to the dust in confusion, to be caught up again and restored to a meaning never before imagined by the subtlest of wordmongers.

The pandits were in ecstasy; they applauded vociferously; and the crowd followed them, deluded into the certainty that they had witnessed, that day, the last shred of the curtains of Truth torn to pieces before their eyes by a prodigy of intellect. The performance of his tremendous feat so delighted them that they forgot to ask themselves if there was any truth behind it after all.

The king's mind was overwhelmed with wonder. The atmosphere was completely cleared of all illusion of music, and the vision of the world around seemed to be changed from its freshness of tender green to the solidity of a high road levelled and made hard with crushed stones.

To the people assembled their own poet appeared a mere boy in comparison with this giant, who walked with such ease, knocking down difficulties at each step in the world of words and thoughts. It became evident to them for the first time that the poems Shekhar wrote were absurdly simple, and it must be a mere accident that they did not write them themselves. They were neither new, nor difficult, nor instructive, nor necessary.

The king tried to goad his poet with keen glances, silently inciting him to make a final effort. But Shekhar took no notice, and remained fixed to his seat.

The king in anger came down from his throne - took off his pearl chain and put it on Pundarik's head. Everybody in the hall cheered. From the upper balcony came a slight sound of the movements of rustling robes and waist- chains hung with golden bells. Shekhar rose from his seat and left the hall. It was a dark night of waning moon. The poet Shekhar took down his MSS from his shelves and heaped them on the floor. Some of them contained his earliest writings, which he had almost forgotten. He turned over the pages, reading passages here and there. They all seemed to him poor and trivial - mere words and childish rhymes!

One by one he tore his books to fragments, and threw them into a vessel containing fire, and said: 'To thee, to thee, O my beauty, my fire! Thou hast been burning in my heart all these futile years. If my life were a piece of gold it would come out of its trial brighter, but it is a trodden turf of grass, and nothing remains of it but this handful of ashes.'The night wore on. Shekhar opened wide his windows. He spread upon his bed the white flowers that he loved, the jasmines, tuberoses and chrysanthemums, and brought into his bedroom all the lamps he had in his house and lighted them. Then mixing with honey the juice of some poisonous root, he drank it and lay down on his bed.

Golden anklets tinkled in the passage outside the door, and a subtle perfume came into the room with the breeze.

The poet, with his eyes shut, said: 'My lady, have you taken pity upon your servant at last and come to see him?'

The answer came in a sweet voice: 'My poet, I have come.

Shekhar opened his eyes - and saw before his bed the figure of a woman.

His sight was dim and blurred. And it seemed to him that the image made of a shadow that he had ever kept throned in the secret shrine of his heart had come into the outer world in his last moment to gaze upon his face.

The woman said: 'I am the Princess Ajita.'

The poet with a great effort sat up on his bed.

The princess whispered into his ear: 'The king has not done you justice. It was you who won at the combat, my poet, and I have come to crown you with the crown of victory.'

She took the garland of flowers from her own neck, and put it on his hair, and the poet fell down upon his bed stricken by death.

Giribala

Giribala is overflowing with exuberance of youth that seems spilling over in spray all around her, - in the folds of her soft dress, the turning of her neck, the motion of her hands, in the rhythm of her steps, now quick now languid, in her tinkling anklets and ringing laughter, in her voice and glances. She would often been seen, wrapt in a blue silk, walking on her terrace, in an impulse of unaccountable restlessness. Her limbs seem eager to dance to the time of an inner music unceasing and unheard. She takes pleasure in merely moving her body, causing ripples to break out in the flood of her young life. She would suddenly pluck a leaf from a plant in the flower-pot and throw it up in the sky, and her bangles would give a sudden tinkle, and the careless grace of her hand, like a bird freed from its cage, would fly unseen in the air. With her swift fingers she would brush away from her dress a mere nothing; standing on tiptoe she would peep over her terrace walls for no cause whatever, and then with a rapid motion turn round to go to another direction, swinging her bunch of keys tied to a corner of her garment. She would loosen her hair in an untimely caprice, sitting before her mirror to do it up again, and then in a fit of laziness would fling herself upon her bed, like a line of stray moonlight slipping through some opening of the leaves, idling in the shadow.

She has no children and, having been married in a wealthy family, has very little work to do. Thus she seems to be daily accumulating her own self without expenditure, till the vessel is brimming over with the seething surplus. She has her husband, but not under her control. She has grown up from a girl into a woman, yet escaping, through familiarity, her husband's notice.

When she was newly married and her husband, Gopinath, was attending his college, he would often play the truant and under cover of the midday siesta of his elders secretly come to make love to Giribala. Though they lived under the same roof, he would create occasions to send her letters on tinted paper perfumed with rosewater, and would even gloat upon some exaggerated grievances of imaginary neglect of love.

Just then his father died and he became the sole owner of his property. Like an unseasoned piece of timber, the immature youth of Gopinath attracted parasites which began to bore into his substance. From now his movements took the course that led him in a contrary direction from his wife.

There is a dangerous fascination to be leaders of men, to which many strong minds have succumbed. To be accepted as the leader of a small circle of sycophants, in his own parlour, has the same fearful attraction for a man who suffers from a scarcity of brains and character. Gopinath assumed the part of a hero among his friends and acquaintances, and tried daily to invent new wonders in all manner of extravagance. He won a reputation among his followers for his audacity of excesses, which goaded him not only to keep up his fame, but to surpass himself at all costs.

In the meanwhile, Giribala, in the seclusion of her lonely youth, felt like a queen who had her throne, but no subjects. She knew she had the power in her hand which could make the world of men her captive; only that world itself was wanting.

Giribala has a maidservant whose name is Sudha. She can sing and dance and improvise verses, and she freely gives expression to her regret that such a beauty as that of her mistress should be dedicated to a fool who forgets to enjoy what he owns. Giribala is never tired of hearing from her the details of her charms, while at the same time contradicting her, calling her a liar and a flatterer, exciting her to swear by all that is sacred that she is earnest in her admiration, which statement, even without the accompaniment of a solemn oath, is not difficult for Giribala to believe.

Sudha used to sing to her a song beginning with the line, 'Let me write myself a slave upon the soles of thy feet,' and Giribala in her imagination could feel that her beautiful feet were fully worthy of bearing inscriptions of everlasting slavery from conquered hearts, if only they could be free in their career of conquest.

But the woman to whom her husband Gopinath has surrendered himself as a slave is Lavanga, the actress, who has the reputation of playing to perfection the part of a maiden languishing in hopeless love and swooning on the stage with an exquisite naturalness. When her husband had not altogether vanished from her sphere of influence, Giribala had often heard from him about the wonderful histrionic powers of this woman and in her jealous curiosity had greatly desired to see Lavanga on the stage. But she could not secure her husband's consent, because Gopinath was firm in his opinion that the theatre was a place not fit for any decent woman to visit.

At last she paid for a seat and sent Sudha to see this famous actress in one of her best parts. The account that she received from her on her return was far from flattering to Lavanga, both as to her personal appearance and her stage accomplishments. As, for obvious reasons, she had great faith in Sudha's power of appreciation, where it was due, Giribala did not hesitate to believe her in her description of Lavanga, which was accompanied by a mimicry of a ludicrous mannerism.

When at last her husband deserted her in his infatuation for this woman, she began to feel qualms of doubt. But as Sudha repeatedly asserted her former opinion with ever greater vehemence, comparing Lavanga to a piece of burnt log dressed up in a woman's clothes, Giribala determined secretly to go to the theatre herself and settle this question for good.

And she did go there one night with all the excitement of a forbidden entry. Her very trepidation of heart lent a special charm to what she saw. She gazed at the faces of the spectators, lit up with an unnatural shine of lamplight; and, with the magic of its music and the painted canvas of its scenery, the theatre seemed to her like a world where society was suddenly freed from its law of gravitation.

Coining from her walled up terrace and joyless home, she had entered a region where dreams and reality had clasped their hands in friendship, over the wine cup of art.

The bell rang, the orchestra music stopped, the audience sat still in their seats, the stage-lights shone brighter, and the curtain was drawn up. Suddenly appeared in the light, from the mystery of the unseen, the shepherd girls of the Vrinda forest, and with the accompaniment of songs commenced their dance, punctuated with the uproarious applause of the audience. The blood began to throb all over Giribala's body, and she forgot for the moment that her life was limited to the circumstances and that she was not free in a world where all laws had melted in music.

Sudha came occasionally to interrupt her with her anxious whispers urging her to hasten back home for the fear of being detected. But she paid no heed to her warning, for her sense of fear had gone.

The play goes on. Krishna has given offence to his beloved Radha and she in her wounded pride refuses to recognize him. He is entreating her, abasing himself at her feet, but in vain. Giribala's heart seems to swell. She imagines herself as offended Radha; and feels that she also has in her this woman's power to vindicate her pride. She had heard what a force was woman's beauty in the world but to-night it became to her palpable.

At last the curtain dropped, the light grew dim, the audience got ready to leave the theatre, but Giribala sat still like one in a dream. The thought that she would have to go home had vanished from her mind. She waited for the curtain to rise again and the eternal theme of Krishna's humiliation at the feet of Radha to continue. But Sudha came to remind her that the play had ended and the lamps would soon be put out.

It was late when Giribala came back home. A kerosene lamp was dimly burning in the melancholy solitude and silence of her room. Near the window upon her lonely bed a mosquito curtain was gently moving in the breeze. Her world seemed to her distasteful and mean like a rotten fruit swept into the dustbin.

From now she regularly visited the theatre every Saturday. The fascination of her first sight of it lost much of its glamour. The painted vulgarity of the actresses and the falseness of their affectation became more and more evident, yet the habit grew upon her. Every time the curtain rose the window of her life's prison-house seemed to open before her and the stage, bordered off from the world of reality by its gilded frame and scenic display, by its array of lights and even its flimsiness of conventionalism, appeared to her like a fairyland where it was not impossible for herself to occupy the throne of the fairy queen.

When for the first time she saw her husband among the audience shouting his drunken admiration for a certain actress she felt an intense disgust and prayed in her mind that a day might come when she might have an opportunity to spurn him away with her contempt. But the opportunity became rarer every day, for Gopinath was hardly ever to be seen at his home now, being carried away, one knew not where, in the centre of a dust-storm of dissipation.

One evening in the month of March, in the light of the full moon, Giribala was sitting on her terrace dressed in her cream-coloured robe. It was her habit daily to deck herself with jewellery as if for some festive occasion. For these cosily gems were like wine to her - they sent heightened consciousness of beauty to her limbs; she felt like a plant in spring tingling with the impulse of flowers in all its branches. She wore a pair of diamond bracelets on her arms, a necklace of rubies and pearls on her neck, and a ring with a big sapphire on the little finger of her left hand. Sudha was sitting near her bare feet admiringly touching them with her hand and expressing her wish that she were a man privileged to offer her life as homage to such a pair of feet.

Sudha gently hummed a lovesong to her and the evening wore on to night. Every body in the household had finished their evening meal, and gone to sleep. When suddenly Gopinath appeared reeking with scent and liquor, and Sudha drawing for cloth-end over her face, hastily ran away from the terrace.

Giribala thought for a moment that her day had come at last. She turned away her face and sat silent.

But the curtain in her stage did not rise and no song of entreaty came from her hero, with the words - 'Listen to the pleading of the moon-light, my love, and hide not thy face.'

In his dry unmusical voice Gopinath said, 'Give me your keys.'

A gust of south wind like a sigh of the insulted romance of the poetic world scattered all over the terrace the smell of the night-blooming jasmines and loosened some wisp of hair on Giribala's cheek. She let go her pride, and got up and said, 'You shall have your keys if you listen to what I have to say.' Gopinath said, I cannot delay. Give me your keys.'

Giribala said, I will give you the keys and everything that is in the safe, but you must not leave me.'

Gopinath said, 'That cannot be. I have urgent business.'

'Then you shan't have the keys,' said Giribala.

Gopinath began to search for them. He opened the drawers of the dressing table, broke open the lid of the box that contained Giribala's toilet requisites, smashed the glass panes of her almirah, groped under the pillows and mattress of the bed, but the keys he could not find. Giribala stood near the door stiff and silent like a marble image gazing at vacancy. Trembling with rage Gopinath came to her and said with an angry growl, 'Give me your keys or you will repent.'Giribala did not answer and Gopinath, pinning her to the wall, snatched away by force her bracelets, necklace and ring, and, giving her a parting kick, went away.

Nobody in the house woke up from his sleep, none in the neighbourhood knew of this outrage, the moonlight remained placid and the peace of the night undisturbed. Hearts can be rent never to heal again amidst such serene silence.

The next morning Giribala said she was going to see her father and left home. As Gopinath's present destination was not known and she was not responsible to anybody else in the house her absence was not noticed.

Vision

I

When I was a very young wife, I gave birth to a dead child, and came near to death myself. I recovered strength very slowly, and my eyesight became weaker and weaker.

My husband at this time was studying medicine. He was not altogether sorry to have a chance of testing his medical knowledge on me. So he began to treat my eyes himself.

My elder brother was reading for his law examination. One day he came to see me, and was alarmed at my condition.

"What are you doing?" he said to my husband. "You are ruining Kumo's eyes. You ought to consult a good doctor at once."

My husband said irritably: "Why! what can a good doctor do more than I am doing? The case is quite a simple one, and the remedies are all well known."

Dada answered with scorn: "I suppose you think there is no difference between you and a Professor in your own Medical College."

My husband replied angrily: "If you ever get married, and there is a dispute about your wife's property, you won't take my advice about Law. Why, then, do you now come advising me about Medicine?"

While they were quarrelling, I was saying to myself that it was always the poor grass that suffered most when two kings went to war. Here was a dispute going on between these two, and I had to bear the brunt of it.

It also seemed to me very unfair that, when my family had given me in marriage, they should interfere afterwards. After all, my pleasure and pain are my husband's concern, not theirs.

From that day forward, merely over this trifling matter of my eyes, the bond between my husband and Dada was strained.

To my surprise one afternoon, while my husband was away, Dada brought a doctor in to see me. He examined my eyes very carefully, and looked grave. He said that further neglect would be dangerous. He wrote out a prescription, and Dada for the medicine at once. When the strange doctor had gone, I implored my Dada not to interfere. I was sure that only evil would come from the stealthy visits of a doctor.

I was surprised at myself for plucking up courage speak to my brother like that. I had always hitherto been afraid of him. I am sure also that Dada was surprised at my boldness. He kept silence for a while, and then said to me: "Very well, Kumo. I won't call in the doctor any more. But when the medicine comes you must take it."

Dada then went away. The medicine came from chemist. I took it - bottles, powders, prescriptions and all - and threw it down the well!

My husband had been irritated by Dada's interference, and he began to treat my eyes with greater diligence than ever. He tried all sorts of remedies. I bandaged my eyes as he told me, I wore his coloured glasses, I put in his drops, I took all his powders. I even drank the cod-liver oil he gave me, though my gorge rose against it.

Each time he came back from the hospital, he would ask me anxiously how I felt; and I would answer: "Oh! much better." Indeed I became an expert in self-delusion. When I found that the water in my eyes was still increasing, I would console myself with the thought that it was a good thing to get rid of so much bad fluid; and, when the flow of water in my eyes decreased, I was elated at my husband's skill.

But after a while the agony became unbearable. My eyesight faded away, and I had continual headaches day and night. I saw how much alarmed my husband was getting. I gathered from his manner that he was casting about for a pretext to call in a doctor. So I hinted that it might be as well to call one in.

That he was greatly relieved, I could see. He called in an English doctor that very day. I do not know what talk they had together, but I gathered that the Sahib had spoken very sharply to my husband.

He remained silent for some time after the doctor had gone. I took his hands in mine, and said: "What an ill-mannered brute that was! Why didn't you call in an Indian doctor? That would have been much better. Do you think that man knows better than you do about my eyes?"

My husband was very silent for a moment, and then said with a broken voice: "Kumo, your eyes must be operated on."

I pretended to be vexed with him for concealing the fact from me so long.

"Here you have known this all the time," said I, "and yet you have said nothing about it! Do you think I am such a baby as to be afraid of an operation?"

At that he regained his good spirits: "There are very few men," said he, "who are heroic enough to look forward to an operation without shrinking."

I laughed at him: "Yes, that is so. Men are heroic only before their wives!"

He looked at me gravely, and said: "You are perfectly right. We men are dreadfully vain."

I laughed away his seriousness: "Are you sure you can beat us women even in vanity?"

When Dada came, I took him aside: "Dada, that treatment your doctor recommended would have done me a world of good; only unfortunately. I mistook the mixture for the lotion. And since the day I made the mistake, my eyes have grown steadily worse; and now an operation is needed."

Dada said to me: "You were under your husband's treatment, and that is why I gave up coming to visit you."

"No," I answered. "In reality, I was secretly treating myself in accordance with your doctor's directions."

Oh! what lies we women have to tell! When we are mothers, we tell lies to pacify our children; and when we are wives, we tell lies to pacify the fathers of our children. We are never free from this necessity.

My deception had the effect of bringing about a better feeling between my husband and Dada. Dada blamed himself for asking me to keep a secret from my husband: and my husband regretted that he had not taken my brother's advice at the first.

At last, with the consent of both, an English doctor came, and operated on my left eye. That eye, however, was too weak to bear the strain; and the last flickering glimmer of light went out. Then the other eye gradually lost itself in darkness.

One day my husband came to my bedside. "I cannot brazen it out before you any longer," said he, "Kumo, it is I who have ruined your eyes."

I felt that his voice was choking with tears, and so I took up his right hand in both of mine and said: "Why! you did exactly what was right. You have dealt only with that which was your very own. Just imagine, if some strange doctor had come and taken away my eyesight. What consolation should I have had then? But now I can feel that all has happened for the best; and my great comfort is to know that it is at your hands I have lost my eyes. When Ramchandra found one lotus too few with which to worship God, he offered both his eyes in place of the lotus. And I hate dedicated my eyes to my God. From now, whenever you see something that is a joy to you, then you must describe it to me; and I will feed upon your words as a sacred gift left over from your vision."

I do not mean, of course, that I said all this there and then, for it is impossible to speak these things an the spur of the moment. But I used to think over words like these for days and days together. And when I was very depressed, or if at any time the light of my devotion became dim, and I pitied my evil fate, then I made my mind utter these sentences, one by one, as a child repeats a story that is told. And so I could breathe once more the serener air of peace and love.

At the very time of our talk together, I said enough to show my husband what was in my heart.

"Kumo," he said to me, "the mischief I have done by my folly can never be made good. But I can do one thing. I can ever remain by your side, and try to make up for your want of vision as much as is in my power."

"No," said I. "That will never do. I shall not ask you to turn your house into an hospital for the blind. There is only one thing to be done, you must marry again."

As I tried to explain to him that this was necessary, my voice broke a little. I coughed, and tried to hide my emotion, but he burst out saying:

"Kumo, I know I am a fool, and a braggart, and all that, but I am not a villain! If ever I marry again, I swear to you - I swear to you the most solemn oath by my family god, Gopinath - may that most hated of all sins, the sin of parricide, fall on my head!"

Ah! I should never, never have allowed him to swear that dreadful oath. But tears were choking my voice, and I could not say a word for insufferable joy. I hid my blind face in my pillows, and sobbed, and sobbed again. At last, when the first flood of my tears was over, I drew his head down to my breast.

"Ah!" said I, "why did you take such a terrible oath? Do you think I asked you to marry again for your own sordid pleasure? No! I was thinking of myself, for she could perform those services which were mine to give you when I had my sight."

"Services!" said he, "services! Those can be done by servants. Do you think I am mad enough to bring a slave into my house, and bid her share the throne with this my Goddess?"

As he said the word "Goddess," he held up my face in his hands, and placed a kiss between my brows. At that moment the third eye of divine wisdom was opened, where he kissed me, and verily I had a consecration.

I said in my own mind: "It is well. I am no longer able to serve him in the lower world of household cares. But I shall rise to a higher region. I shall bring down blessings from above. No more lies! No more deceptions for me! All the littlenesses and hypocrisies of my former life shall be banished for ever!"

That day, the whole day through, I felt a conflict going on within me. The joy of the thought, that after this solemn oath it was impossible for my husband to marry again, fixed its roots deep in my heart, and I could not tear them out. But the new Goddess, who had taken her new throne in me, said: "The time might come when it would be good for your husband to break his oath and marry again." But the woman, who was within me, said: "That may be; but all the same an oath is an oath, and there is no way out." The Goddess, who was within me, answered: "That is no reason why you should exult over it." But the woman, who was within me, replied: "What you say is quite true, no doubt; all the same he has taken his oath." And the same story went on again and again. At last the Goddess frowned in silence, and the darkness of a horrible fear came down upon me.

My repentant husband would not let the servants do my work; he must do it all himself. At first it gave me unbounded delight to be dependent on him thus for every little thing. It was a means of keeping him by my side, and my desire to have him with me had become intense since my blindness. That share of his presence, which my eyes had lost, my other senses craved. When he was absent from my side, I would feel as if I were hanging in mid-air, and had lost my hold of all things tangible.

Formerly, when my husband came back late from the hospital, I used to open my window and gaze at the road. That road was the link which connected his world with mine. Now when I had lost that link through my blindness, all my body would go out to seek him. The bridge that united us had given way, and there was now this unsurpassable chasm. When he left my side the gulf seemed to yawn wide open. I could only wait for the time when he should cross back again from his own shore to mine.

But such intense longing and such utter dependence can never be good. A wife is a burden enough to a man, in all conscience, and to add to it the burden of this blindness was to make his life unbearable. I vowed that I would suffer alone, and never wrap my husband round in the folds of my all-pervading darkness.

Within an incredibly short space of time I managed to train myself to do all my household duties by the help of touch and sound and smell. In fact I soon found that I could get on with greater skill than before. For sight often distracts rather than helps us. And so it came to pass that, when these roving eyes of mine could do their work no longer, all the other senses took up their several duties with quietude and completeness.

When I had gained experience by constant practice, I would not let my husband do any more household duties for me. He complained bitterly at first that I was depriving him of his penance.

This did not convince me. Whatever he might say, I could feel that he had a real sense of relief when these household duties were over. To serve daily a wife who is blind can never make up the life of a man.

II

My husband at last had finished his medical course. He went away from Calcutta to a small town to practise as a doctor. There in the country I felt with joy, through all my blindness, that I was restored to the arms of my mother. I had left my village birthplace for Calcutta when I was eight years old. Since then ten years had passed away, and in the great city the memory of my village home had grown dim. As long as I had eyesight, Calcutta with its busy life screened from view the memory of my early days. But when I lost my eyesight I knew for the first time that Calcutta allured only the eyes: it could not fill the mind. And now, in my blindness, the scenes of my childhood shone out once more, like stars that appear one by one in the evening sky at the end of the day.

It was the beginning of November when we left Calcutta for Harsingpur. The place was new to me, but the scents and sounds of the countryside pressed round and embraced me. The morning breeze coming fresh from the newly ploughed land, the sweet and tender smell of the flowering mustard, the shepherd-boy's flute sounding in the distance, even the creaking noise of the bullock-cart, as it groaned over the broken village road, filled my world with delight. The memory of my past life, with all its ineffable fragrance and sound, became a living present to me, and my blind eyes could not tell me I was wrong. I went back, and lived over again my childhood. Only one thing was absent: my mother was not with me.

I could see my home with the large peepul trees growing along the edge of the village pool. I could picture in my mind's eye my old grandmother seated on the ground with her thin wisps of hair untied, warming her back in the sun as she made the little round lentil balls to be dried and used for cooking. But somehow I could not recall the songs she used to croon to herself in her weak and quavering voice. In the evening, whenever I heard the lowing of cattle, I could almost watch the figure of my mother going round the sheds with lighted lamp in her hand. The smell of the wet fodder and the pungent smoke of the straw fire would enter into my very heart. And in the distance I seemed to hear the clanging of the temple bell wafted up by the breeze from the river bank.

Calcutta, with all its turmoil and gossip, curdles the heart. There, all the beautiful duties of life lose their freshness and innocence. I remember one day, when a friend of mine came in, and said to me: "Kumo, why don't you feel angry? If I had been treated like you by my husband, I would never look upon his face again."

She tried to make me indignant, because he had been so long calling in a doctor.

"My blindness," said I, "was itself a sufficient evil. Why should I make it worse by allowing hatred to grow up against my husband?"

My friend shook her head in great contempt, when she heard such old-fashioned talk from the lips of a mere chit of a girl. She went away in disdain. But whatever might be my answer at the time, such words as these left their poison; and the venom was never wholly got out of the soul, when once they had been uttered.

So you see Calcutta, with its never-ending gossip, does harden the heart. But when I came back to the country all my earlier hopes and faiths, all that I held true in life during childhood, became fresh and bright once more. God came to me, and filled my heart and my world. I bowed to Him, and said:

"It is well that Thou has taken away my eyes. Thou art with me."

Ah! But I said more than was right. It was a presumption to say: "Thou art with me." All we can say is this: "I must be true to Thee." Even when nothing is left for us, still we have to go on living.

III

We passed a few happy months together. My husband gained some reputation in his profession as a doctor. And money came with it.

But there is a mischief in money. I cannot point to any one event; but, because the blind have keener perceptions than other people, I could discern the change which came over my husband along with the increase of wealth.

He had a keen sense of justice when he was younger, and had often told me of his great desire to help the poor when once he obtained a practice of his own. He had a noble contempt far those in his profession who would not feel the pulse of a poor patient before collecting his fee. But now I noticed a difference. He had become strangely hard. Once when a poor woman came, and begged him, out of charity, to save the life of her only child, he bluntly refused. And when I implored him myself to help her, he did his work perfunctorily.

While we were less rich my husband disliked sharp practice in money matters. He was scrupulously honourable in such things. But since he had got a large account at the bank he was often closeted for hours with some scamp of a landlord's agent, for purposes which clearly boded no good.

Where has he drifted? What has become of this husband of mine, - the husband I knew before I was blind; the husband who kissed me that day between my brows, and enshrined me on the throne of a Goddess? Those whom a sudden gust of passion brings down to the dust can rise up again with a new strong impulse of goodness. But those who, day by day, become dried up in the very fibre of their moral being; those who by some outer parasitic growth choke the inner life by slow degrees, - such wench one day a deadness which knows no healing.

The separation caused by blindness is the merest physical trifle. But, ah! it suffocates me to find that he is no longer with me, where he stood with me in that hour when we both knew that I was blind. That is a separation indeed!

I, with my love fresh and my faith unbroken, have kept to the shelter of my heart's inner shrine. But my husband has left the cool shade of those things that are ageless and unfading. He is fast disappearing into the barren, waterless waste in his mad thirst for gold.

Sometimes the suspicion comes to me that things not so bad as they seem: that perhaps I exaggerate because I am blind. It may be that, if my eyesight were unimpaired, I should have accepted world as I found it. This, at any rate, was the light in which my husband looked at all my moods and fancies.

One day an old Musalman came to the house. He asked my husband to visit his little grand-daughter. I could hear the old man say: "Baba, I am a poor man; but come with me, and Allah will do you good." My husband answered coldly: "What Allah will do won't help matters; I want to know what you can do for me."

When I heard it, I wondered in my mind why God had not made me deaf as well as blind. The old man heaved a deep sigh, and departed. I sent my maid to fetch him to my room. I met him at the door of the inner apartment, and put some money into his hand.

"Please take this from me," said I, "for your little grand-daughter, and get a trustworthy doctor to look after her. And pray for my husband."

But the whole of that day I could take no food at all. In the afternoon, when my husband got up from sleep, he asked me: "Why do you look so pale?"

I was about to say, as I used to do in the past: "Oh! It's nothing "; but those days of deception were over, and I spoke to him plainly.

"I have been hesitating," I said, "for days together to tell you something. It has been hard to think out what exactly it was I wanted to say. Even now I may not be able to explain what

I had in my mind. But I am sure you know what has happened. Our lives have drifted apart."

My husband laughed in a forced manner, and said: "Change is the law of nature."

I said to him: "I know that. But there are some things that are eternal."

Then he became serious.

"There are many women," said he, "who have a real cause for sorrow. There are some whose husbands do not earn money. There are others whose husbands do not love them. But you are making yourself wretched about nothing at all."

Then it became clear to me that my very blindness had conferred on me the power of seeing a world which is beyond all change. Yes! It is true. I am not like other women. And my husband will never understand me.

IV

Our two lives went on with their dull routine for some time. Then there was a break in the monotony. An aunt of my husband came to pay us a visit.

The first thing she blurted out after our first greeting was this: "Well, Krum, it's a great pity you have become blind; but why do you impose your own affliction on your husband? You must get him to another wife."

There was an awkward pause. If my husband had only said something in jest, or laughed in her face, all would have been over. But he stammered and hesitated, and said at last in a nervous, stupid way: "Do you really think so? Really, Aunt, you shouldn't talk like that."

His aunt appealed to me. "Was I wrong, Kumo?"

I laughed a hollow laugh.

"Had not you better," said I, "consult some one more competent to decide? The pickpocket never asks permission from the man whose pocket he is going to pick."

"You are quite right," she replied blandly. "Abinash, my dear, let us have our little conference in private. What do you say to that?"

After a few days my husband asked her, in my presence, if she knew of any girl of a decent family who could come and help me in my household work. He knew quite well that I needed no help. I kept silence.

"Oh! there are heaps of them," replied his aunt. "My cousin has a daughter who is just of the marriageable age, and as nice a girl as you could wish. Her people would be only too glad to secure you as a husband."

Again there came from him that forced, hesitating laugh, and he said: "But I never mentioned marriage."

"How could you expect," asked his aunt, "a girl of decent family to come and live in your house without marriage?"

He had to admit that this was reasonable, and remained nervously silent.

I stood alone within the closed doors of my blindness after he had gone, and called upon my God and prayed: "O God, save my husband."

When I was coming out of the household shrine from my morning worship a few days later, his aunt took hold of both my hands warmly.

"Kumo, here is the girl," said she, "we were speaking about the other day. Her name is Hemangini. She will be delighted to meet you. Hemo, come here and be introduced to your sister."

My husband entered the room at the same moment. He feigned surprise when he saw the strange girl, and was about to retire. But his aunt said: "Abinash, my dear, what are you running away for? There is no need to do that. Here is my cousin's daughter, Hemangini, come to see you. Hemo, make your bow to him."

As if taken quite by surprise, he began to ply his aunt with questions about the when and why and how of the new arrival.

I saw the hollowness of the whole thing, and took Hemangini by the hand and led her to my own room. I gently stroked her face and arms and hair, and found that she was about fifteen years old, and very beautiful.

As I felt her face, she suddenly burst out laughing and said: "Why! what are you doing? Are you hypnotising me?"

That sweet ringing laughter of hers swept away in a moment all the dark clouds that stood between us. I threw my right arm about her neck.

"Dear one," said I, "I am trying to see you." And again I stroked her soft face with my left hand.

"Trying to see me?" she said, with a new burst of laughter. "Am I like a vegetable marrow, grown in your garden, that you want to feel me all round to see how soft I am?"

I suddenly bethought me that she did not know I had lost my sight.

"Sister, I am blind," said I.

She was silent. I could feel her big young eyes, full of curiosity, peering into my face. I knew they were full of pity. Then she grew thoughtful and puzzled, and said, after a short pause:

"Oh! I see now. That was the reason your husband invited his aunt to come and stay here."

"No!" I replied, "you are quite mistaken. He did not ask her to come. She came of her own accord."

Hemangini went off into a peal of laughter. "That's just like my aunt," said she. "Oh I wasn't it nice of her to come without any invitation? But now she's come, you won't get her to move for some time, I can assure you!"

Then she paused, and looked puzzled.

"But why did father send me?" she asked. "Can you tell me that?"

The aunt had come into the room while we were talking. Hemangini said to her: "When are you thinking of going back, Aunt?"

The aunt looked very much upset.

"What a question to ask!" said she, "I've never seen such a restless body as you. We've only just come, and you ask when we're going back!"

"It is all very well for you," Hemangini said, "for this house belongs to your near relations. But what about me? I tell you plainly I can't stop here." And then she held my hand and said: "What do you think, dear?"

I drew her to my heart, but said nothing. The aunt was in a great difficulty. She felt the situation was getting beyond her control; so she proposed that she and her niece should go out together to bathe.

"No! we two will go together," said Hemangini, clinging to me. The aunt gave in, fearing opposition if she tried to drag her away.

Going down to the river Hemangini asked me: "Why don't you have children?"

I was startled by her question, and answered: "How can I tell? My God has not given me any. That is the reason."

"No! That's not the reason," said Hemangini quickly. "You must have committed some sin. Look at my aunt. She is childless. It must be because her heart has some wickedness. But what wickedness is in your heart?"

The words hurt me. I have no solution to offer for the problem of evil. I sighed deeply, and said in the silence of my soul: "My God! Thou knowest the reason."

"Gracious goodness," cried Hemangini, "what are you sighing for? No one ever takes me seriously."

And her laughter pealed across the river.

V

I found out after this that there were constant interruptions in my husband's professional duties. He refused all calls from a distance, and would hurry away from his patients, even when they were close at hand.

Formerly it was only during the mid-day meals and at night-time that he could come into the inner apartment. But now, with unnecessary anxiety for his aunt's comfort, he began to visit her at all hours of the day. I knew at once that he had come to her room, when I heard her shouting for Hemangini to bring in a glass of water. At first the girl would do what she was told; but later on she refused altogether.

Then the aunt would call, in an endearing voice: "Hemo! Hemo! Hemangini." But the girl would cling to me with an impulse of pity. A sense of dread and sadness would keep her silent. Sometimes she would shrink towards me like a hunted thing, who scarcely knew what was coming.

About this time my brother came down from Calcutta to visit me. I knew how keen his powers of observation were, and what a hard judge he was. I feared my husband would be put on his defence, and have to stand his trial before him. So I endeavoured to hide the true situation behind a mask of noisy cheerfulness. But I am afraid I overdid the part: it was unnatural for me.

My husband began to fidget openly, and asked how long my brother was going to stay. At last his impatience became little short of insulting, and my brother had no help for it but to leave. Before going he placed his hand on my head, and kept it there for some time. I noticed that his hand shook, and a tear fell from his eyes, as he silently gave me his blessing.

I well remember that it was an evening in April, and a market-day. People who had come into the town were going back home from market. There was the feeling of an impending storm in the air; the smell of the wet earth and the moisture in the wind were all-pervading. I never keep a lighted lamp in my bedroom, when I am alone, lest my clothes should catch fire, or some accident happen. I sat on the floor in my dark room, and called upon the God of my blind world.

"O my Lord," I cried, "Thy face is hidden. I cannot see. I am blind. I hold tight this broken rudder of a heart till my hands bleed. The waves have become too strong for me. How long wilt thou try me, my God, how long?"

I kept my head prone upon the bedstead and began to sob. As I did so, I felt the bedstead move a little. The next moment

Hemangini was by my side. She clung to my neck, and wiped my tears away silently. I do not know why she had been waiting that evening in the inner room, or why she had been lying alone there in the dusk. She asked me no question. She said no word. She simply placed her cool hand on my forehead, and kissed me, and departed.

The next morning Hemangini said to her aunt in my presence: "If you want to stay on, you can. But I don't. I'm going away home with our family servant."

The aunt said there was no need for her to go alone, for she was going away also. Then smilingly and mincingly she brought out, from a plush case, a ring set with pearls.

"Look, Hemo," said she, "what a beautiful ring my Abinash brought for you."

Hemangini snatched the ring from her hand.

"Look, Aunt," she answered quickly, "just see how splendidly I aim." And she flung the ring into the tank outside the window.

The aunt, overwhelmed with alarm, vexation, and surprise, bristled like a hedgehog. She turned to me, and held me by the hand.

"Kumo," she repeated again and again, "don't say a word about this childish freak to Abinash. He would be fearfully vexed."

I assured her that she need not fear. Not a word would reach him about it from my lips.

The next day before starting for home Hemangini embraced me, and said: "Dearest, keep me in mind; do not forget me."

I stroked her face over and over with my fingers, and said: "Sister, the blind have long memories."

I drew her head towards me, and kissed her hair and her forehead. My world suddenly became grey. All the beauty and laughter and tender youth, which had nestled so close to me, vanished when Hemangini departed. I went groping about with arms outstretched, seeking to find out what was left in my deserted world.

My husband came in later. He affected a great relief now that they were gone, but it was exaggerated and empty. He pretended that his aunt's visit had kept him away from work.

Hitherto there had been only the one barrier of blindness between me and my husband. Now another barrier was added, - this deliberate silence about Hemangini. He feigned utter indifference, but I knew he was having letters about her.

It was early in May. My maid entered my room one morning, and asked me: "What is all this preparation going on at the landing on the river? Where is Master going?"

I knew there was something impending, but I said to the maid: "I can't say."

The maid did not dare to ask me any more questions. She sighed, and went away.

Late that night my husband came to me.

"I have to visit a patient in the country," said he. "I shall have to start very early to-morrow morning, and I may have to be away for two or three days."

I got up from my bed. I stood before him, and cried aloud: "Why are you telling me lies?"

My husband stammered out: "What - what lies have I told you?"

I said: "You are going to get married."

He remained silent. For some moments there was no sound in the room. Then I broke the silence:

"Answer me," I cried. "Say, yes."

He answered, "Yes," like a feeble echo.

I shouted out with a loud voice: "No! I shall never allow you. I shall save you from this great disaster, this dreadful sin. If I fail in this, then why am I your wife, and why did I ever worship my God?"

The room remained still as a stone. I dropped on the floor, and clung to my husband's knees.

"What have I done?" I asked. "Where have I been lacking? Tell me truly. Why do you want another wife?"

My husband said slowly: "I will tell you the truth. I am afraid of you. Your blindness has enclosed you in its fortress, and I have now no entrance. To me you are no longer a woman. You are awful as my God. I cannot live my every day life with you. I want a woman - just an ordinary woman - whom I can be free to chide and coax and pet and scold."

Oh, tear open my heart and see! What am I else but that, - just an ordinary woman? I am the same girl that I was when I was newly wed, a girl with all her need to believe, to confide, to worship.

I do not recollect exactly the words that I uttered. I only remember that I said: "If I be a true wife, then, may God be my witness, you shall never do this wicked deed, you shall never break your oath. Before you commit such sacrilege, either I shall become a widow, or Hemangini shall die."

Then I fell down on the floor in a swoon. When I came to myself, it was still dark. The birds were silent. My husband had gone.

All that day I sat at my worship in the sanctuary at the household shrine. In the evening a fierce storm, with thunder and lightning and rain, swept down upon the house and shook it. As I crouched before the shrine, I did not ask my God to save my husband from the storm, though he must have been at that time in peril on the river. I prayed that whatever might happen to me, my husband might be saved from this great sin.

Night passed. The whole of the next day I kept my seat at worship. When it was evening there was the noise of shaking and beating at the door. When the door was broken open, they found me lying unconscious on the ground, and carried me to my room.

When I came to myself at last, I heard some one whispering in my ear: "Sister."

I found that I was lying in my room with my head on Hemangini's lap. When my head moved, I heard her dress rustle. It was the sound of bridal silk.

O my God, my God! My prayer has gone unheeded! My husband has fallen!

Hemangini bent her head low, and said in a sweet whisper: "Sister, dearest, I have come to ask your blessing on our marriage."

At first my whole body stiffened like the trunk of a tree that has been struck by lightning. Then I sat up, and said, painfully, forcing myself to speak the words: "Why should I not bless you? You have done no wrong."

Hemangini laughed her merry laugh.

"Wrong!" said she. "When you married it was right; and when I marry, you call it wrong!"

I tried to smile in answer to her laughter. I said in my mind: "My prayer is not the final thing in this world. His will is all. Let the blows descend upon my head; but may they leave my faith and hope in God untouched."

Hemangini bowed to me, and touched my feet. "May you be happy," said I, blessing her, "and enjoy unbroken prosperity."

Hemangini was still unsatisfied.

"Dearest sister," she said, "a blessing for me is not enough. You must make our happiness complete. You must, with those saintly hands of yours, accept into your home my husband also. Let me bring him to you."

I said: "Yes, bring him to me."

A few moments later I heard a familiar footstep, and the question, "Kumo, how are you?"

I started up, and bowed to the ground, and cried: "Dada!"

Hemangini burst out laughing.

"You still call him elder brother?" she asked. "What nonsense! Call him younger brother now, and pull his ears and cease him, for he has married me, your younger sister."

Then I understood. My husband had been saved from that great sin. He had not fallen.

I knew my Dada had determined never to marry. And, since my mother had died, there was no sacred wish of hers to implore him to wedlock. But I, his sister, by my sore need bad brought it to pass. He had married for my sake.

Tears of joy gushed from my eyes, and poured down my cheeks. I tried, but I could not stop them. Dada slowly passed his fingers through my hair. Hemangini clung to me, and went on laughing.

I was lying awake in my bed for the best part of the night, waiting with straining anxiety for my husband's return. I could not imagine how he would bear the shock of shame and disappointment.

When it was long past the hour of midnight, slowly my door opened. I sat up on my bed, and listened. They were the footsteps of my husband. My heart began to beat wildly. He came up to my bed, held my band in his.

"Your Dada," said he, "has saved me from destruction. I was being dragged down and down by a moments madness. An infatuation had seized me, from which I seemed unable to escape. God alone knows what a load I was carrying on that day when I entered the boat. The storm came down on river, and covered the sky. In the midst of all fears I had a secret wish in my heart to be drowned, and so disentangle my life from the knot which I had tied it. I reached Mathurganj. There I heard the news which set me free. Your brother had married Hemangini. I cannot tell you with what joy and shame I heard it. I hastened on board the boat again. In that moment of self-revelation I knew that I could have no happiness except with you. You are a Goddess."

I laughed and cried at the same time, and said: "No, no, no! I am not going to be a Goddess any longer I am simply your own little wife. I am an ordinary woman."

"Dearest," he replied, "I have also something I want to say to you. Never again put me to shame by calling me your God."

On the next day the little town became joyous with sound of conch shells. But nobody made any reference to that night of madness, when all was so nearly lost.

The Kingdom of Cards

Once upon a time there was a lonely island in a distant sea where lived the Kings and Queens, the Aces and the Knaves, in the Kingdom of Cards. The Tens and Nines, with the Twos and Threes, and all the other members, had long ago settled there also. But these were not twice-born people, like the famous Court Cards.

The Ace, the King, and the Knave were the three highest castes. The fourth Caste was made up of a mixture of the lower Cards. The Twos and Threes were lowest of all. These inferior Cards were never allowed to sit in the same row with the great Court Cards.

Wonderful indeed were the regulations and rules of that island kingdom. The particular rank of each individual had been settled from time immemorial. Every one had his own appointed work, and never did anything else. An unseen hand appeared to be directing them wherever they went,—according to the Rules.

No one in the Kingdom of Cards had any occasion to think: no one had any need to come to any decision: no one was ever required to debate any new subject. The citizens all moved along in a listless groove without speech. When they fell, they made no noise. They lay down on their backs, and gazed upward at the sky with each prim feature firmly fixed for ever.

There was a remarkable stillness in the Kingdom of Cards. Satisfaction and contentment were complete in all their rounded wholeness. There was never any uproar or violence. There was never any excitement or enthusiasm.

The great ocean, crooning its lullaby with one unceasing melody, lapped the island to sleep with a thousand soft touches of its wave's white hands. The vast sky, like the outspread azure wings of the brooding mother-bird, nestled the island round with its downy plume. For on the distant horizon a deep blue line betokened another shore. But no sound of quarrel or strife could reach the Island of Cards, to break its calm repose.

In that far-off foreign land across the sea, there lived a young Prince whose mother was a sorrowing queen. This queen had fallen from favour, and was living with her only son on the seashore. The Prince passed his childhood alone and forlorn, sitting by his forlorn mother, weaving the net of his big desires. He longed to go in search of the Flying Horse, the Jewel in the Cobra's hood, the Rose of Heaven, the Magic Roads, or to find where the Princess Beauty was sleeping in the Ogre's castle over the thirteen rivers and across the seven seas.

From the Son of the Merchant at school the young Prince learnt the stories of foreign kingdoms. From the Son of the Kotwal he learnt the adventures of the Two Genii of the Lamp. And when the rain came beating down, and the clouds covered the sky, he would sit on the threshold facing the sea, and say to his sorrowing mother: "Tell me, mother, a story of some very far-off land."

And his mother would tell him an endless tale she had heard in her childhood of a wonderful country beyond the sea where dwelt the Princess Beauty. And the heart of the young Prince would become sick with longing, as he sat on the threshold, looking out on the ocean, listening to his mother's wonderful story, while the rain outside came beating down and the grey clouds covered the sky.

One day the Son of the Merchant came to the Prince, and said boldly: "Comrade, my studies are over. I am now setting out on my travels to seek my fortunes on the sea. I have come to bid you good-bye."

The Prince said; "I will go with you."

And the Son of Kotwal said also: "Comrades, trusty and true, you will not leave me behind. I also will be your companion."

Then the young Prince said to his sorrowing mother; "Mother, I am now setting out on my travels to seek my fortune. When I come back once more, I shall surely have found some way to remove all your sorrow."

So the Three Companions set out on their travels together. In the harbour were anchored the twelve ships of the merchant, and the Three Companions got on board. The south wind was blowing, and the twelve ships sailed away, as fast as the desires which rose in the Prince's breast.

At the Conch Shell Island they filled one ship with conchs. At the Sandal Wood Island they filled a second ship with sandal-wood, and at the Coral Island they filled a third ship with coral.

Four years passed away, and they filled four more ships, one with ivory, one with musk, one with cloves, and one with nutmegs.

But when these ships were all loaded a terrible tempest arose. The ships were all of them sunk, with their cloves and nutmeg, and musk and ivory, and coral and sandal-wood and conchs. But the ship with the Three Companions struck on an island reef, buried them safe ashore, and itself broke in pieces.

This was the famous Island of Cards, where lived the Ace and King and Queen and Knave, with the Nines and Tens and all the other Members—according to the Rules.

Up till now there had been nothing to disturb that island stillness. No new thing had ever happened. No discussion had ever been held.

And then, of a sudden, the Three Companions appeared, thrown up by the sea,—and the Great Debate began. There were three main points of dispute.

First, to what caste should these unclassed strangers belong? Should they rank with the Court Cards? Or were they merely lower-caste people, to be ranked with the Nines and Tens? No precedent could be quoted to decide this weighty question.

Secondly, what was their clan? Had they the fairer hue and bright complexion of the Hearts, or was theirs the darker complexion of the Clubs? Over this question there were interminable disputes. The whole marriage system of the island, with its intricate regulations, would depend on its nice adjustment.

Thirdly, what food should they take? With whom should they live and sleep? And should their heads be placed south-west, north-west, or only north-east? In all the Kingdom of Cards a series of problems so vital and critical had never been debated before.

But the Three Companions grew desperately hungry. They had to get food in some way or other. So while this debate went on, with its interminable silence and pauses, and while the Aces called their own meeting, and formed themselves into a Committee, to find some obsolete dealing with the question, the Three Companions themselves were eating all they could find, and drinking out of every vessel, and breaking all regulations.

Even the Twos and Threes were shocked at this outrageous behaviour. The Threes said; "Brother Twos, these people are openly shameless!" And the Twos said: "Brother Threes, they are evidently of lower caste than ourselves!" After their meal was over, the Three Companions went for a stroll in the city.

When they saw the ponderous people moving in their dismal processions with prim and solemn faces, then the Prince turned to the Son of the Merchant and the Son of the Kotwal, and threw back his head, and gave one stupendous laugh.

Down Royal Street and across Ace Square and along the Knave Embankment ran the quiver of this strange, unheard-of laughter, the laughter that, amazed at itself, expired in the vast vacuum of silence.

The Son of the Kotwal and the Son of the Merchant were chilled through to the bone by the ghost-like stillness around them. They turned to the Prince, and said: "Comrade, let us away. Let us not stop for a moment in this awful land of ghosts."

But the Prince said: "Comrades, these people resemble men, so I am going to find out, by shaking them upside down and outside in, whether they have a single drop of warm living blood left in their veins."

The days passed one by one, and the placid existence of the Island went on almost without a ripple. The Three Companions obeyed no rules nor regulations. They never did anything correctly either in sitting or standing or turning themselves round or lying on their back. On the contrary, wherever they saw these things going on precisely and exactly according to the Rules, they gave way to inordinate laughter. They remained unimpressed altogether by the eternal gravity of those eternal regulations.

One day the great Court Cards came to the Son of the Kotwal and the Son of the Merchant and the Prince.

"Why," they asked slowly, "are you not moving according to the Rules?"

The Three Companions answered: "Because that is our Ichcha (wish)."

The great Court Cards with hollow, cavernous voices, as if slowly awakening from an age-long dream, said together: "Ich-cha! And pray who is Ich-cha?"

They could not understand who Ichcha was then, but the whole island was to understand it by-and-by. The first glimmer of light passed the threshold of their minds when they found out, through watching the actions of the Prince, that they might move in a straight line in an opposite direction from the one in which they had always gone before. Then they made another startling discovery, that there was another side to the Cards which they had never yet noticed with attention. This was the beginning of the change.

Now that the change had begun, the Three Companions were able to initiate them more and more deeply into the mysteries of Ichcha. The Cards gradually became aware that life was not bound by regulations. They began to feel a secret satisfaction in the kingly power of choosing for themselves.

But with this first impact of Ichcha the whole pack of cards began to totter slowly, and then tumble down to the ground. The scene was like that of some huge python awaking from a long sleep, as it slowly unfolds its numberless coils with a quiver that runs through its whole frame.

Hitherto the Queens of Spades and Clubs and Diamonds and Hearts had remained behind curtains with eyes that gazed vacantly into space, or else remained fixed upon the ground.

And now, all of a sudden, on an afternoon in spring the Queen of Hearts from the balcony raised her dark eyebrows for a moment, and cast a single glance upon the Prince from the corner of her eye.

"Great God," cried the Prince, "I thought they were all painted images. But I am wrong. They are women after all."

Then the young Prince called to his side his two Companions, and said in a meditative voice; "My comrades! There is a charm about these ladies that I never noticed before. When I saw that glance of the Queen's dark, luminous eyes, brightening with new emotion, it seemed to me like the first faint streak of dawn in a newly created world."

The two Companions smiled a knowing smile, and said: "Is that really so, Prince?"

And the poor Queen of Hearts from that day went from bad to worse. She began to forget all rules in a truly scandalous manner. If, for instance, her place in the row was beside the Knave, she suddenly found herself quite accidentally standing beside the Prince instead. At this, the Knave, with motionless face and solemn voice, would say: "Queen, you have made a mistake."

And the poor Queen of Hearts' red cheeks would get redder than ever. But the Prince would come gallantly to her rescue and say: "No! There is no mistake. From to-day I am going to be Knave!"

Now it came to pass that, while every one was trying to correct the improprieties of the guilty Queen of Hearts, they began to make mistakes themselves. The Aces found themselves elbowed out by the Kings. The Kings got muddled up with the Knaves. The Nines and Tens assumed airs as though they belonged to the Great Court Cards. The Twos and Threes were found secretly taking the places specially resented for the Fours and Fives. Confusion had never been so confounded before.

Many spring seasons had come and gone in that Island of Cards. The Kokil, the bird of Spring, had sung its song year after year. But it had never stirred the blood as it stirred it now. In days gone by the sea had sung its tireless melody. But, then, it had proclaimed only the inflexible monotony of the Rule. And suddenly its waves were telling, through all their flashing light and luminous shade and myriad voices, the deepest yearnings of the heart of love!

Where are vanished now their prim, round, regular, complacent features? Here is a face full of love-sick longing. Here is a heart heating wild with regrets. Here is a mind racked sore with doubts. Music and sighing, and smiles and tears, are filling the air. Life is throbbing; hearts are breaking; passions are kindling.

Every one is now thinking of his own appearance, and comparing himself with others. The Ace of Clubs is musing to himself, that the King of Spades may be just passably good-looking. "But," says he, "when I walk down the street you have only to see how people's eyes turn towards me." The King of Spades is saying; "Why on earth is that Ace of Clubs always straining his neck and strutting about like a peacock? He imagines all the Queens are dying of love for him, while the real fact is—" Here he pauses, and examines his face in the glass.

But the Queens were the worst of all. They began to spend all their time in dressing themselves up to the Nines. And the Nines would become their hopeless and abject slaves. But their cutting remarks about one another were more shocking still.

So the young men would sit listless on the leaves under the trees, lolling with outstretched limbs in the forest shade. And the young maidens, dressed in pale-blue robes, would come walking accidentally to the same shade of the same forest by the same trees, and turn their eyes as though they saw no one there, and look as though they came out to see nothing at all. And then one young man more forward than the rest in a fit of madness would dare to go near to a maiden in blue. But, as he drew near, speech would forsake him. He would stand there tongue-tied and foolish, and the favourable moment would pass.

The Kokil birds were singing in the boughs overhead. The mischievous South wind was blowing; it disarrayed the hair, it whispered in the ear, and stirred the music in the blood. The leaves of the trees were murmuring with rustling delight. And the ceaseless sound of the ocean made all the mute longings of the heart of man and maid surge backwards and forwards on the full springtide of love.

The Three Companions had brought into the dried-up channels of the Kingdom of Cards the full flood-tide of a new life.

And, though the tide was full, there-was a pause as though the rising waters would not break into foam but remain suspended for ever. There were no outspoken words, only a cautious going forward one step and receding two. All seemed busy heaping up their unfulfilled desires like castles in the air, or fortresses of sand. They were pale and speechless, their eyes were burning, their lips trembling with unspoken secrets.

The Prince saw what was wrong. He summoned every one on the Island and said: "Bring hither the flutes and the cymbals, the pipes and drums. Let all be played together, and raise loud shouts of rejoicing. For the Queen of Hearts this very night is going to choose her Mate!"

So the Tens and Nines began to blow on their flutes and pipes; the Eights and Sevens played on their sackbuts and viols; and even the Twos and Threes began to beat madly on their drums.

When this tumultous gust of music came, it swept away at one blast all those sighings and mopings. And then what a torrent of laughter and words poured forth! There were daring proposals and locking refusals, and gossip and chatter, and jests and merriment. It was like the swaying and shaking, and rustling and soughing, in a summer gale, of a million leaves and branches in the depth of the primeval forest.

But the Queen of Hearts, in a rose-red robe, sat silent in the shadow of her secret bower, and listened to the great uproarious sound of music and mirth, that came floating towards her. She shut her eyes, and dreamt her dream of lore. And when she opened them she found the Prince seated on the ground before her gazing up at her face. And she covered her eyes with both hands, and shrank back quivering with an inward tumult of joy.

And the Prince passed the whole day alone, walking by the side of the surging sea. He carried in his mind that startled look, that shrinking gesture of the Queen, and his heart beat high with hope.

That night the serried, gaily-dressed ranks of young men and maidens waited with smiling faces at the Palace Gates. The Palace Hall was lighted with fairy lamps and festooned with the flowers of spring. Slowly the Queen of Hearts entered, and the whole assembly rose to greet her. With a jasmine garland in her hand, she stood before the Prince with downcast eyes. In her lowly bashfulness she could hardly raise the garland to the neck of the Mate she had chosen. But the Prince bowed his head, and the garland slipped to its place. The assembly of youths and maidens had waited her choice with eager, expectant hush. And when the choice was made, the whole vast concourse rocked and swayed with a tumult of wild delight. And the sound of their shouts was heard in every part of the island, and by ships far out at sea. Never had such a shout been raised in the Kingdom of Cards before.

And they carried the Prince and his Bride, and seated them on the throne, and crowned them then and there in the Ancient Island of Cards.

And the sorrowing Mother Queen, on the 'far-off island shore on the other side of the sea, came sailing to her son's new kingdom in a ship adorned with gold.

And the citizens are no longer regulated according to the Rules, but are good or bad, or both, according to their Ichcha.

Living or Dead?

The widow in the house of Saradasankar, the Ranihat zemindar, had no kinsmen of her father's family. One after another all had died. Nor had she in her husband's family any one she could call her own, neither husband nor son. The child of her brother-in-law Saradasankar was her darling. Far a long time after his birth, his mother had been very ill, and the widow, his aunt Kadambini, had fostered him. If a woman fosters another's child, her love for him is all the stronger because she has no claim upon him-no claim of kinship, that is, but simply the claim of love. Love cannot prove its claim by any document which society accepts, and does not wish to prove it; it merely worships with double passion its life's uncertain treasure. Thus all the widow's thwarted love went out to wards this little child. One night in Sraban Kadambini died suddenly. For some reason her heart stopped beating. Everywhere else the world held on its course; only in this gentle little breast, suffering with love, the watch of time stood still for ever.

Lest they should be harassed by the poike, four of the zemindar's Brahmin servants took away the body, without ceremony, to be burned. The burning-ground of Ranihat was very far from the village. There was a hut beside a tank, a huge banian near it, and nothing more. Formerly a river,

now completely dried up, ran through the ground, and part
of the watercourse had been dug out to make a tank for the
performance of funeral rites. The people considered the tank
as part of the river and reverenced it as such.

Taking the body into the hut, the four men sat down to
wait for the wood. The time seemed so long that two of the
four grew restless, and went to see why it did not come. Nitai
and Gurucharan being gone, Bidhu and Banamali remained to
watch over the body.

It was a dark night of Sraban. Heavy clouds hung In a
starless sky. The two men sat silent in the dark room. Their
matches and lamp were useless. The matches were damp, and
would not light, for all their efforts, and the lantern went out.

After a long silence, one said: "Brother, it would be good if
we had a bowl of tobacco. In our hurry we brought none."

The other answered: "I can run and bring all we want."

Understanding why Banarnali wanted to go (From fear of
ghosts, the burning-ground being considered haunted.), Bidhu
said: "I daresay! Meanwhile, I suppose I am to sit here alone!"

Conversation ceased again. Five minutes seemed like an
hour. In their minds they cursed the two, who had gone to fetch
the wood, and they began to suspect that they sat gossiping
in some pleasant nook. There was no sound anywhere, except
the incessant noise of frogs and crickets from the tank. Then
suddenly they fancied that the bed shook slightly, as if the dead
body had turned on its side. Bidhu and Banamali trembled,
and began muttering: "Ram, Ram." A deep sigh was heard in
the room. In a moment the watchers leapt out of the hut, and
raced for the village.

After running about three miles, they met their colleagues
coming back with a lantern. As a matter of fact, they had gone
to smoke, and knew nothing about the wood. But they declared
that a tree had been cut down, and that, when it was split up, it
would be brought along at once. Then Bidhu and Banamali told
them what had happened in the hut. Nitai and Gurucharan

scoffed at the story, and abused Bidhu and Banamali angrily for leaving their duty.

Without delay all four returned to the hut. As they entered, they saw at once that the body was gone; nothing but an empty bed remained. They stared at one another. Could a jackal have taken it? But there was no scrap of clothing anywhere. Going outside, they saw that on the mud that had collected at the door of the but there were a woman's tiny footprints, newly made. Saradasankar was no fool, and they could hardly persuade him to believe in this ghost story. So after much discussion the four decided that it would be best to say that the body had been burnt.

Towards dawn, when the men with the wood arrived they were told that, owing to their delay, the work had been done without them; there had been some wood in the but after all. No one was likely to question this, since a dead body is not such a valuable property that any one would steal it.

Every one knows that, even when there is no sign, life is often secretly present, and may begin again in an apparently dead body. Kadambini was not dead; only the machine of her life had for some reason suddenly stopped.

When consciousness returned, she saw dense darkness on all sides. It occurred to her that she was not lying in her usual place. She called out "Sister," but no answer came from the darkness. As she sat up, terror-stricken, she remembered her death-bed, the sudden pain at her breast, the beginning of a choking sensation. Her elder sister-in-law was warming some milk for the child, when Kadambini became faint, and fell on the bed, saying with a choking voice: "Sister, bring the child here. I am worried." After that everything was black, as when an inkpot is upset over an exercise-book. Kadambini's memory and consciousness, all the letters of the world's book, in a moment became formless. The widow could not remember whether the child, in the sweet voice of love, called her "Auntie," as if for the last time, or not; she could not remember whether, as she left the world she knew for death's endless unknown journey, she had received a parting gift of affection, love's passage-money for the silent land. At first, I fancy, she thought the lonely dark place was the House of Yama, where there is nothing to see, nothing to hear, nothing to do, only an eternal watch. But when a cold damp wind drove through the open door, and she heard the croaking of frogs, she remembered vividly and in a moment all the rains of her short life, and could feel her kinship with the earth. Then came a flash of lightning, and she saw the tank, the banian, the great plain, the far-off trees. She remembered how at full moon she had sometimes come to bathe in this tank, and how dreadful death had seemed when she saw a corpse on the burning-ground.

Her first thought was to return home. But then she reflected: "I am dead. How can I return home? That would bring disaster on them. I have left the kingdom of the living; I am my own ghost!" If this were not so, she reasoned, how could she have got out of Saradasankar's well-guarded zenana, and come to this distant burningground at midnight? Also, if her funeral rites had not been finished, where had the men gone who should burn her? Recalling her death-moment in Saradasankar's brightly-lit house, she now found herself alone in a distant, deserted, dark burning. ground. Surely she was no member of earthly society! Surely she was a creature of horror, of ill-omen, her own ghost!

At this thought, all the bonds were snapped which bound her to the world. She felt that she had marvellous strength, endless freedom. She could do what she liked, go where she pleased. Mad with the inspiration of this new idea, she rushed from the but like a gust of wind, and stood upon the burning ground. All trace of shame or fear had left her.

But as she walked on and on, her feet grew tired, her body weak. The plain stretched on endlessly; here and there were paddy-fields; sometimes she found herself standing knee-deep in water.

At the first glimmer of dawn she heard one or two birds cry from the bamboo-clumps by the distant houses. Then terror seized her. She could not tell in what new relation she stood to the earth and to living folk. So long as she had been on the plain, on the burning-ground, covered by the dark night of Sraban, so long she had been fearless, a denizen of her own kingdom. By daylight the homes of men filled her with fear. Men and ghosts dread each other, for their tribes inhabit different banks of the river of death.

Her clothes were clotted in the mud; strange thoughts and walking by night had given her the aspect of a madwoman; truly, her apparition was such that folk might have been afraid of her, and children might have stoned her or run away. Luckily, the first to catch sight of her was a traveller. He came up, and said: "Mother, you look a respectable woman. Wherever are you going, alone and in this guise?"

Kadambini, unable to collect her thoughts, stared at him in silence. She could not think that she was still in touch with the world, that she looked like a respectable woman, that a traveller was asking her questions.

Again the min said: "Come, mother, I will see you home. Tell me where you live."

Kadambini thought. To return to her father-in-law's house would be absurd, and she had no father's house. Then she remembered the friend of her childhood. She had not seen Jogmaya since the days of her youth, but from time to time they had exchanged letters. Occasionally there had been quarrels between them, as was only right, since Kadambini wished to make it dear that her love for Jogmaya was unbounded, while her friend complained that Kadambini did not return a love equal to her own. They were both sure that, if they once met, they would be inseparable.

Kadambini said to the traveller: "I will go to Sripati's house at Nisindapur."

As he was going to Calcutta, Nisindapur, though not near, was on his way. So he took Kadambini to Sripati s house, and the friends met again. At first they did not recognise one another, but gradually each recognised the features of the other's childhood.

"What luck!" said Jogmaya. "I never dreamt that I should see you again. But how hate you come here, sister? Your father-in-law's folk surely didn't let you go!"

Kadambini remained silent, and at last said: "Sister, do not ask about my father-in-law. Give me a corner, and treat me as a servant: I will do your work."

"What?" cried Jogmaya. "Keep you like a servant! Why, you are my closest friend, you are my - " and so on and so on.

Just then Sripati came in. Kadambini stared at him for some time, and then went out very slowly. She kept her head uncovered, and showed not the slightest modesty or respect. Jogmaya, fearing that Sripati would be prejudiced against her friend, began an elaborate explanation. But Sripati, who readily agreed to anything Jogmaya said, cut short her story, and left his wife uneasy in her mind.

Kadambini had come, but she was not at one with her friend: death was between them. She could feel no intimacy for others so long as her existence perplexed her and consciousness remained. Kadambini would look at Jogmaya, and brood. She would think: "She has her husband and her work, she lives in a world far away from mine. She shares affection and duty with the people of the world; I am an empty shadow. She is among the living; I am in eternity."

Jogmaya also was uneasy, but could not explain why. Women do not love mystery, because, though uncertainty may be transmuted into poetry, into heroism, into scholarship, it cannot be turned to account in household work. So, when a woman cannot understand a thing, she either destroys and forgets it, or she shapes it anew for her own use; if she fails to deal with it in one of these ways, she loses her temper with it. The greater Kadambini's abstraction became, the more impatient was Jogmaya with her, wondering what trouble weighed upon her mind.

Then a new danger arose. Kadambini was afraid of herself; yet she could not flee from herself. Those who fear ghosts fear those who are behind them; wherever they cannot see there is fear. But Kadambini's chief terror lay in herself, for she dreaded nothing external. At the dead of night, when alone in her room, she screamed; in the evening, when she saw her shadow in the lamp-light, her whole body shook. Watching her fearfulness, the rest of the house fell into a sort of terror. The servants and Jogmaya herself began to see ghosts.

One midnight, Kadambini came out from her bedroom weeping, and wailed at Jogmaya's door: "Sister, sister, let me lie at your feet! Do not put me by myself!"

Jogmaya's anger was no less than her fear. She would have liked to drive Kadambini from the house that very second. The good-natured Sripati, after much effort, succeeded in quieting their guest, and put her in the next room.

Next day Sripati was unexpectedly summoned to his wife's apartments. She began to upbraid him: "You, do you call yourself a man? A woman runs away from her father-in-law, and enters your house; a month passes, and you haven't hinted that she should go away, nor have I heard the slightest protest from you. I should cake it as a favour if you would explain yourself. You men are all alike."

Men, as a race, have a natural partiality for womankind in general, foe which women themselves hold them accountable. Although Sripati was prepared to touch Jogmaya's body, and swear that his kind feeling towards the helpless but beautiful Kadambini was no whit greater than it should be, he could not prove it by his behaviour. He thought that her father-in-law's people must have treated this forlorn widow abominably, if she could bear it no longer, and was driven to take refuge with him. As she had neither father nor mother, how could he desert her? So saying, he let the matter drop, far he had no mind to distress Kadambini by asking her unpleasant questions.

His wife, then, tried other means of her sluggish lord, until at last he saw that for the sake of peace he must send word to Kadambini's father-in-law. The result of a letter, he thought, might not be satisfactory; so he resolved to go to Ranihat, and act on what he learnt.

So Sripati went, and Jogmaya on her part said to Kadambini "Friend, it hardly seems proper for you to stop here any longer. What will people say?"

Kadambini stared solemnly at Jogmaya, and said: "What have I to do with people?"

Jogmaya was astounded. Then she said sharply: "If you have nothing to do with people, we have. How can we explain the detention of a woman belonging to another house?"

Kadambini said: "Where is my father-in-law's house?"

"Confound it!" thought Jogmaya. "What will the wretched woman say next?"

Very slowly Kadambini said: "What have I to do with you? Am I of the earth? You laugh, weep, love; each grips and holds his own; I merely look. You are human, I a shadow. I cannot understand why God has kept me in this world of yours."

So strange were her look and speech that Jogmaya understood something of her drift, though not all. Unable either to dismiss her, or to ask her any more questions, she went away, oppressed with thought.

It was nearly ten o'clock at night when Sripati returned from Ranihat. The earth was drowned in torrents of rain. It seemed that the downpour would never stop, that the night would never end.

Jogmaya asked: "Well?"

"I've lots to say, presently."

So saying, Sripati changed his clothes, and sat down to supper; then he lay dawn for a smoke. His mind was perplexed.

His wife stilled her curiosity for a long time; then she came to his couch and demanded: "What did you hear?"

"That you have certainly made a mistake."

Jogmaya was nettled. Women never make mistakes, or, if they do, a sensible man never mentions them; it is better to take them on his own shoulders. Jogmaya snapped: "May I be permitted to hear how?"

Sripati replied: "The woman you have taken into your house is not your Kadambini."

Hearing this, she was greatly annoyed, especially since it was her husband who said it. "What! I don't know my own friend? I must come to you to recognise her! You are clever, indeed!"

Sripati explained that there was no need to quarrel about his cleverness. He could prove what he said. There was no doubt that Jogmaya's Kadambini was dead.

Jogmaya replied: "Listen! You've certainly made some huge mistake. You've been to the wrong house, or are confused as to what you have heard. Who told you to go yourself? Write a letter, and everything will be cleared up."

Sripati was hurt by his wife's lack of faith in his executive ability; he produced all sorts of proof, without result. Midnight found them still asserting and contradicting. Although they were both agreed now that Kadambini should be got out of the house, although Sripati believed that their guest had deceived his wife all the time by a pretended acquaintance, and Jogmaya that she was a prostitute, yet in the present discussion neither would acknowledge defeat. By degrees their voices became so loud that they forgot that Kadambini was sleeping in the next room.

The one said: "We're in a nice fix! I tell you, I heard it with my own ears!" And the other answered angrily: "What do I care about that? I can see with my own eyes, surely."

At length Jogmaya said: "Very well. Tell me when Kadambini died." She thought that if she could find a discrepancy between the day of death and the date of some letter from Kadambini, she could prove that Sripati erred.

He told her the date of Kadambini's death, and they both saw that it fell on the very day before she came to their house. Jogmaya's heart trembled, even Sripati was not unmoved.

Just then the door flew open; a damp wind swept in and blew the lamp out. The darkness rushed after it, and filled the whole house. Kadambini stood in the room. It was nearly one o'clock, the rain was pelting outside.

Kadambini spoke: "Friend, I am your Kadambini, but I am no longer living. I am dead."

Jogmaya screamed with terror; Sripati could speak.

"But, save in being dead, I have done you no wrong. If I have no place among the living, I have none among the dead. Oh! whither shall I go?"

Crying as if to wake the sleeping Creator in the dense night of rain, she asked again: "Oh! whither shall I go?"

So saying Kadambini left her friend fainting in the dark house, and went out into the world, seeking her own place.

It is hard to say how Kadambini reached Ranihat. At first she showed herself to no one, but spent the whole day in a ruined temple, starving. When the untimely afternoon of the rains was pitch-black, and people huddled into their houses for fear of the impending storm, then Kadambini came forth. Her heart trembled as she reached her father-in-law's house; and when, drawing a thick veil over her face, she entered, none of the doorkeepers objected, since they took her for a servant. And the rain was pouring down, and the wind howled.

The mistress, Saradasankar's wife, was playing cards with her widowed sister. A servant was in the kitchen, the sick child was sleeping in the bedroom. Kadambini, escaping every one's notice, entered this room. I do not know why she had come to her father-in-law's house; she herself did not know; she felt only that she wanted to see her child again. She had no thought where to go next, or what to do.

In the lighted room she saw the child sleeping, his fists clenched, his body wasted with fever. At sight of him, her heart became parched and thirsty. If only she could press that tortured body to her breast! Immediately the thought followed: "I do not exist. Who would see it? His mother loves company, loves gossip and cards. All the time that she left me in charge, she was herself free from anxiety, nor was she troubled about him in the least. Who will look after him now as I did?"

The child turned on his side, and cried, half-asleep: "Auntie, give me water." Her darling had not yet forgotten his auntie! In a fever of excitement, she poured out some water, and, taking him to her breast, she gave it him.

As long as he was asleep, the child felt no strangeness in taking water from the accustomed hand. But when Kadambini satisfied her long-starved longing, and kissed him and began rocking him asleep again, he awoke and embraced her. "Did you die, Auntie?" he asked.

"Yes, darling."

"And you have come back? Do not die again."

Before she could answer disaster overtook her. One of the maidservants coming in with a cup of sago dropped it, and fell down. At the crash the mistress left her cards, and entered the room. She stood like a pillar of wood, unable to flee or speak. Seeing all this, the child, too, became terrified, and burst out weeping: "Go away, Auntie," he said, "go away!"

Now at last Kadambini understood that she had not died. The old room, the old things, the same child, the same love, all returned to their living state, without change or difference between her and them. In her friend's house she had felt that her childhood's companion was dead. In her child's room she knew that the boy's "Auntie" was not dead at all. In anguished tones she said: "Sister, why do you dread me? See, I am as you knew me."

Her sister-in-law could endure no longer, and fell into a faint. Saradasankar himself entered the zenana. With folded hands, he said piteously: "Is this right? Satis is my only son. Why do you show yourself to him? Are we not your own kin? Since you went, he has wasted away daily; his fever has been incessant; day and night he cries: 'Auntie, Auntie.' You have left the world; break these bonds of maya (Illusory affection binding a soul to the world). We will perform all funeral honours."

Kadambini could bear no more. She said: "Oh, I am not dead, I am not dead. Oh, how can I persuade you that I am not dead? I am living, living!" She lifted a brass pot from the ground and dashed it against her forehead. The blood ran from her brow. "Look!" she cried, "I am living!" Saradasankar stood like an image; the child screamed with fear, the two fainting women lay still.

Then Kadambini, shouting "I am not dead, I am not dead," went down the steps to the zenana well, and plunged in. From the upper storey Saradasankar heard the splash.

All night the rain poured; it poured next day at dawn, was pouring still at noon. By dying, Kadambini had given proof that she was not dead.